Praise for Kate Alcott's

THE **DARING LADIES** OF **LOWELL**

"Riveting. . . . In this book, and in real life, there's no story—or change—if people don't push the boundaries of what is acceptable, or give voice to uncomfortable truths."
—*The Huffington Post*

"Alcott draws from dramatic events indelibly etched in history and offers a fresh perspective. . . . Alcott's work will attract historical romance fans, who will be entertained by the antics of the daring ladies who leave everything they know and embrace less-than-ideal conditions to gain their freedom."
—*Library Journal* (starred review)

"The carefully detailed life in the Massachusetts cotton mills gives Alcott's latest a ring of authenticity. Add to this well-drawn characters, a sensational trial, a forbidden romance and a young woman's struggle for independence and you have a compelling read. Alcott is a splendid story-teller who knows exactly how to capture reader attention with a perfect combination of history and romance."
—*RT Book Reviews*

"Captures the spirit and courage of the young women who dared to work at factory jobs. Kate Alcott draws on the true story of a murdered mill girl for this captivating story of loyalty, friendship, and love—most of all, love."
—Sandra Dallas, author of *Alice's Tulips*

Kate Alcott

THE **DARING LADIES** OF **LOWELL**

Kate Alcott is the pseudonym of journalist Patricia O'Brien, who has written several books, both fiction and nonfiction. As Kate Alcott, she is the author of *The Dressmaker*, a *New York Times* bestseller. She lives with her husband in Washington, DC.

katealcott.com

ALSO BY KATE ALCOTT

The Dressmaker

THE
DARING LADIES
OF
LOWELL

THE

DARING LADIES

OF

LOWELL

A NOVEL

Kate Alcott

ANCHOR BOOKS

A DIVISION OF RANDOM HOUSE LLC

NEW YORK

FIRST ANCHOR BOOKS EDITION, OCTOBER 2014

The Library of Congress has cataloged the Doubleday edition as follows:
Alcott, Kate.
The daring ladies of Lowell / Kate Alcott. — First edition.
pages cm.
1. Young women—Fiction.   2. Friendship—fiction.   I. Title.
PR6101.L426D33 2013
823'.92—dc23   2013010093

**Anchor Books Trade Paperback ISBN: 978-0-345-80256-9
eBook ISBN: 978-0-385-53650-9**

Book design by Pei Loi Koay

www.anchorbooks.com

Printed in the United States of America
10 9 8 7 6 5 4 3 2 1

For Deborah Howell

FRIEND AND JOURNALIST

1941–2010

THE
DARING LADIES
OF
LOWELL

CHAPTER ONE

LOWELL, MASSACHUSETTS

MARCH 1832

*A*lice stepped gingerly into the darkened dormitory, holding her breath against the unexpected. An oil lamp flickered, turned so low she could see no more than a line of cots squeezed together in a long, narrow room. The air was close, aromatic with the scent of warm bodies.

"Who are you?" demanded a sleepy voice.

"Alice Barrow. I'm from New Hampshire, here to work." It didn't seem enough, but she was worn to the bone from her long coach ride to this gritty, bustling mill town that promised so much.

"Lordy, another one." This was a second voice, bouncy and light, with a hint of mischief. "Move over, girls. Here we go again."

"They shouldn't be waking us. She's got to take the far bed, I'm not giving up this one," declared the first voice, now on the edge of indignation.

"Calm down, Mary-o, there's one empty."

Alice began climbing over the still, shadowy figures, unnerved by their smothered giggles and deliberate pokes from unseen feet. She counted: she had to crawl over five almost invisible people before she got to the last bed in this small dormitory. "What's your name?" she said into the dim light, in the direction of the most friendly voice.

"I'm Lovey. Welcome to Boott Boardinghouse, number fifty-two, your new home. You're in Dormitory A; six of us now. They'd better not try squeezing in another bed."

Then more gently, "You've come a long way to get here this late. Hope they fed you."

"Parsnips and potatoes." Alice's stomach lurched slightly. She untied her green cloak and folded it carefully at the end of the bed. Her bandbox, more books in it than clothes.

"Not feeling too good, I'll bet. The potatoes were turning black at breakfast." Lovey broke into giggles.

"Don't listen to her," piped up a calm new voice. "She's a bit of a wag; sports with every new girl that comes along. There's nothing wrong with the potatoes, Lovey just likes to make trouble. Anyway, nice to meet you. I'm Tilda, hope you don't snore."

Alice felt for the blanket covering her bed; it seemed warm enough. Her eyes were adjusting. The girl named Lovey was two cots down, sitting up now, her thin shoulders sheathed in what appeared to be a white muslin gown. The figure between them lay huddled under a gray coverlet, ignoring them as she whispered to herself.

"That's Jane," Lovey said casually. "Congregationalist, you know. Always praying, for people like me, mostly. Maybe you do too, unless you're one of those revivalists who weep and sing all the time. Why are you here?"

Alice replied with carefully rehearsed firmness. "To earn enough money to help my father with his bills and save so I never have to work on a farm again. At three dollars a week, I can do it."

She must keep repeating that to herself. It was all that had kept her steady when she left home.

"Get to spend any for fun?"

"A little. Enough."

"There's no such thing as enough, not with the starvation wages here," Lovey muttered.

"Nobody's starving," said the one named Tilda, audibly smothering a yawn. "Stop grumbling, Lovey—let the girl sleep. You can complain in the morning." Her easy tone seemed effective, for Lovey said no more.

Alice pulled back the covers, easing herself into bed. There was no use hunting for her nightdress; the girl named Mary-o would just complain again. And no use saying more to the one named Lovey, either. It didn't matter. She shivered, but not from cold. The most important day of her life was almost over, and she wanted now only to rest. She had done it, she had made the leap. No more cleaning up cow dung, no more twisting the necks of squawking chickens. She was a factory girl now; she'd soon be working the looms and making money. Tomorrow it would begin.

Alice closed her eyes, dropping her head onto a thin pillow. No one was talking; she could drift and let go.

A sound intruded. A slight, hiccupping sob, a sound so lonely that it pulled at her heart. "Who's that?" she asked in a whisper to Lovey.

"That's Ellie, our bobbin girl. A hard worker, better than most."

"How old is she?"

"Nine or ten."

"Why is she crying?"

"Her legs. A bobbin girl does a lot of running. We take turns rubbing them for her."

"Can't anyone comfort her now?"

"She wants Delia, her sister. But Delia's on kitchen duty until midnight this week."

An unease floated over Alice, so ephemeral she could give it no shape or words, nor push it away. The bobbin girl's weary cry followed her into her dreams, and somewhere, somehow, it ceased. Only then did she join the others, still invisible, in deep sleep.

*T*he piercing shriek of the factory whistle at 4:30 a.m. was the loudest sound she had ever heard. It made her teeth ache. She lifted her head from the pillow, blinking at the sight of girls flinging themselves out of bed, pulling off nightdresses, putting on blue work shifts, and heading for the door. No washing up? She saw a basin and pitcher behind the door, but no one approached it.

"You're late already, hurry up." The lighthearted voice of the night before was husky in the morning chill. She looked into Lovey's face, which didn't quite match what she had imagined in the dark. It was all motion: thin and lively, not exactly pretty, but with a mouth that smiled easily and eyes that flicked restlessly about. She looked capable of switching moods with great speed. Right now, her eyes showed impatience.

"Breakfast, rotten or not, in five minutes," Lovey said, clapping her hands together. "I can see I'm going to have to push you along."

With a twinge of annoyance, Alice pulled on the smock she had been issued last night and ran her fingers through her long, chocolate-brown hair. "Nobody has to push me along. I'm ready," she said.

Lovey shook her head. "Pull your hair up, twist it tight. Here's a knitting needle to hold it." She grabbed a needle from a bag filled with yarn and held out her hand.

"I don't like braiding my hair up." Really, who was this person ordering her around?

Lovey's eyes darkened. "Just do it."

Alice jammed the needle through her sloppily twisted bun with more force than necessary. She wasn't going to get in an argument with anyone on her first day.

*T*he boardinghouse dining room, papered in a tight gold-and-brown windowpane pattern, was immense and claustrophobic at the same time. On the narrow mantel, perched perilously close to the edge, sat a worn-looking chiming clock. A watercolor of a child playing with a rag doll hung slightly askew next to the swinging door that led to the kitchen. There were five tables covered in oilcloth, with up to ten girls from each of the dormitories squeezed in, chattering at the top of their voices as they took turns ladling out breakfast from a tureen filled with pumpkin mush. A kitchen girl was squeezing through the crowd handing out slabs of fried codfish. Alice looked around and saw not a single seat was empty.

"There's quite a few of us at number fifty-two, six to each dormitory. I don't know half of them, but we're all about the same age. How old are you?"

"I turned twenty last week," Alice said.

"Ah, I'm an old lady, then. I'm twenty-three." Lovey nodded toward the table. "Just nudge somebody over, only ten minutes for breakfast," she said. "Move over, Tilda, make room for Alice." She gave the placid, plump Tilda a small shove, tipping the chair. Tilda almost fell off.

"You can be so rude," Tilda said indignantly.

"If your bottom weren't so big, there'd be room for two," Lovey murmured.

A sudden sharp voice cut through the chatter. "That's enough from you, Lovey." A large, pale woman emerged from the kitchen. Her chin looked permanently dusted with fine, dark hair, and her nose was round as a potato. She planted herself across the kitchen entrance. "We've got a new girl this morning, so show your manners." She nodded in Alice's direction. "It's Alice Barrow, right?"

Alice nodded.

"Your papers say you've worked spinning and weaving on hand looms."

Alice nodded again, quickly. "I'm quite good at it," she said.

"Don't get overconfident; running these machines is much harder than handwork. The foreman said to tell you you're being tried out on the looms today. Tilda will teach you." The woman's gaze swept now around the table. "So what's the most important thing she should know? Who wants to answer?" After a pause, "Don't all jump up at once, now."

"Make sure the bobbin doesn't run out of thread; if it does you have to stop the machine, and that's money lost," Tilda said.

"Your money gets docked, too," Lovey murmured to Alice. "Fewer jingling coppers in the paymaster's money box."

"Who is she?" Alice asked, once the woman was out of earshot.

"That's Mrs. Holloway, the house mistress. She worked the looms until she got too old, so now she keeps busy making a ton of rules. You break them, you are out."

Almost on cue, Mrs. Holloway turned back and pointed to a cardboard sign hanging next to the fireplace. "There are the rules," she said. "Read them and heed them. And know this—we'll have no loose girls at Lowell. Your conduct here at the mill and in town will be watched. And church is mandatory, Saint Anne's Episcopal."

"But I'm not religious."

"Makes no difference," Mrs. Holloway said.

Lovey's arm shot up, her eyes bright. "Mrs. Holloway, are you going to tell her about the rule saying she has to tithe every week? A little extra for the church and mill owners out of her pay envelope?"

A nervous, thin giggle spread across the room.

Mrs. Holloway shot Lovey a cross look. "One day you'll push me too far, Lovey Cornell. Get yourself a biscuit, that's all for now. Breakfast is over." As one, the crowd of girls shoved back their chairs and stood, some cramming biscuits into their pockets as quickly as they could.

Alice looked longingly at the warm pumpkin mush, still steaming, but the girls were straightening aprons and lining up to leave the building.

"Here," hissed Lovey. She threw Alice a biscuit.

Outside, Alice inhaled deeply, glad to be free of the closeness of the boardinghouse. The cold air shocked her fully awake. She looked around. She was in a square lined in brick, a huge clock tower rising grandly to the still-dark sky, hurrying with the others toward a wooden bridge that crossed the Merrimack River. The boardinghouses, eight rows of them built of the same red brick as the square, stood directly across the bridge from the factory. They had tall chimneys, gabled dormers, and precisely spaced windows lined up as snappily as soldiers on review; no hint of the crowded conditions within. Tall pines graced each side of the road leading away from the boardinghouses into Lowell, their branches bare but plentiful, offering promise. Everything offered promise. The road itself beckoned. Alice knew that if they took a right turn, over the next hill, there was a company store and small shops selling sweets and real leather shoes. Beyond that sat the Lowell Bank with the majestic solid marble pillars she had been told about. A real bank that whispered promises for those who saved their money. You had to give it to them first, but she understood how that would work. She couldn't see all this, not yet, but she knew it was there.

"You shouldn't tantalize yourself, peeking toward town; that's for Saturday afternoon," Lovey said, glancing at her. "Hear the water?"

Alice nodded; the sound of the rushing water had built to a roar. "I've never heard a river flow so fast," she shouted.

"It's coming down a thirty-foot drop from Pawtucket Falls," Lovey shouted back. They were on the bridge now, Alice nervously watching the water gurgling beneath her feet.

"See the wheel?" Lovey pointed ahead to a huge, rapidly turning wheel, larger and more breathtaking than any Alice had ever seen. "The water makes the wheel turn, and that makes the looms work, and the cloth from that turns into your three dollars a week, and that means you're not stuck on a farm all your life," she said cheerfully. "That's all you need to know."

Alice stopped suddenly, turning to the huge brick-and-mortar structure ahead of her that straddled the river. The cotton mill, all six stories of it. Already alive and humming. She saw men lifting and hauling dozens of canvas bags from three carts lined up by the ground-floor entrance, trudging into the mill, their backs bent.

"That's the raw cotton; they scrub it first," Lovey said, following her gaze. "Takes real strength, so women don't work on that floor."

Alice's eyes traveled upward. She was awed by the sight as she listened to Lovey's brisk introduction. Everything was done here. On each floor, there were machines that performed one step of a complicated process: the cleaning of the cotton, the carding to untangle the strands, the drawing to make the fibers strong, the spinning of thread, the weaving—all part of the magic of creating cloth. She thought of her homespun dress, so roughly made; she was almost dizzy in the presence of such progress.

She and Lovey hurried with the others into the factory, the girls scattering to their various posts. Alice covered her ears. If the roar of the water had been loud outside, the clattering of almost one thousand machines inside was deafening.

"Get over here, girl!" yelled a man beckoning to her, his voice bellowing hoarsely over the clattering machinery. She saw Tilda smiling encouragingly. This was Jonah Briggs, the mill foreman, a stocky man with heavy, dark eyebrows. He wore a blue work shirt already drenched in sweat. She moved quickly and stood straight, ready for instruction. The heavy, moist heat was tickling her throat.

"I run this place; you answer to me," he said. "Tilda will show you what to do. Pay attention; you don't get coddled around here." He pointed upward to a huge moving leather belt cutting through to the floor above. "See that thing? It's powered by the water from below up to the machines on each floor, then back down again. It's always moving, and it weighs nine hundred pounds. You don't want to get your hand caught in it, or you'll be squashed against the ceiling, hear me?"

Alice nodded. She felt a bit light-headed.

Tilda was all business now, her fingers moving with deft speed.

Alice watched closely and was rewarded with Tilda handing off a loom to her by ten in the morning. It was all she could handle so far; Tilda took care of six at once.

The other girls worked just as fast—and even with the roar of the machines, they carried on shouting conversations.

"You going to the next Lyceum lecture?" Tilda called out to the one named Mary-o, whose face was not as fretful as her voice had been last night.

"It costs too much, I don't need more bills," she answered cheerily. "And I want to get a pretty dress in town; I'm tired of homespun."

Another girl, with a tangled mass of curly red hair and freckles scattered across her nose, piped up. "Well, I hear one of these days we're getting a grand mystery lecturer. And I hear the handsome Samuel Fiske is coming to town for it; in fact, the whole Fiske family is planning to show up. Now those mill owners don't come poking around up here unless they've got someone special to show off."

Down the line, Lovey suddenly was alert. "Are you sure, Delia? He's coming? The son of old Hiram? And his brother, Jonathan— the one who winks at me when he visits? I'm setting my cap for *that* one, and don't anybody get in my way!"

Jane frowned, looking around nervously. "Don't talk like that, Lovey," she said. "You know Hiram Fiske wouldn't allow that for one minute."

"Oh, Jane, you're so serious," Lovey shot back.

They all laughed, never stopping their weaving, watching their machines, moving among them with expert timing.

"A Lyceum lecture?" Alice asked, trying not to get distracted.

"It's a great event," said Tilda. "Wonderful speakers come and talk about everything under the sun. You get to learn all sorts of things, as long as you can stay awake; you know, after a thirteen-hour day. We get speakers frequently. The one they're talking about is still months away."

A buzz of voices at the far end of the room. "You know why?

Guess who the mystery speaker is," came a shout. "President Jackson, what do you think of *that*? Just heard it from the foreman. No wonder it merits a visit from the Fiskes."

A sudden scream pierced the cacophony, a high, curdling sound that froze all in place.

"Oh, God," Tilda moaned. "It's Delia. We warned her to pin her hair up."

The revolving cylinder pulling the huge rubber belt that ran from the first floor to the top of the mill had caught a swaying tendril from the head of the girl with the red hair, snapping it up tight, hoisting her off her feet, and yanking her upward.

Alice saw Delia's toes desperately searching for traction on the floor. She sprinted toward her as Lovey ran from the opposite direction. Alice grabbed a pair of scissors sitting on a nearby work table and tossed them to Lovey.

"Cut!" she screamed. She hoisted Delia's body around her hips, lifting her to take pressure off, realizing to her horror the belt was still moving. She held the girl higher. Lovey had pulled herself up on a loom and lifted the scissors high over her head. A flash of the blades and a large swatch of thick red hair fell to the ground.

The tug upward was inexorable. "Hurry," Alice panted. She was already on her tiptoes. How long could she hold the girl?

Another flash of the scissors, then another. Hair fell to the floor in two final hunks, and suddenly Alice felt Delia's body slump down on her. She was free.

Only then did the belt, with a sickening screech, grind to a halt.

"What took you so long?" Lovey yelled at Jonah Briggs.

"Where the damn hell did you think I was?" Briggs roared back. "I was in the next room, I don't fly!"

Delia was gasping, great ragged inhalations, trying to get her breath again. Her eyes were scared and bulging. She looked curiously older than the others without her hair, as if she had come out from beneath an artful wig.

Lovey put an arm around her and led her to a bench under one of the closed windows. "Well, at least you didn't break your neck," she said gently.

Alice noticed the bobbin girl standing in the doorway, her arms burdened with a bundle of freshly filled bobbins for the spinning floor, her mouth open.

"Delia!" the child wailed. She seemed unable to move.

Alice scooped her up and took her over to the bench where Delia rested. "Don't worry," Alice said, realizing the child could be no older than eight.

"She's my *sister;* I'm Ellie."

"I think she'll be all right, Ellie." It sounded like inadequate comfort, but the redheaded girl on the bench was alive and breathing better. Delia reached out to the child, and they shared a wordless hug.

"She's gonna have a mighty sore neck for a while," the foreman said. "Serves her right."

"Will she lose her job?" Ellie asked, her voice tight and off pitch. "She can't lose her job."

"Actually, nothing much really happened, I would say." Lovey was staring at the foreman as she spoke. "I can't imagine our Mr. Briggs would want to spend any time fussing over this."

The foreman hesitated. Carelessness was to be punished: mill rules. But he'd be up for punishment, too; it had happened on his watch.

"My dear Mr. Briggs, we are your friends, you know."

Lovey's voice had turned saucy, warm with a dash of vinegar.

The foreman's gaze turned bold as his eyes surveyed her body. He still hadn't said anything. Lovey gave him a slow wink, then a faint curve of a smile.

"Well, I guess she just got a bad haircut," he said with a shrug, walking away. "One of you can walk her back to the boardinghouse. And get her a cap."

The minute he disappeared, Lovey gave Delia a quick kiss on the forehead, then looked over at Alice. "You know, you're supposed to throw scissors handles first," she said. And then she grinned.

And in that moment, whatever the risk—and she knew there would be risks—Alice decided she wanted Lovey Cornell as a friend.

CHAPTER TWO

*T*hat night Alice was almost too exhausted to lift a spoon. She had to force herself into her seat in the boardinghouse dining room before reaching gratefully for a slab of cheese and bread and eyeing a bubbling pot of beans in the middle of the table. She was suddenly ravenous.

The table was quieter than it had been at breakfast. Alice looked toward the other end and saw Delia slip into a chair, her head kept down. A rough knit cap was pulled tight around the girl's ears, hiding the stubby remains of her ginger hair. A dull-red stain was visible behind her right ear.

"You're bleeding," Alice ventured.

Delia's hand flew to her ear. "It's nothing," she said quickly.

"Oh, but it should have a dressing." No one said anything, and Alice could sense the hovering presence of Mrs. Holloway behind her. Maybe she was violating some unspoken rule.

"All mill accidents are small ones," Lovey said cheerfully, breaking the silence. "We're too competent a crew to risk our jobs over little things. Right, girls?"

"You're making fun, again," Mary-o said.

"Well, isn't an almost-scalping a good joke on us all?"

"Enough." Mrs. Holloway looked unsettled. "Nothing bad happened. This was carelessness, pure carelessness, on Delia's part. Isn't that right, Delia?"

"Yes, ma'am," Delia murmured.

"Pass your soup bowls to me. And get in the habit of proper laundering of your clothes; I'm tired of seeing chemises scattered about. You need to be dressed properly when the president graces us with a visit."

"Have faith, Mrs. Holloway, that's several fortnights away. We can scrub and iron everything by then, I'm sure. Is our Lyceum attendance mandatory, then?" Lovey asked innocently.

The clatter of bowls being passed to Mrs. Holloway gave her a few moments before answering. "It is indeed," she finally said. "But you'll all be given new green silk parasols to carry when the president greets you, which should please you."

"I love green," Mary-o said happily.

"Can we keep them?" Lovey asked.

"We will reserve them for special occasions." Mrs. Holloway's voice was tensing.

"And I assume we each have to pay the usual fifty cents to attend?"

The room fell silent again as Mrs. Holloway carefully put down a bowl and folded her hands, looking directly at Lovey. "What is your point, please?" she said.

"I think we're being trotted out to make the mill owners look good in President Jackson's eyes, that's all. And when it's for their benefit, we shouldn't have to pay."

"Well, perhaps you should raise that issue with the Fiske family. Several of them, including old Hiram Fiske, will be there."

"Perhaps I shall." Lovey's eyes held, for an instant, a dangerous glitter.

*A*lice wasn't quite sure what to do after the tables were cleared. A few girls disappeared into their respective dormitories, then reemerged with baskets of rolled yarn and knitting needles and drifted into the great keeping room. Jane could be heard complaining about somebody's britches tossed on the floor near her bed. Alice peeked in and saw her plumping up her pillow and scrubbing out the communal washbasin, grumbling away to herself.

"When Jane's not praying, she's nagging us about the mess. She can't stand disorder of any kind," Lovey said drily. "Not of the mind and certainly not on the floor."

Alice followed the others into the keeping room. They called it the parlor, which seemed a fancy name, but it was of generous size. An old but lavishly patterned wool rug, worn thin in spots, reached almost to the corners. There was plenty of room for several chairs and even a settee covered in a rough-textured linen. The girls carrying their baskets of yarn were settling into the chairs, their chatter lively. Little Ellie sat cross legged on the carpet, playing with jackstraws. Alice spied an unexpectedly ornate desk tucked into one corner of the room with a magazine lying open on it, the reader's place held by a glass paperweight in the shape of a pineapple. She looked closer at the title on the cover and, yes, it read *The Lowell Offering*. Her fingers itched to pick it up. It meant the story spread from farm to farm along the coast was true: there *was* in the magic town of Lowell a literary magazine the mill girls wrote themselves. Girls like herself could write and publish poetry and stories without pretending to be male; no need to hide. She reached for it, then hesitated. It was a rude thing to do, to ignore the fact that some absent reader had staked her claim with the paperweight.

In the center of the room was an ancient grand piano, clearly the proudest item of all. The keys were yellowed, and one foot pedal looked broken, but two girls were already vying to sit in the straight-backed chair substituting for a piano bench.

Mrs. Holloway opened the front door at the sound of a discreet knock. An elderly man, lugging a sackful of books, stepped inside, tipping his hat and nodding to the mill girls. "Finally got Walter

Scott's *Fair Maid of Perth*, first one up here gets it," he announced with a grin.

"He brings us the lending library," Lovey said, seeing Alice's confusion. "He's a very popular man. A good number of the girls are readers here. Not me, I'm too twitchy to sit still long."

One of the girls began to play, a simple tune that Alice recognized but couldn't place. At home, she rarely heard the piano. She looked around to speak again to Lovey, but Lovey had slipped outside. Alice hesitated, then quietly opened the door and followed her. Lovey was sitting on the front steps, looking up at the sky.

"How did you know so fast what had to be done today?" Lovey asked, without turning around.

"I saw a woman's hair get caught in a tractor's rotating shaft. One of the farmhands cut it off with a knife and pulled her out," Alice said.

"Was she hurt?"

"They got her out too late." Alice closed her eyes at the memory; would that she could have then.

"How old were you?"

"Ten."

Lovey was silent for a long moment. Then, still not turning around, she pointed to the sky. "Full moon," she said. "It dims the stars, but it's still nice. Now look carefully—what do you see?"

Alice stared at the milky planet, puzzled. "Nothing, really."

"Oh dear, where is your sense of romance? Look harder. See? On the left is a man, and on the right is a woman. They're kissing."

Bemused, Alice looked again. And there they were, two lovers on the moon; she had never seen them before, and now she would see them forever.

"Do you mind if I sit with you?" she asked.

"I would have no objection."

Shivering, Alice sat down on the step and looked around. The moonlight had bathed the rough-surfaced road leading to the mill in a silvery glow that was almost otherworldly. Like a painting, she thought. She felt a quick moment of longing for the brushes and small pots of paint she had been forced to leave behind at the family farm. Her father would probably throw them out, but at least she had saved the books.

"You're wondering why I was provoking Mrs. Holloway, I suppose."

"I'm just trying to figure out how things work here. I knew you were angry."

"Perceptive. About what?"

"I would be much obliged if you told me." Alice was freezing now, and her arms were aching from the day's work. She needed to find her place here, to know when to keep her head down, when to seize opportunity. She would not dwell on it; it would rob her of the thrill of having pushed her way out of a narrow life. But it was the next step, and the one after that, that mattered now. She glanced at Lovey's profile against the porch light. She didn't look as if she could be defeated by anything.

"There's plenty to be angry about," Lovey said. "None of us wants to lose our jobs, so we can't say much, but look how they treated Delia. The mill isn't safe, but we don't have any way of fixing things, and the Fiskes—those pompous people—know it. They're hypocrites, too. All that cotton making them rich comes from the labor of slaves, but none of them wants to think about that."

"But without the cotton—"

"We wouldn't have the jobs that make *us* feel rich, right?"

"Are you afraid—"

"Of being fired? Yes, but I've been fired before." Lovey's tone was matter-of-fact. "They'll try to do it again. It won't be banishment by Mrs. Holloway; she just likes to threaten. She's one of those sorrowful widows without a penny; not such a bad person, actually."

"What would you do?"

"Go to another mill where they don't know me. The important thing is not to care; that's what keeps me free."

Alice reflected on that for a moment. To not care was the spice of life for a permanent wanderer, but it wasn't for her.

"Where is your home?" she asked.

Lovey turned her face full toward Alice's, putting it into shadow. "I grew up in Fall River, but I'm not welcome there, according to my father. You might watch being around me, Alice—I'm a bad influence." She laughed. The sound of it was like water bubbling in a pot on low, light and airy, with a tease at the end.

"Where do you *feel* at home?" Alice asked.

"I don't know such a place."

"Not here?"

Lovey sat silently, picking at a fingernail. "Sometimes. The girls are a good sort."

"I don't know such a place, either, at least not yet," Alice said. "I'm seen as something of a troublemaker where I come from."

"Really?" Lovey glanced at her with renewed interest. "Tell me. I love troublemaker stories. Where were you born?"

"On a farm, same as you, I suppose. My father tried being a blacksmith for a while, but he couldn't make a go of it. We ended up as tenant farmers." Alice paused at the memory of watching her father, a grin on his face, pounding an iron bar over a fiercely hot fire. It would bend to his will; it always did. And so did I, she thought. Well, mostly.

"Did you go to school?"

"I finished secondary school. Won my certificate of completion last June." She hoped Lovey wouldn't see her pride as boasting.

"So why are you here? Helping out your father sounds a little too noble to be the whole story."

"I want to be independent. To be on my own and do things I

choose to do," Alice said. "I never fit in on the farm. Some of the neighbors in our village were glad to see me go."

"Why?"

"I made them nervous. Once I took a single board and a rope and fixed it so I could swing from a tree out over a cliff. It was glorious, until the landlord's daughter tried it and the rope broke."

"I hope this story doesn't have a bad end."

Alice smiled. "I grabbed her; we slid down the side of the cliff a short way, but we were fine."

"And you lived to tempt fate another day."

"I left, truly, because I couldn't bear it anymore. I had a suitor, but he was too content with his lot for me. Marrying him meant never leaving farm life. I heard about the mill, and I knew it was going to be the only way I could escape, but . . ." She paused. Memories of that last night at home were excruciating. Her father had ordered her to stay, shouting from the kitchen even as she packed. Yes, he had lost the blacksmith shop. Yes, he was a miserable farmer, but it was her duty to stay, he said.

She couldn't.

"My father said he would be ruined financially if I didn't stay and marry Jebediah."

"So you ran. Maybe we are a little alike."

Alice hugged her knees close and bowed her head. "I told my father I could help better by working in the mill, but I don't think he will ever forgive me."

"Do you think about what you want after this?" Lovey asked, nodding toward the mill.

Alice nodded. Most people would laugh, but she sensed Lovey would not. "It's just a dream, but I want to paint, even sculpt, some-day," she said.

"What does that feel like?" Lovey asked almost shyly.

"It's hard to explain—but I love holding a brush, dipping it into pots of color, touching it to paper or canvas, and seeing something appear, something I made, nobody else." It didn't have to be painting in front of an easel; she would bargain with fate on that.

"How do you get time?"

"At night, when my father was sleeping. I would make cameos." She drew in a deep breath. "I love making cameos, catching the light just right, making someone's face come alive. Maybe, even if I'm not good enough, I could teach children to paint, to reach out, to hold a brush with confidence—oh, I'm talking too much."

"No, no, I love hearing about it. Now, if you're teaching those children, be sure to tell them not to let anyone, man or woman, tell them they're wasting their time."

Alice laughed. "I will. Now, what about you?"

"I want what I lost," Lovey said, almost dreamily. "There was a man, and I was quite sure we were going to be married; he had proposed, after all. But I made a dreadful mistake. He left me, decrying the fact that I was no longer a virgin." Her words were without inflection. "It was a scandal at home. My father said, 'You learned your lesson too late. No man will buy a cow if he can get the milk for free.' Fancy that, he called me a *cow*."

"What a cruel and stupid thing to say!"

"Well, thank you," Lovey replied, casting Alice a slightly surprised but gratified smile. "Many people would agree with him."

"Could you defend yourself?"

"Not very well. I've had more practice since."

The distance between them seemed to be shrinking. She could confide her own remembered blows here. "When I was a child, my father kept saying I would come to a bad end if I didn't stop fighting him."

"Well, and here you are," Lovey said merrily. "I'll tell you a secret. I write my mother letters, and she never writes back."

"Is she sick?"

"No, she just doesn't care."

"That's worse than terrible," Alice said. Lovey's mood had darkened so abruptly, she wondered if she was about to cry. But no, just a long sigh, and the two girls sat for a while again in companionable silence.

"I want other things, too. I don't know, I like to punch little holes in puffed-up people." Lovey flashed a wry smile. "Now there's a plan for life, wouldn't you say?"

"Of course. You could run for president, maybe."

This time they chuckled in unison. Then Lovey said something unexpected. "Do you think bad girls are redeemable?"

"Yes."

"All of them?"

"I'm not religious at all. I don't think anyone's going to hell, if that's what you mean," Alice said. Coming to that decision had started another argument with her father last year; hard to tell which one was the final spark that had sent her packing for Lowell.

"I rather like the Methodists better than the Calvinists on that sort of thing; at least they offer salvation. The others, you probably know how *they* are—bad is bad, and no redemption. Poor old Mary-o is enthralled with those new revivalists who like to dance themselves into a frenzy praising God. People are swooning over their preachers. She talked me into going to one of their camp meetings last month."

"What was it like?" The Methodists Alice knew back home cluck-clucked about the self-proclaimed revivalists roaming through New England who claimed church membership; either that or made jokes about them.

"Much hollering and singing. I promised to go again, mainly because of the preacher, very intense. He's intelligent, more than you can say of most of them. Poor Mary-o, she thinks she's making progress trying to convert me. I haven't the heart to tell her it won't work." The laughter again; that sound of bubbling water. "Want to come with us?"

Alice hesitated. She had had quite enough religious fervor from her father. "I don't know, I'll think about it."

"Fine, let's not stay so serious," Lovey said, jumping to her feet. "Let's go inside and sing along with Mary-o's piano playing." She cupped an ear to the sound of the piano. "My heavens, I think we're hearing 'Rise Gentle Moon' for the hundredth time; she loves that one." She gathered her skirts, adding with another laugh, "I'm not really making fun; I'm very fond of Mary. She's a decent sort and no hypocrite."

She stopped, her hand on the front doorknob. "So?" she asked, glancing up at the moon. "Do you see the man and the woman?"

Alice smiled, her spirits up. "Yes," she said. "I see them."

"Good, I would have been a bit worried if you hadn't. Isn't it nice that somewhere, if not here, people can be in love?"

*T*he week went by slowly, so slowly Alice at times despaired. Her aching arms and burning feet grew worse each day as she struggled to master working the loom. The ringing in her ears from the constant clatter and banging of the machines wouldn't stop. Thirteen long hours a day. Yet her determination was building as she watched the other girls. She would become as good as they were; she would train herself, and soon she would be able to handle six looms at a time, too. Every day she carefully cleaned away the wispy particles of cotton and dust from her loom, wishing only that she could open a window to clear them from the air. Impossible, she was told. The air had to remain moist inside or the cotton would dry out, and anyone who opened a window ran the risk of being fired.

At night it was back to the boardinghouse for beans, pancakes, applesauce; finally, sleep. Sometimes the girls went straight to bed, but most lingered in the parlor. Alice, claiming a rocker, began rereading her mother's old copy of Sir Walter Scott's *Ivanhoe*, too tired to take on more than a few pages at a time. But she always managed to thumb through *The Lowell Offering*. Stories, poems—it made her proud to be a mill girl.

The best moments were sitting out on the porch with Lovey. She was filled with funny, mocking stories that made Alice laugh and forget her aching muscles. They discovered they both hated plums and loved the color blue, and they both had once excelled at doing cartwheels. On the fourth day, Lovey challenged Alice to a contest on the frozen grass, to see who could do the most cartwheels in succession. With laughter and clapping from the other girls gathered on the porch—and ignoring her burning feet and aching arms—Alice won. Oh, how free it felt!

And every night she would drift off to sleep to the sound of Jane murmuring prayers, of Tilda's knitting needles clicking long past lights-out, of Delia, her head still covered in a cap, snoring faintly with her little sister cradled in one arm. Since the accident, the child would sleep only with her sister, never apart.

Alice felt a measure of new contentment. Just a drop at a time, but it was real.

*F*inally, payday. When the closing whistle shrieked on Saturday at noon, Alice shut down her loom, awash in relief. She had done well. Now came the reward. A buoyancy of spirit swept the room. Laughing and joking, the girls shoved cold hands into the pockets of their coats and half ran out of the mill, across the bridge, heading toward the stairs of the Boott Boardinghouse. The lights were on in the parlor. Their precious time off had arrived.

"Look!" Mary-o spread her arms up to the sky. "It's snowing!"

Small flakes of snow were indeed drifting lazily to the ground.

"Ah," Lovey said, tipping her face to the sky as the snow began falling faster. "Fancy this, the Fiskes have ordered a March snowfall to dress the town up!"

Tilda gave a rich chortle, leaned down, cupped a handful of

flakes into a meager ball, and threw it at Lovey. "But we make the snowballs!" she cried.

And then in an instant they were all laughing and ducking and running for the porch—a group of girls who, Alice realized to her delighted surprise, had somehow not forgotten how to play.

*W*ithin an hour the short flurry of snow had turned the ground to mud, bringing moans of frustration from the puddle-jumping girls as they walked together into town.

Alice drank in everything. To the right of the road, there was a small park carved out of rolling terrain with picnic tables and benches. A child's rocking horse, its colors faded, stood still, waiting for spring. Just past the park was a school, another building fashioned solidly from red brick. Next to it rose the white steeple of a church—could this be Saint Anne's? Alice looked questioningly at Lovey, who nodded, not even needing to hear the question.

The closer they got to town, the busier the road grew. Carriages with drivers seated high, smartly cracking whips with a light touch, clattered by. A cluster of women in crisp suits and hats was gathered around a small pastry shop, examining its wares through a glass window. The door was open, and the fragrance of freshly baked bread wafted through the street. Across from the pastry shop was a pharmacy, its mortar-and-pestle sign so shiny and bright, it could have come directly from the U.S. Mint. In fact, the entire town looked new and vigorous, and all faces were as bright as the glittering signs and storefronts.

Alice inhaled deeply, not joining the grumbles from the other girls about the mud. She was here, finally, in the town of Lowell, the magical place girls whispered about back home. She was part of it now, with a week's wages in her pocket.

Lovey abruptly gave her a hard nudge.

"Look, over there, by the bank," she said.

Alice followed her gaze and saw two men standing in front of the arched stone entrance of the imposing Fiske Bank, nodding greetings to the mill workers filing past them into the grand building. Even from a distance, the taller man had a large, well-carved face and exuded a gravity of manner. He wore a black greatcoat with velvet buttons and carried his hat in his hand, revealing dark, well-trimmed sideburns. He stood stiff as a soldier, bobbing slightly as the mill girls passed by.

The younger man couldn't have been more different. He had a ruddy complexion, displaying broad shoulders under his linen shirt and wide green cravat as, coatless, he exchanged hearty greetings with men in the crowd.

"The one with the coat is Samuel, and the cheerful-looking one is Jonathan," Lovey said. "I don't think they like each other much, but the family trots them out together to make everybody feel grateful once in a while. Aren't you lucky? You get to see both of them at the same time. Now watch this."

Grabbing Alice's hand, Lovey quickened her step and marched up the steps of the bank. "Good morning, Mr. Fiske," she said with almost-languorous ease to the man in the linen shirt, twirling her parasol. "You do remember me, I presume?"

Jonathan Fiske seemed startled but almost instantly flashed her a smile. "Of course," he said with a slight bow. "Do remind me, where have we met?"

"Nowhere, actually. But you have on several occasions winked at me."

A quick guffaw, a sly glance in his brother's direction, then a move closer to Lovey. "Well, I shall do so again. No harm in winking, right? And who's your friend?"

"This is Alice, new to the town. Feel free to wink at her, too, from time to time."

A mortified Alice tried to pull free, but Lovey held firm to her hand, a reckless light in her eyes. Her bit of theater was drawing attention. Townspeople glanced over their shoulders, then bent their heads together, whispering. Heads were shaking; here and there a snicker.

"It appears this young lady wants to enter the bank," said Samuel Fiske, his deep voice cutting through the murmurings as he looked toward Alice.

"Indeed, I want to open an account," Alice said, freeing her hand from Lovey's and tipping her chin high. She felt sharply aware of her faded coat with its threadbare collar.

"Well, then, welcome. We certainly won't stand in your way." Samuel Fiske opened the massive carved door and gave her a stiff little bow, his manner, she imagined, like that of a host ushering a customer into a tearoom. She caught a flash in his eyes as he shot a cold glance at his younger brother.

"Just having a bit of fun," Jonathan said, annoyed, his flirtatious grin disappearing. He turned back to Lovey, leaned down, and whispered something in her ear.

*W*hy did you do that to me?" Alice said furiously after Lovey later joined her inside.

"It was just a lark—my goodness, are you really upset? I'm sorry, I feel like tweaking their noses every now and then. What's wrong with a little flirting?"

"Not with them. We *work* for them."

"So what? I like surprising the important men of industry."

"I'd rather surprise them by learning everything I can and moving up in the world."

"Alice, don't tell me you're shrinking back like some little mouse," Lovey said.

Alice shook her head emphatically. "My mother taught me to take risks and be brave when it *counted*, not just to play."

She regretted her words instantly when she saw the expression on Lovey's face.

"My mother—," Lovey began, looking a bit lost. She stopped.

"Maybe we're both trying to be brave but in different ways," Alice amended.

"I'm sorry for drawing you in like that," Lovey said slowly. "It matters to me that you like me. Please forgive me."

They stood awkwardly in the crowded room, hovering at some kind of crossroads. Lovey clasped her hands in front of her so tightly, the tips of her fingers were white.

"I'm being self-righteous," Alice said finally. "I'm sorry, too."

The look of relief on Lovey's face held no artifice. "Thank you," she said.

Alice held up a small green passbook, unable to contain her pride. "See this?" she said. "I just deposited my pay, and I will add a dollar every week. My father *will* get out of debt, and I *will* be independent."

"I'm happy for you," Lovey said. "I've never had the discipline myself. But—oh dear, I hope you saved a little for shopping in the company store." Her usual teasing mode was back again.

"Maybe," Alice said cautiously. "Will I be able to buy something worthwhile for a dollar?"

"Come with me," Lovey replied, breaking into a grin. "I will be your guide."

*T*he company store was dazzling. Alice walked the aisles, amazed at the array of velvet bonnets, colorful shawls. She stared a long time at a showcase of bracelets adorned with glittering chips of colored glass, then watched as the other girls tried things on, preening and laughing in front of oval gilt-edged mirrors. Lovey was admiring a bangle of gold and silver on her wrist, her eyes dancing.

Then Mary-o was twirling on her toes in front of them. "Isn't this beautiful?" she said. She had donned one of the scarves, a beautiful piece, made of light silk shimmering with many shades of blue. "When I went home the first time, all the neighbors sniffed and held up their noses," she confided. "I was a factory girl, not genteel enough for them, nobody important. But now they see me as a grand city lady, coming home with new fashions and ideas. Now I am somebody," she finished proudly, twirling again in the beautiful shawl.

"She will buy the shawl," Lovey murmured. "And then complain all week that she has no money."

Guiltily, Alice stared at an array of splendid bonnets and fingered the dollar in her pocket. She reached out, lifting one from its stand, holding it aloft. What gave it that shape—was it wired buckram? Yes. It had an arched crown and sloping sides that formed a halo over a woman's face. The outer covering looked like tan silk, with edging strips of brown velvet. The bonnet was topped with a sheer cream-colored bow that matched the ties for under the chin. Alice caught her breath. She had never seen anything like this.

"It's muslin, of course," Mary-o said. "But it looks a little like silk, no one except you will ever know. Here, try it on."

The girls watched silently as Alice put on the hat and Mary-o tied the strings in an artful bow. "Look at yourself in the glass," she said.

Alice stared; she was not used to seeing her own reflection. She hardly registered her wide-spaced deep-blue eyes; her precise, delicate features. She noted only that her smile was one of startled pleasure; she was looking at the bonnet.

"It's the most splendid thing I've ever seen," breathed Mary-o.

Lovey turned to the salesclerk behind the counter. "How much for this hat?" she asked.

"It's a copy of a very expensive one that is the latest fashion," the clerk replied. "The buckram on this one isn't as sturdy, of course. But it is a great bargain."

"How much?" Alice repeated.

"Fifty cents."

Her hand went into her pocket. Would there ever again be a moment quite like this? Out came the dollar, which she flattened smooth onto the display case.

"Then I shall buy it," she said in a firm voice.

"I have no box; you'll have to wear it home. And mind the weather, any rain or snow will ruin it."

"I will quite possibly never take it off."

Lovey laughed that full rich laugh again, enough to buoy them all as they left the store and headed back to the boardinghouse.

$\mathcal{A}$n errant puff of wind caught them halfway home, swirling under the brim of Alice's hat, tugging it enough to loosen the ties and blow it aloft. She snatched for it in vain. "No!" she cried, horrified. The bonnet was heading for a brown puddle of mud; it was gone. She couldn't bear it and closed her eyes.

"Ma'am?" A reedy, hesitant voice.

Alice's eyes shot open. A tall, gaunt man with long limbs and thinning white hair in a coat with sleeves that exposed bony wrists was standing next to the puddle, her hat safely in his hand.

"Thank you," she said gratefully. He seemed in a hurry; he mumbled something, handed her the hat, and started to move on.

"Hello there, Dr. Stanhope," Lovey said breezily. "You certainly came along at the right time."

"Yes, Miss . . ." He seemed at a loss for words, glancing from one girl to another.

"Cornell. Don't you remember us? You gave us all those nasty smallpox injections a few weeks ago."

"Indeed. Good day," he said firmly, nodding his head and walking quickly away, leaning on a cane. He walked in something of a jerky fashion, like a marionette on strings. Perhaps it was because of the cane, or perhaps he was just conscious of the bemused stares following him.

"He's a strange one," Lovey said. "Not exactly crusty, but as reserved as a stone."

"Who is he?" Alice asked.

"Benjamin Stanhope, the company doctor. How he ever got this job, I don't know. Taking care of hundreds of women? He can't stand to connect with anybody. I'll wager he's never lifted the skirts of a female patient to see what goes on past her britches, that's what I think."

Delia tittered. "Lovey, how shocking of you. Well, he's all we've got. He gives us pills, anyhow. And he saved Alice's hat; that speaks well for him. Let's get home, and, Alice, tie those strings tighter this time."

The winter sun faded quickly as they trudged on through the town, down a cobblestone road, past a row of neat houses built especially for the mill agents. How warm and cozy they looked, with lights glowing inside. Alice spied a woman through one window, reading under an astral lamp. She looked content, calm, without worry. Someday that will be me, she promised herself silently. Someday. She held tight to the ties of her bonnet, now knotted firmly under her chin, as she climbed the stairs of the boardinghouse. Her elegant hat would not escape again.

CHAPTER THREE

*A*lice heard it first in her dreams. Coughing. Dry, tired coughing, the deep kind that leaves one's chest heavy and sore. She didn't want to be pulled from sleep. Weeks now of working at the mill had taught her to jealously guard her rest. But the coughing pulled her awake. She lay, stiff, listening. Weary heaves, smothered, as if into a pillow.

Then a stirring; Alice squinted. Lovey was standing, wraithlike in her white nightgown, holding Tilda's head up with one hand, a cup of water in the other. Tilda moaned in her half sleep as Lovey whispered something to her. She took a sip, then fell back onto her pillow.

"Is she sick?" Alice whispered over slumbering Jane's form as Lovey crawled back into her bed.

"Probably, but she won't admit it."

"She should go to the doctor."

"She can't do that; he'll tell the owners."

"Why?"

Lovey pulled herself up onto one elbow, her voice patient. "You know they don't want sick girls here; it makes them look bad. The doctor has to report right away when it happens. We're supposed to be the young, healthy workers of modern industry, remember? She'd be sacked immediately."

"That's outrageous, they owe us decency."

Lovey sighed. "You're beginning to sound like me."

*T*ilda was determinedly bright, though pale, the next morning as the girls took turns washing up, filling pitcher after pitcher with water at the basin. Sunday meant leisurely scrubbing. It meant good manners; lowered voices; stockings without holes. Sunday was church. The sermon at Saint Anne's usually set everybody dozing.

Jane was standing last in line for the water basin, her thin hands clasped tight. "None of you take worshipping the Lord seriously enough," she declared.

"Mainly me, of course," Lovey said.

"Yes, mainly you. And I'm suspecting that you'll be searching the pews to see if Jonathan Fiske is down from Boston. Am I right?" Her voice turned disapproving. "You flirt with him every chance you get; we've seen you. Don't you have any sense of decorum?"

"Decorum? Janie, you think that bothers me? I'm announcing right now, I'm going to disappear for an hour or so today, and don't any of you tell," Lovey replied. She winked to the others, as if it were the most ordinary plan in the world.

"That's much too daring," Delia breathed, a look of concern on her face as she tried to dry Ellie's newly washed hair with a damp towel.

"You'll come to a bad end," mumbled Jane. "And if you're the one who brought crackers in here last night, you should clean them up, or we'll have mice."

"Oh, leave me be," Lovey said impatiently. "There's little enough fun in our lives." She grabbed a wet washcloth from the soapy water and hung it on the clothesline strung across that corner of the room. "Anyway, I'm getting some religion. I'm going to the Methodist camp meeting with Mary-o tomorrow night; anyone want to come?"

"Again?" blurted Jane. The others were silent.

Lovey laughed. "Last time, I assure you. I just want to flirt with the preacher. At least he won't be warning of fire and brimstone."

"Those revivalists make cheap promises." Jane was standing her ground.

"They talk about glory; your God is all about hell. Plus, they're more entertaining."

The silence grew uneasy, broken only when Lovey shrugged and sauntered out, heading for the dining room.

*H*ow do you feel?" Alice asked as quietly as she could of Tilda at breakfast.

Tilda sat across from her, spooning in mush as if the utensil weighed ten pounds. "Much better, thank you," she said. But she rested the spoon on the lip of the bowl and seemed at a loss for what to do next.

"You should try to eat more," Alice began, and stopped. Vacant, empty words to someone as exhausted looking as Tilda.

Dutifully, Tilda picked up the spoon and plunged it into the mush. "Some good news for you," she said, her lips widening into a bright smile. "Coming tomorrow, I'm giving you more looms. You've become quite fast, and you should be proud."

Before Alice could respond, Mrs. Holloway broke in. "You'll need to wait until Tuesday," she said as she put a platter of bacon on the table. "Alice has to get one of those smallpox injections tomorrow morning."

"Aren't you lucky," Lovey teased. "You get to pay a visit to the dashing Dr. Stanhope. Remember—he won't look directly at you, so be sure he aims right and gives you the shot in your arm and not somewhere embarrassing."

Tilda started to giggle, triggering a coughing fit. She pushed back from the table and hurried to the front door, banging it shut behind her.

No one else moved. Not quite knowing why, Alice pushed her chair back against the rough floorboards and followed.

Half doubled over, holding on to the ice-covered railing, Tilda was coughing so deeply it sounded as if her insides were being wrenched apart.

"I'm all right," she gasped. "I just have to get it out."

"Get what out?"

"The cotton."

"The *what*?"

Tilda's hand went to her mouth. A second later she slowly spread her fingers wide, staring at its contents. A white ball.

"You are coughing up cotton?" Alice asked. Cotton. The fiber the mill girls spun, carded, wove into wonderful patterns and weaves. The magical source of their emancipation from the farm.

"We all do, sooner or later," Tilda said calmly. She tossed the cotton ball into the bushes and turned back into the house, leaving Alice speechless, shivering on the porch.

*T*he doctor's surgery was housed in a small building with closed shutters off the main road, on the edge of town. Alice stepped through the front door Monday morning into a vacant, silent room permeated with a faint, acrid smell. She had never had one of these vaccinations, and wasn't sure she wanted it, but had been told there was no choice. So that was that. She would concentrate on other things to ask the doctor.

A door creaked open. The same strangely constructed man who had rescued her hat stood staring at her from behind large spectacles, looking alarmed.

"May I inquire as to what you want?" he asked, not unkindly.

"I'm told I must have a smallpox vaccination," she said.

"Well, indeed." He seemed uncertain what to do next. The white doctor's jacket hanging on his frame was too immaculately clean, and Alice wondered how many people actually came to see this strange man. "Come in." He gestured toward the door, fixing his gaze on the far wall of the sparsely furnished room as she entered. "It will only take a moment."

She winced as the needle went in, her heart pounding. Such a strange way to be kept free of disease. "It is safe, isn't it?" she asked timidly as Benjamin Stanhope withdrew the needle from her arm.

He gave her a hint of a smile. "Everybody asks that, right after the injection," he said. "But yes, it is. It saves many lives, and we're fortunate to have it." His voice had become less jerky.

"What is in it?" she said, staring at her arm.

"It's miraculous, really. It's material taken from a cowpox lesion. A little bit of it gives immunity. All the work of a brilliant man, Edward Jenner, about forty years ago—"

"Could I ask you about something else?"

A flicker of alarm in his eyes. She suddenly had the crazy idea of saying, Nothing to do with what is under my skirt. Lovey would have said it in an instant, and she would have gotten away with it, too.

"It's the air in the mill," Alice put forward instead.

"The air in the mill?"

"Yes. You know, the quality of it." Surely she wasn't telling him something new.

"Well, yes. It does leave something to be desired," he said. His voice sounded as if it needed oiling.

"One of the girls in the boardinghouse coughed up cotton yesterday." She waited, searching his face for some shock.

But Dr. Stanhope's expression held steady, barely changing. "Yes," he said.

"You aren't surprised?"

"It happens every now and then."

"So what can be done about it? What will happen?"

He began dismantling his injection equipment, wiping the needle with a cloth and putting it back into a narrow leather box resting on a table. "Most will be fine," he said. "You are a young and healthy group of women."

"And the others?"

"Lung problems, perhaps." He snapped the leather case closed, stood, and replaced it on a shelf above the table, his back to Alice.

"Is it because of the bad air?" Pulling responses from this man was getting frustrating. She rubbed her arm, which was getting sore.

"All of you there are breathing in lint, especially the girls who suck thread through the eye of the shuttles that feed the thread into the looms. I understand they do it to get the job done faster."

Alice remembered watching Tilda performing exactly this maneuver, lauding its efficiency. She thought of her own scratchy throat in the steaming hot room where she worked, the constant tickle and the constant wish that she could open a window. And she remembered something. "The girls were joking last week about something they called the kiss of death. Is that—"

"Yes, that's what they call it."

She caught her breath. "Does that describe it correctly?"

Reluctantly, he turned to face her. "I call it one of the hazards of mill work," he said.

"Doctor—wouldn't it be the right thing to tell the mill owners how dangerous it is?"

"Miss . . . Miss—"

"Barrow."

"Miss Barrow, any health alarm could deprive the girls of their jobs. In this time of economic want? You would want me to do this?"

His indignation sounded practiced, almost as if he were reading from some handbook. This wasn't hard to decipher—the man was afraid of losing his own job. He worked for the mill owners, same as she did, and Tilda, and all the others. "I wish you felt you could," she said.

Wordlessly he unbuttoned his crisp white coat and hung it on a hook on the back of the surgery door, smoothing out the very few wrinkles marring its spotless surface. Underneath he wore the same coat exposing his knobby wrists that Alice recognized from when he had saved her hat.

She couldn't leave without saying something more. "It will only get worse, won't it?" she asked.

He ran a hand through his hair; pink scalp was showing through the white strands. His voice suddenly sharpened. "I'm a doctor who does his best, and that's all I need to say to you." Regaining his composure, he added, "Good day, Miss . . . ah—"

"Barrow."

"Yes, of course."

"Good day, Dr. Stanhope." She donned her coat and walked out of the surgery, pulling the door shut behind her as hard as she dared

*I*t was a Monday night, perfectly ordinary, except for the fact that there were two empty places at the dinner table.

"Where are Mary and Lovey?" Ellie asked, her voice carrying around the table.

"Hush, they went to a meeting," her sister replied.

"Who knows what goes on in those tents the revivalists put up," mumbled Mrs. Holloway. "Those girls are—"

"They'll be fine," Alice interjected. The chilly edge to her voice halted the conversation. Why did she feel she had to speak up? Perhaps because there was so often a tut-tut tone to any conversation about Lovey, who was a bit of a risk taker, yes, but as generous as anybody. The other girls didn't always appreciate that. Anyhow, Alice was still brooding over her encounter with the spineless doctor. There was nothing to do about it at the moment. But at least Lovey would patiently listen to her complaints. She wanted to talk to her now. Where was she?

*M*idnight. No Lovey or Mary-o. Alice sat up in the parlor, sleepless, worrying. She could hear the rhythmic breathing of the others from the dormitory and wondered if they, too, were listening. Mrs. Holloway had padded around the house at ten o'clock, her face set tight with strain, peering out the window from time to time before finally turning out all the lights.

"It's long past my bedtime, and I'm locking up for the night," she finally said. "If there's any mischief going on, we know who's causing it, don't we? I swear, that girl Lovey has no common sense." After some hesitation, she left one lamp on in the parlor. "I don't want them freezing out there," she said when she saw Alice watching her.

"They'll come," Alice said.

Mrs. Holloway stared out the window into the blackness. "We do always want to hope for the best, don't we?" she said.

"No, I truly mean it, they will be here soon."

Mrs. Holloway stared into the distance, her thoughts on broader territory. "Young women, taking foolish chances, old story," she said tiredly. "I didn't take well to a harness, either, but there's no telling that to the young." She turned and left the room.

*A*t a quarter past the hour, Alice heard movement on the porch. Slipping out of bed, she hurried to open the door. A shivering Mary-o and Lovey looked up from where they sat on the steps.

"Thank God," Mary-o whispered.

"We have to get up in only four more hours," Alice sputtered. "How could you stay out so late?"

"Don't scold," Lovey said. Her cheeks were flushed, her eyes dancing.

"Weren't you worried? You broke a major rule, you could be sacked," Alice protested.

"Please forgive us," Mary-o said, her voice contrite.

"What happened?"

Mary-o stole a furtive glance at Lovey. "We got separated; I couldn't find her."

"It just ran late," Lovey cut in, yanking at Mary-o's hand. The three of them walked into the house, standing in the weak light of one lamp.

"I've been so afraid we would be thrown out of here," Mary-o began. "I—"

"Stop it, Mary," Lovey said, her voice lightly careless. "We had a good time, now pick your chin off the ground and let's go to bed."

Mary-o straightened. "Well, *you* did, more than me." She sniffed.

"Lovey—" Alice ventured, touching her friend's hand.

Lovey's hand softened under her touch for a second, then pulled away. And she would say no more.

*T*he next morning, nothing seemed different. Lovey had hollows under her eyes but laughed and joked at breakfast with the others, ignoring the stony manner of Mrs. Holloway, while Mary-o ate in silence. There were glances exchanged, but no one asked questions, and neither Lovey nor Mary-o discussed their late-night return. By some unspoken group agreement, that event hadn't happened.

Alice had little time to dwell on this at the mill, for Tilda did indeed hand over to her a second loom that day, and tending two of them for the first time left her breathless. There would be a way through all the questions. It would just take time.

*T*he weeks streamed by, the days beginning to blur, each much the same as another. Almost every night, Alice and Lovey gravitated to the front steps, enjoying the warm summer breezes and then the crisp fall air. Lovey was always in great spirits. She would sneak out extra cookies from the kitchen, and they would argue the merits of sugar versus gingerbread, talking and munching. Lovey teased Alice for being a bit too proper, and Alice confessed to a cautionary approach to rules. "You know what you need to do?" Lovey declared one day. "You need to steal a cookie. It's your turn."

The next night Alice dumped half-a-dozen cookies in her friend's lap.

"You see? You can filch things, too."

"I learned from an expert."

"Do you think we should have to start work so early?"

It was habit now, for both of them, to pick any topic and introduce it at any time, and they were always, always able to discuss it together. They could be talking about labor reform, Sir Walter Scott's *Ivanhoe,* or the best way to seam up a shirtwaist. It didn't matter. To feel free to think and argue and explore was new to Alice and made her euphoric. She had not known a friendship like this.

"I wish I had stayed in school," Lovey said one night, staring up at the moon. "I'd like to learn things—history, things like that."

"You know many things I don't know, especially how to navigate life in Lowell. Sometimes I think you want people to believe you are always reckless and not too smart, and I know that isn't true. Why?"

Lovey's reply was light and self-mocking. "It's my costume," she said. Then she simply grew quieter, seeming to draw into herself more. She could suddenly not *be* there, be oddly distracted, her mind somewhere else.

"Where are you?" Alice teased, waving a hand in front of her friend's face.

Lovey grinned. "Wandering in my head," she replied. "But you wander in your books. What are you reading?" She pointed at the book of poetry in Alice's hands. "Is it yours? You brought so many."

Alice sighed. Probing her friend was like poking at a drop of quicksilver. "It's mine now, I guess," she said, staring down at the creased and faded pages of her mother's favorite book of poetry. It was in such forlorn shape because Alice had left it out in the leaky barn one night when it rained. And she would never forget her mother's gentle scolding.

"For your punishment, you must memorize them all," she had said. And so Alice had, and now she would always love poetry. Which was precisely what her mother had hoped would happen, she told Lovey.

"You never talk about her," Lovey said. "I figured there was some bad story, but from what you're saying, if she were my mother, I'd be thrilled."

"She died last year." The words filled her throat, thickening her breath.

"I'm sorry, I'm truly sorry." Then with a touch of surprise, Lovey said, "Why haven't you told me before?"

"I didn't want to say it out loud."

"Makes it final, I suppose."

Alice nodded.

Lovey was silent for a moment. "It must have been wonderful to have a mother who read," she offered.

"That's all I have left of her, the books she loved." There weren't that many left, but Alice hadn't been about to leave a single one in her father's farmhouse for him to throw away.

"You told me she taught you to stand up for yourself," Lovey said. "That's a good legacy, I'd say."

"Yes." There would be no awkward platitudes from Lovey, for which she was grateful. But Lovey's next comment startled her.

"I wish there had been someone who loved me."

"Oh, Lovey, there must—"

Lovey cut her off. "Who wrote the poems?" she asked.

"A woman named Elizabeth Barrett Browning. They're quite wonderful, especially the ones about love."

"Is it sinful love? That's always interesting."

"Love isn't sinful." Alice pointed to a sonnet and read the first two lines, then handed the book to Lovey. *If thou must love me, let it be for nought, except for love's sake only.*

Lovey read in silence, absorbed as she began to turn the pages. "May I copy some of these?" she asked.

"Only if you promise to memorize them."

Lovey broke into a wide grin. "You just watch me," she said. "Lovey is going to learn about love."

There was something strange about the way she said it. "Are you all right?" Alice asked. "Something—"

The swift tenderness of Lovey's glance stopped her. "You really do care, don't you? I'm fine, Alice. Remember, I'm the one who is always fine."

"You seem pale. The cotton—"

"Not me." Lovey patted her rib cage. "Lungs of an ox," she said with a laugh.

CHAPTER FOUR

DECEMBER 1832

*W*ell, finally. I was beginning to wonder if the whole thing was some kind of joke," Lovey said as they stared at the notice pinned on the mill bulletin board one morning.

"President Jackson is really coming," Mary-o said, her eyes shining. "My goodness, it's tonight!"

The big event had been postponed three times already, and all of them had begun to doubt whether it was ever going to happen.

"What will you wear?" shouted Tilda to Alice above the clattering machines as the day came near its end.

"My beautiful hat," Alice shouted back. She had spent nothing at the store for weeks. She wasn't about to miss the president.

"And that's all?" teased Tilda.

"Have to keep saving my money," Alice said with a smile. She shook her head, rubbing her ears, all the while watching the low-hanging whale-oil lamps swinging above the looms.

"You're hearing crickets in your head, right?" Tilda shouted cheerfully. "It happens to all of us."

Just like the cotton balls, Alice thought.

"Look!" Tilda was pointing at Lovey, who was working four looms today, moving expertly back and forth, peering at scraps of paper she had attached to one of the machines, frowning in concentration.

"What are you doing?" Mary-o yelled.

"I'm memorizing," Lovey yelled back. "'How do I love thee, let me count the ways'!"

They all laughed as the closing whistle sounded. Only twelve hours of work today, and weren't they lucky? The overseer for the mill had announced this morning, a bit grudgingly, that it was a gesture of respect for the visit of President Andrew Jackson.

Or perhaps, some agreed, it was out of fear that the mill girls would otherwise fall asleep in their chairs at tonight's splendid event.

Lyceum Hall looked as if it had been carved from a single block of cool stone, then crowned with a soaring steeple. Looming high on a hill above Lowell, it had the lines of a church, but it was more impressive than any church Alice had ever seen. She felt inspired. She mustn't keep saving or sending every penny home. She must come here to learn. She would take notes and absorb all the knowledge she could. She would do everything necessary to pull herself up in the world. She and Lovey would do it together.

There was a flurry of movement as the mill girls lined up and began marching into the hall, two by two, through the huge double doors. "Sit up straight, be attentive," a portly overseer announced as he wiped perspiration from his brow. "You're important tonight. Old Mr. Fiske wants you to be the living examples of his magnificent new model of industry, do you understand?"

"We're important," Jane recited, standing up straight.

"Do you think the mills would close without us?" murmured Mary-o, her eyes wide.

"Heavens, no," said Lovey. "They'd just bring in the Irish."

It wasn't said with her usual easy humor. Alice wondered if the other girls had even noticed.

Inside, arched stained-glass windows rose from floor to ceiling for the length of the hall. Alice could not take her eyes off them. Even now, after dark, the windows—lit from behind by lanterns— cast rich hues of red and blue and orange, flooding the hall with glowing light. Rainbows seemed to dance off the mahogany floors. It was as grand as a palace, she was sure.

"Look," Tilda whispered, nodding toward the stage. "They're all here, the whole family. Even Hiram Fiske and the daughter, Daisy. Look at her, she's a pretty thing and she knows it."

An old man sat to the left of a large podium, straight and tall. His hair was white, his well-groomed mustache a perfect snowy match. Rumors were he would soon retire. But now he gazed at the line of mill girls filing into their seats with the approving eye of a general reviewing his troops.

Alice knew the story. Hiram Fiske—with several partners—had built the Lowell mill after Francis Cabot Lowell died. It was Lowell who had toured the cotton mills of Britain, memorizing their structure and machines and techniques. Not allowed to make notes, he had kept the information all in his head—and brought back to America a new industry. And this was the man who had known him, worked with him. Aged though he was, Hiram Fiske certainly didn't look to Alice like someone who would tolerate being pushed aside.

The young woman sitting to his right wore a peach-colored silk gown that perfectly set off her fair, translucent skin. She fanned herself vigorously, looking calmly bored, her thoughts somewhere else.

And there was Samuel Fiske. He stood erect, hands clasped behind his back in what seemed to be an effort at ease, looking both in demeanor and clothing as prepared for a funeral as for a wedding. His eyebrows were dark and thick, which she hadn't noticed before. He had an ample mouth held in mannered reserve. He looked fully trained to take on the role of responsibility expected of an elder son.

She wished she could see him smile. His expression now was quite serious as he leaned sideways to whisper something in his father's ear.

Hiram frowned slightly, nodding his head, continuing to watch the girls with their matching parasols moving into their seats, giving them a wintry smile.

"He approves of us; that's good. If we had decent working conditions, all would be splendid," Lovey murmured. She tossed back her hair in a careless gesture that immediately drew Jonathan Fiske's eye.

"Lovey, no, not tonight. Please don't court attention," warned Delia, looking quickly right and left, her voice strained. Alice thought she knew why. Delia had been upset when Mrs. Holloway insisted that Ellie could not go to hear President Jackson. A child would disturb the decorum; she would have to stay in the boardinghouse. The cook would watch her. Company orders. She did not budge from her stance even when Delia's protests grew increasingly fevered. Lovey had given Delia a warning nudge—not good to cause a scene.

"Have you been hearing the same stories I've been hearing?" Lovey said now. "One of the men downstairs was combing cotton and got his hand caught in the carding machine yesterday. Lost two fingers."

Alice's gaze shifted back to Samuel; surely he hadn't recognized her. But there was a flicker when their eyes caught. Embarrassed, she looked away.

Lovey suddenly yanked hard at her shoulder. "Take off your hat before she sees you," she hissed, pointing urgently to Daisy Fiske.

Alice looked. Was Daisy wearing the same hat? Yes. She fumbled with the ribbons under her chin, but it was too late. Daisy Fiske was staring directly at her with startled indignation.

"Yours looks every bit as good as hers, and she paid much more than fifty cents," Lovey whispered lightly. "Anyhow, you weren't looking to make her your friend."

Alice sank into her seat, unnerved by Daisy Fiske's frosty glare. She glanced up again only once, this time at Samuel. For an instant she thought she saw a faint smile on his face, but it disappeared; she had only imagined it.

*T*hat mill girl, where did she get my hat?" Daisy Fiske whispered to her brothers. Her small mouth, the color of rosebuds, was pinched tight, with her lower lip protruding a bit more than usual. "Doesn't she know that it is *not* appropriate for her?"

"Sorry, my dear sister—you can't say, 'Off with her head,' and you can't confiscate her hat," Jonathan said, trying to hold back laughter.

"I'm certain it's a poorly made copy, no one will think it's yours," Samuel retorted. He was weary of his sister's flaring temper; surely she was past the age where her behavior could be excused as "a little spoiled." His fingers flexed and intertwined, a nervous habit of sorts, his prelude to calming Daisy's flare-ups, wondering—not for the first time—about women and their moods.

"Everyone is noticing," Daisy complained. "I've been made a laughingstock."

The sound of Hiram Fiske stamping his cane twice on the floor stopped her from saying more. The old man stood and walked slowly to the podium, raising his hand for silence.

"Ladies and gentlemen," he announced. "I have the great pleasure tonight to welcome Andrew Jackson, the president of the United States. He visits us today to see firsthand the visionary work we here in Lowell have undertaken—while giving unheard-of opportunity to these young women before us now." His gaze briefly took in the array of mill girls before him. Then, with a theatrical gesture, Hiram extended his arm in the direction of the heavy curtains. "Make no mistake about it—we are changing the economics and the culture of this country. Ladies and gentlemen—President Jackson."

A tall man with a long, craggy face and a thin, tightly sculpted mouth strode forward to enthusiastic applause.

"No praising of the president," Jonathan whispered to his brother. "But then we know Father doesn't trust him."

"Jackson is not always a reliable friend of industry."

"At least he doesn't balk at using southern cotton; helps to have a slave owner in the White House."

"We have no need for satisfaction there," Samuel retorted.

"You're always fighting the truth. We can't say our hands are clean, can we?"

Samuel felt a familiar knot in his stomach. He did not reply.

Jackson spoke for close to an hour, something about banking. The huge crowd listened respectfully, but there was impatient stirring in the seats as he wound down. Alice felt her eyelids growing heavy. Tomorrow would be another long day.

"Before I leave, I must say I am intrigued by these pretty women before me," Jackson said. "Such bright, intelligent faces! This town is truly becoming a showpiece for respectable female employment, isn't that right, young ladies?"

He stared down at Alice and the others. Startled, they nodded.

"So now"—he bowed in the Fiske family's direction—"I would like to ask these pioneers a few questions. Do my hosts have any objections?"

Hiram looked pointedly at Jackson before giving a curt shake of his head. "No objections," he said.

"Outperformed," Jonathan muttered.

Jackson's eyes looked coldly amused. Clearly, he liked Hiram no better than Hiram liked him.

"My dear," he said, beckoning at Mary-o, who jumped up, vainly trying to hide the knitting in her lap. It slipped with a clatter to the floor. "What do you like best about working at the Lowell mill?"

"The money," she stammered.

"Not the camaraderie? New friends?"

"We sleep mostly when we're not working." A hiss from Lovey told Mary-o this was not a good answer, and she saw Hiram Fiske frown directly at her. "I mean—no, I mean . . ." Tears began to well.

Alice reached up and squeezed Mary-o's hand, trying to give her courage. President Jackson, eyes narrowed, caught the gesture.

"You, young lady—yes, you," he said, nodding toward Alice. "What do you think?"

Alice stood slowly, standing very stiff and straight. "Sir, we like the bank," she said after pausing to calm her voice. She must do this right. "We make our own money, and we can save it in our own names. And nobody else can touch it."

"That's the girl with my bonnet," Daisy said to Samuel. "Why is she speaking out like that? What does she know?"

"She's new to Lowell, I think. She opened an account at our bank earlier this year." Rather brave, Samuel thought, for the girl to speak up without being flustered in this daunting environment.

Daisy raised an eyebrow. "Really? And why did you notice her?"

Samuel was spared an answer when Jackson spoke again.

"A laudable accomplishment, my dear. And what is your name?"

"Alice Barrow." She was a bit dizzy at her own impulsiveness, conscious of all eyes upon her.

"So, Miss Barrow—let's hear more. What do you like *least*?"

Alice glanced quickly at the Fiske family, concentrating on Samuel, who leaned forward in his seat, as if awaiting her reply. Why did she think she could take a chance and be honest? She would ponder that later.

"Some of our working conditions, sir," she said.

A sigh rippled through the hall, giving her shivers.

"And what might they be?"

"The cotton fibers—" She stopped.

"The cotton fibers?" Jackson's eyes glittered slightly, a small smile on his lips.

"There are so many of them in the air."

"Why is that a problem?"

"The girls breathe them in!" yelled a man's voice from the back of the hall.

"I see. Anything else?"

What could she say? The long hours, the mandatory tithing? No. "Sometimes the machinery doesn't . . ." She hesitated. She didn't dare speak of the dangers, not here. "Can be hard to use."

A roll of approving whispers was spreading through the hall. "Tell him more," the same male voice shouted from the back. "About the accidents!"

Hiram Fiske jumped to his feet. "Thank you, Miss Barrow," he said, walking quickly to the podium, clapping a familiar arm around Jackson. "We mustn't use up any more of President Jackson's time. Sir, we are honored by your presence. Thank you for your visit, it will be long remembered." He raised both arms above his head. "A hand, please, for the president of the United States."

Amid the ensuing applause, Hiram escorted Jackson from the stage.

Alice caught a fleeting glimpse of the president's expression—she detected a self-satisfied smile and wondered: had she been manipulated? And Hiram's face? Stony. She shivered, not for the first time.

*F*or heaven's sake, just fire her," Daisy said. "She spoke out of turn."

Hiram Fiske, hands clasped behind his back, stopped pacing up and down in their suite of rooms at the Lowell Inn and viewed his daughter somberly. His jacket had been discarded and tossed over the arm of a high-backed chair in one swift motion as he walked into the room. The buttons on his waistcoat were clearly at maximum effort, straining over his ample girth. His color was too high.

"That would be unwise. There was real dissatisfaction in that crowd tonight, and it was triggered by that damnable Jackson. Making her a scapegoat would not resolve anything," Hiram seethed.

"Oh, give her a pretty dress or something, she'll be grateful for a treat." Jonathan tried to hide a yawn, sneaking a look at his pocket watch.

"You have things to do?" Daisy asked archly. "And with whom, Jonathan? One of Jackson's 'bright, intelligent faces'? Not that any of those girls looked all that bright and intelligent to me."

"Stop teasing," he retorted. "What I do is my own business."

Hiram ignored them both. "We're becoming a target for those who would organize our laborers, and I want it stopped."

"We could plant spies in the mill," Jonathan said.

"That's useless; they're always spotted, sooner or later."

"Did something happen between you and Jackson when you left the stage?" Samuel asked.

"Yes."

"What?"

"That bastard wanted to hear complaints, he as much as admitted it. He's trying to force my hand, pressing me to show my 'democratic values.' What he really wants is to embarrass us." Hiram fell into a glum silence.

Samuel walked over to the fire and picked up a poker to prod the smoldering embers. The flames burst upward, healthy and cheering. He stared at them, thinking. It would help to do something—something unexpected that might soothe the discontent they had witnessed that night.

"You look serious, Samuel. Any ideas?"

"I'm thinking about how to show those 'democratic values,'" Samuel said, still staring into the fire. He loosened his vest, replaced the poker, and turned to face his father. "What if we invite one of the mill workers to our home for a dinner meeting?"

"What kind of idea is *that*?" Jonathan said.

"A democratic one, actually."

Hiram looked thoughtfully at his elder son. "I don't want any malcontents haranguing me, and certainly not in my home."

"We would have control over who was invited," Samuel said. "It would show our concern and give them a hearing."

Hiram didn't respond immediately. He crossed his arms and walked over to the window, staring out for a few moments at the town he had built. He turned around slowly. "It could work," he said. "But we must retain control."

"So how do we guarantee that?" Jonathan said.

"We could invite a mill girl," Hiram said. "A girl would be more manageable than a man. We could feed her, listen to her, make her feel important." His face brightened. "I like this."

"She could be something of an emissary, perhaps."

Hiram shot his elder son an appreciative look as he resumed pacing. His face was brightening. "Yes, someone who could placate troublemakers with a little authority after getting a hearing in our home. A bit of orchestrated democracy."

"I'd make it that girl who spoke up," Samuel said. He remembered his first encounter with the flustered young woman intent on opening a bank account. There had been some grit there.

"Then we'll do it."

"Oh, you must be joking," Daisy said, letting out a thin, incredulous laugh. "You missed your nap today, you really should—"

Hiram stared hard at his daughter. "Do not patronize me," he said in a voice that brought them all straight. "I am the one who makes decisions here. I remind you, that hasn't changed."

"Yes, Father."

There was a momentary silence in the room.

"Well, if you want someone to approach that girl for you, I nominate Samuel." Jonathan yawned again, then grinned in his brother's direction. "Stalwart Samuel, that's who."

"Why Samuel?" Hiram asked.

"Because he knows that girl."

"I don't know her at all," Samuel interjected.

"You helped her open an account at our bank, isn't that true?"

"I didn't *help* her, and you know it."

"Right." Jonathan's eyes flashed a challenge. "What you were really doing was rescuing her from me. Guiding her away, opening the door, tipping your hat—trying not to let her be sullied by association with your dastardly brother."

"Damn it, you are impossible."

"And you, sir, are a stiff, proper prig."

Hiram slammed his fist on a table. "May I remind you gentlemen who you *are*?" he said evenly.

"I'm just saying the truth," Jonathan said.

"Far from it," barked his father. The anger under his words silenced both sons. "You are indulging yourselves. The members of this family do not cheapen themselves by indulging in petty quarrels. We *teach* civility; we don't destroy it. Do you hear me?"

"Yes, sir," Jonathan replied.

Hiram pointed at him. "You're the one always on the edge of trouble," he continued. "Don't think I don't know about your escapades with those mill girls. I had to send the last one packing. Will you get it through your head? Our reputation depends on offering *respectability*."

Jonathan wilted into his chair, saying nothing.

"Samuel"—Hiram nodded toward his elder son—"I don't care whether you know this girl or not. I care what you do for me now."

"Just let me know what that is, Father," Samuel said. His fingers curled tight, gripping the back of a chair. He should be above stupid flare-ups with his brother by now. But Jonathan still managed to push him beyond what he was willing to endure.

"I want you to find out where this girl lives, and I want you to invite her to meet with us in Boston. What was her name?"

"Alice Barrow."

"Good. We will discuss the problems she has mentioned and tell her we will work together to continue to make this mill a fine place for young women to establish their independence."

"Very good, we will yank her out of enemy territory and take over her concerns," Jonathan said.

"If she wears that hat of hers, I'm not coming," Daisy broke in.

Hiram did not take his eyes off of his elder son. "Well?" he said.

"I'll do whatever you want, of course."

Hiram broke into a grin. "This will be a fine family example of democracy at work," he said. "I'll tell your mother to expect an overnight guest next week. That should give her time to calm her nerves."

"We don't know yet if the girl will be willing," Samuel objected.

The others stood still, staring at him. His father had a shocked expression on his face; Jonathan's mouth curved in amusement; his sister simply looked blank.

A strange feeling—contrary to his nature, he had just displayed a radical point of view. The girl, whoever she was, had a choice.

Samuel stood out on the balcony after all the others were asleep, gazing at the stars that cradled the town in an arc of light. He breathed deeply. The air was crisp and cold.

He loved this town. There was something here, something not easily confined—a sense of possibility and energy. It excited him. It was tantalizing in part because it both affirmed and contradicted the brilliantly ordered nature of the place. His father had produced an economic model of both grace and precision. But something unpredictable was flowing through the veins of this country, something not nearly as contained as the Merrimack River. His family had done much good. He knew it was his job to carry on the family legacy. But how, was the question. His thoughts turned to the woman who had stood so straight in the hall, not shy about answering a question from one so lofty as the president of the United States. She did indeed show grit. Yes, that was the right word, and it was a trait he admired. One to be fostered in those who worked for the family's mill. Again he took a deep breath. Whether his mother raised a fuss or not over hosting a mill girl, he was glad it was going to happen—with the girl's consent, of course.

$\mathcal{A}$lice once again lay sleepless in her bed, staring up at the ceiling. The other girls had chattered on about her bravery in answering President Jackson's questions, and all she could think of was how her words might imperil her future. She wanted to talk to Lovey, but she was already asleep. "I'm not brave," she whispered out loud. "I'm a bit frightened, and that's the fact of it." As she finally drifted off, the one comforting thought was the memory of Samuel Fiske's face. He might not be a friend, but she sensed a kindness to him, or was she fooling herself? Enough.

$\mathcal{T}$he clock was striking three when her eyes flew open. She lay still, listening. A splash of something against the window. Gravel. She crawled out of bed and looked outside. Lovey was standing there, a warning finger to her mouth. "Let me in," she whispered. She gestured toward the kitchen door.

Alice crept carefully across the beds and tiptoed downstairs to the door. The lock clicked as she turned the key, and she prayed no one had heard.

"Did you know I was gone?" Lovey whispered from the porch, shivering. "I bundled all the pillows to make it look like I was sleeping."

"You fooled me," Alice said. Her worry spilled into anger. "What are you doing, risking everything to sneak out like this? How could you be so thoughtless?"

The sober look in Lovey's eyes silenced her. "I deceived you, I'm sorry. I'm trying to resolve a problem," she said.

"That's too vague. Where were you? Flirting with Jonathan Fiske?"

"Flirting?" Lovey tried to laugh, but there was no mirth in her voice. "I can't explain it properly, not yet, but I will. Please stay by me, Alice."

"I wish I understood you better."

Something quivered in the air; Lovey seemed to be on the cusp of telling her what it was. But all she said was "Please."

Alice was still trying to bank her anger. "I'll stand by you, no question about that. But these late-night vanishing scenes of yours are more than bold; they are reckless."

"I frighten myself, truth be told." Lovey briefly closed her eyes, then looked at Alice.

Her voice was so small and lost, Alice made no attempt to answer. She simply took her friend's hand and held it tight.

CHAPTER FIVE

*T*he weather was turning sharp, with high winds howling around the girls' heads as they crunched down into their coats and hurried across the bridge over the Merrimack River the day after President Jackson's appearance. Lovey pulled out a handful of torn pages from her pocket and hung them onto her looms. They flapped and fluttered as the machinery began to turn and work began.

"The foreman will notice; you've got too many pages," Tilda warned, looking worried. "We can sneak them in here, but he can't pretend not to see what you've posted."

"What are you reading?" Mary-o asked. "More love poems?"

"No, the story of the prodigal son," Lovey replied. Her eyes danced a bit too brightly.

"The Bible? You tore up the Bible?" Jane said incredulously. "That is sacrilegious."

"It is? Why?" Lovey looked confused. It took a second for the others to realize she wasn't joking.

"It's all right; most churches say it isn't," Alice said quickly. "I read it somewhere." She couldn't care less about whether tearing up a Bible was sacrilegious; she wanted to erase the vulnerability on Lovey's face.

The sound of shouting suddenly erupted from the end of the

room, drawing all eyes. An angry Jonah Briggs was trying to bar the entry of a hefty man who was pushing back successfully. The man's face was florid, its color heightened by a bright, twisted scar stretching from the folds of his neck to his ear. His feet were huge, and he used them to advantage, kicking hard at Briggs.

"Who the hell do you think you are? You can't come in here," Briggs yelled as he fell backward.

A humorless grin spread over the man's face. "I can't? Well, looks to me like I already have." He pressed forward, walking slowly now, peering into every face with the look of a hungry dog seeking food.

Delia moaned, motioning Ellie, who had just changed a bobbin on the shuttle, toward her. Ellie obeyed instantly, moving as quickly as she could.

"Who is he?" Alice said.

"Tom Appleton," Delia whispered.

"Who is that?"

"He's my husband. Tom wants Ellie. Oh, God, he'll take Ellie."

"Why does he want your sister?"

"She isn't my sister, she's my daughter." Delia put her arms around Ellie, her knuckles turning white as she pulled the girl close.

"Oh, my goodness," said Mary-o, putting her hand against her heart. "That's not allowed."

"I had no choice." Delia's voice was stronger now, even though pushed through gritted teeth.

The intruder was making his way steadily from one loom to the next, stopping only to shove the angry foreman back again into a corner with a whack.

The first one to move was Lovey. "Somebody take over my looms; look busy," she commanded. Then she lifted her skirts. "Ellie, crawl under. I won't move."

Ellie sank to her knees and scrambled forward, obeying without a word.

"There you are," the man said calmly, spying Delia. That grin again. "Lost your hair, I see. Not much left of you without it, is there? What made you think you could get away with this?"

"You don't want her. You just want to hurt me."

"For leaving? I would've kicked you out, soon enough. Give me the kid, she's my property."

"She's not property." Delia's voice stopped quaking.

Tom Appleton, in a slow, easy motion, took her by the arm and twisted, hard. Delia let out a cry.

Briggs pulled himself from the floor and grabbed Appleton around the neck. Alice and the others came out of their shock and started pulling Delia away from Appleton's grasp, shouting and screaming for help. Only Lovey stood still, concentrating, working one loom as if nothing were happening.

"What's going on here?"

Appleton and the others turned in the direction of the voice. Samuel Fiske stood in the doorway.

"I'm here for my kid," Appleton said.

"I don't care who you are, you are not authorized to be here. Get out."

"I don't need any authorization to get my kid." Appleton wasn't grinning anymore. "This here woman is a runaway wife, I have rights."

"Not to abuse her."

"I have the right to do anything I want, and I want my kid."

Delia found her voice. "She's not here. I sent her to live with my sister."

Appleton purred his reply. "You think I won't find her? I will. And she'll catch it for leaving the farm."

Lovey stood silent, her skirt swaying slightly.

"I see no child here," Samuel said, moving farther into the room. "I repeat—get out. Now. And leave Lowell immediately."

"Who the hell are you?"

"Samuel Fiske."

Appleton blinked. The swagger seemed suddenly punched out of him. "Look, you own the place, and I don't want no trouble with the Fiskes," he muttered.

The foreman, back in charge, grabbed the man by the collar and forced him to the door.

The girls were now all staring at Samuel. He quickly decided that proffering an invitation to the woman named Alice Barrow to join the family in Boston seemed a bit awkward at the moment.

"I don't think you'll see any more of him," he said.

"Thank you," Delia said, holding a wrinkled handkerchief to her face, dabbing at her eyes. "Thank you for not letting him hurt me."

"I could do no less," he said, shifting uncomfortably.

Another voice cut in. "Regardless, sir. You could have let him do what he wanted to do, and the law would back him up. We all thank you."

He recognized that voice. Alice Barrow was looking directly at him, which gave him a swift opening. "Miss Barrow, when your shift is over, I would like to speak to you in the central office, if you will," he said.

She nodded, eyes widening slightly.

As he turned to go, a small girl crawled out from under Lovey's skirts. "Mama," she cried, her face stained with tears, as she ran into Delia's arms.

Everyone froze. "Too soon, Ellie," whispered Lovey.

Alice tried to find her voice. Lovey had been brave; now she had to be. "Mr. Fiske," she said, "will you follow your kindness by refraining from firing our friend for being a mother?"

Samuel blinked. It was a challenge, not an obsequious request—no bobbing, smiling faces here. Yet there were rules. Only single, unwed women could work in the Lowell mill, that was his father's dictate; married women and mothers were too easily distracted.

"There are rules—" he began. He stopped at the determined look in Alice's eyes. No desperation, no supplication.

It really wasn't that hard a decision after all. "I do not believe I saw any child," he finally said. He tipped his hat, turned, and left the room.

*T*he overseer's office was a plain affair: straight-backed chairs, a narrow desk listing slightly, heavy curtains turned gray by age. Ushered in by a secretary, Alice found herself facing Samuel Fiske. She had forced his hand; he would have every reason to retaliate. He must be bringing some response to her speaking out at the Lyceum meeting, and she had made it worse. But she would do it again; if she and the others didn't stand up for one another, who would? She braced herself: perhaps now she was about to be discreetly ushered out of the mill.

"Miss Barrow, I'm here to ask for your cooperation in satisfying concerns you and your coworkers seem to have about working here," he began.

"Cooperation?"

"Yes. We believe—our family—that there are ways to resolve some of these issues and would like to discuss them with you." He paused. The girl looked dumbfounded. Perhaps she wasn't as quick as she had seemed last night; he wasn't saying anything astounding, surely. He couldn't help noting how her dark hair was looped upward in soft, casual curves, then swept into a topknot, exposing a long and graceful neck. Not a fashionable style, if his sister's tastes were any guide. But quite attractive.

"Mr. Fiske, I am not sure what you want from me."

"Your presence, Miss Barrow. At a—meeting."

"What kind of a meeting?"

"To discuss—" He took a deep breath. "I wonder if you will oblige us by coming to dinner at our family home on Beacon Hill next Wednesday. We want to give you the larger picture of what the future is for the cotton mill in America."

"And you want from me the smaller picture of what the present is for those of us who work here."

"Yes, that's it." There was nothing wrong with this woman's brain.

Alice stared at him. There was a flush on his cheeks—was he actually discomfited by her? What an extraordinary invitation. What could she say? What *should* she say? There was, of course, only one possible response.

"Well, then. I accept."

"Excellent." Samuel was already pulling on his leather gloves, a look of relief on his face. "I will arrange for a carriage to pick you up midday Wednesday and bring you to Boston."

She hesitated. "Mr. Fiske, what if that man who threatened Delia comes back?"

"I don't think you have to worry about him. The foreman got his name and checked him out with the police. He's no suffering husband and father, he's served jail time for starving his horses and breaking a few noses in various bar fights. He goes back to jail if he tries anything here again."

$\mathcal{H}$e invited you to *Boston*? To the Fiske *home*?" The girls around the dining room table looked at Alice, mouths agape. She pushed away her plate with its unappetizing meat loaf, wondering about its faintly pungent smell. Good thing she had held off telling her friends until dinner. The news would have swept through the mill in half an hour, and she still wasn't sure what she had agreed to.

She nodded, passing a cookie to Ellie, who sat in her mother's lap, exhausted, blue eyes fogging over with sleep. If Samuel Fiske could be trusted, there would be no more need for subterfuge, no more pretending she was Delia's little sister—not at the boarding-house, anyhow. Mrs. Holloway had initially bridled when she heard the story, a look of alarm on her face. "I'm not risking my job for this," she muttered.

"But my dear Mrs. Holloway, if Samuel Fiske saw nothing out of place, why should you?" Lovey asked. "You weren't there. What could possibly connect you to today's events?"

Mrs. Holloway puzzled that out quickly. "It's true, I see nothing different," she said with a rare smile. "It's the same as always."

"Very perceptive of you, Mrs. Holloway." Lovey beamed.

Alice watched Ellie eat the cookie, still working to get her bearings. "I don't know what it is that they think I can tell them," she said. "I'm no representative for the mill girls, or anybody else."

"Tell them about Mama losing her hair," Ellie said, her eyes flying wide open. "Tell them they should make safer machines. That nice man today will help."

And would it be so? It sounded so simple, voiced by a child. That was the deception of simplicity, of course. Most adults scorned it.

*T*he weather had softened, although clouds still covered the stars tonight, but Alice and Lovey, bundled up, sat out on the front steps in companionable silence.

"They invited you," Lovey finally said softly. "They invited you, like a guest."

"Not like a guest, it's different."

"But you'll sit at their table and eat from their china plates, and you won't have to reach for food. There will be maids standing by, asking if you need anything, anything at all, and their job is to get it for you." Her voice was dreamy. "You know something? No one would ever invite me."

"That's—"

"Hush, Alice. You know it's true. It wouldn't matter what I do, I wouldn't be respectable enough."

"They would be wrong."

"You really are my friend, aren't you." It wasn't a question.

"Yes, I am. And I want to help you. Lovey, where do you go when you're out late at night?"

Silence. Alice could hear someone in the parlor pumping away on the old piano, some tune she didn't recognize, but there was clapping and laughter, mixed with the clatter of dishes being washed coming from the kitchen. Above their heads on the porch, tucked away in the eaves, a motionless robin huddled over her eggs, now used to the comings and goings of the boardinghouse. Everything was normal, but not the silence from Lovey.

"I don't think friends should be burdened with problems other than their own," Lovey finally said.

"I suppose that's true if you don't trust your friends." She couldn't help the barb. And yes, she was frustrated.

"I respect *your* secrets, Alice. I don't have to know all of them. I'm asking no questions."

Alice started to speak, but Lovey put her finger to her friend's lips. "The thing is, I've got to help myself," she said. "I have to do that first."

"What could be braver than hiding that child today from that awful man?"

Even in the darkness, Alice could see Lovey's faint smile. "Oh, I'm good at that sort of thing. I'm just not that good at figuring out consequences."

"And that's what you're going to leave me with?"

"For now." Lovey's voice was gentle. "For now." She reached out a hand as Alice started to rise. "Please don't be cross. I'll tell you everything when you come back from Boston, but I have to do something first. I promise."

Alice sighed. "Soon?" she said.

"Soon."

CHAPTER SIX

L ovey was halfway up the dimly lit stairway that led to the top
floor of the mill, balancing somewhat precariously on the narrow step, bouncing impatiently on her toes. She gestured to Alice.
"Come on," she urged. "We only have half an hour."

Alice hesitated a fraction of a second before following her up.
She had never seen the top floor. She glanced quickly as they passed
the third landing, where the roving, spinning, dressing, warping,
and drawing in were done, wishing she could watch for a while.
But Lovey kept climbing, and then there they were, standing in a
strangely quiet room. Women sat on benches with cloth before them,
weaving in patterns. "It's left thread to harness one and right thread
to harness two, and you bloody well have to concentrate, because you
can't let them cross or the pattern will be ruined," Lovey whispered.

Alice watched, fascinated. The pattern weavers were the most-
skilled mill workers of all. They wove the highly prized calico cloth,
which was not, as Lovey had taken pains to tell her, the cheap coarse
muslin the English called calico. The weavers here were creating
densely intricate patterns of vines and branches in indigo blue woven
through with graceful curls of white. She and Lovey shouldn't be
here, this was a secret process; it was strictly off-limits. The Fiskes
had no intention of allowing a competitor to steal their procedures.

But here she was, feeling some envy. How quickly and deftly these women worked. What beautiful patterns they were creating. Could she ever be good enough to work up here?

*Y*ou are going to represent us at the Fiske home, and you should be properly dressed," Lovey had announced that morning. "I know somebody on the third floor, and she says they have seamstresses making beautiful dresses—for the rich, of course, and that's supposed to be a secret, too."

Lovey leaned closer, her eyes shining. "We're getting one for you to wear."

"I can't do that," Alice had protested.

"Then what are you going to wear? Your homespun? Your apron from the mill?"

"She can borrow my Sunday dress," Mary-o said.

Lovey shook her head, but not unkindly. "It isn't fashionable enough."

And so here they were, she and Lovey, standing in a corner, trying to be inconspicuous. A few of the women looked up curiously but then turned back to their work. They had quotas, too.

Lovey pulled Alice to the back of the room. One of the pattern weavers, looking a little nervous, was waiting behind a curtain. Two dresses hung from a peg.

"They have flaws and can't be sold, so they're supposed to be taken apart," Lovey explained hurriedly. "But I think they're quite handsome anyhow. Look, this one has those new ballooning sleeves." She smoothed her hand over the closest one. "What keeps them so puffed up?"

"Down feathers," said her friend, looking right and left. "They're called gigot sleeves, truly the very latest."

Alice ran her hand down the cloth of the skirt. The weaving was lovely work, not calico, but blended threads of pink and red in

a muted floral design. She gazed at the simple lines of the bodice—
trimmed with a carefully worked collar and small glass buttons—
and could hardly believe it. She had never worn anything so quietly
elegant.

"You have to return it the next day," Lovey's friend said quickly.
"So, choose, please. I'll tuck it in a little for you if you need it."

"This one," she said.

Lovey giggled. "You haven't even looked at the other one."

"I don't need to; I like this one."

*T*here was much gaiety in the boardinghouse that afternoon. Alice
and Lovey had to smuggle the dress into the dormitory without
catching Mrs. Holloway's eye, and everyone seemed delighted by
the conspiracy.

"We can hide it under a mattress," Tilda said, eyeing the volumi-
nous skirt doubtfully.

"No, no, it must hang, best under the drapery," Mary-o protested.

Jane objected. "The first thing *someone* here has to do"—she
glared at Lovey—"is dust those filthy curtains and scrub down the
wall behind them."

"Jane, is anything ever clean enough for you?" Lovey asked.

But Jane had already donned an apron and was soaking a rag in
the washbasin, wringing it out, ready to scrub the wall behind the
limp curtains. "Nothing gets done here unless I do it myself," she
complained.

Lovey held the dress, watching her, while Mary-o watched for
Mrs. Holloway. Then Lovey leaned over to Alice. "Here, hold this,
I'll be back in a few minutes," she whispered, and disappeared out
the door.

When Jane declared the wall clean enough, they carefully hid
the dress behind the folds of the drapery and stepped back. It was
virtually invisible.

"For once, this place is clean," Jane said, rebuttoning her sleeves and hanging her apron. "I'm going to get the mail." She turned and left the room; the others started to follow.

Lovey slipped in, her eyes dancing. She looked around the impressively tidy dormitory and held up something in her hand for the others to see. A wrinkled pair of knickers.

"Knickers?" Mary-o said.

Lovey put a finger to her lips, then carefully deposited the knickers on top of Jane's pillow.

"Let's go to the parlor, quick," Lovey whispered. "She'll be back, she's always forgetting something."

They were barely out of there when, sure enough, Jane went hurrying back for her knitting. Heads down, giggling, they waited. And when they heard Jane's explosive shriek, they broke into laughter; they couldn't contain it, none of them, especially when Jane came storming in, holding the pair of knickers with two fingers and tossed them into Lovey's lap.

"Janie, Janie, it's just a joke," Lovey protested, seeing Jane was nearly in tears.

"You're all just making fun of me, and I don't like it."

Lovey took her hand. "I promise, I will wash these on the scrub board, and I will make sure no bits of food collect on the floor ever again. I swear it." She paused and saw Jane would need a touch more coaxing.

"I'm sorry," she said.

Jane blew her nose quite vigorously. "I guess I'm a bit hard on the rest of you. You can't help it if you weren't taught to my standards."

"Ah, well." Lovey sighed. "We do our best."

Alice and Lovey sat out on the porch quite late that night. Together they studied and argued over an idea Lovey had been working on, an article she had titled "A Manifesto for Mill Girls." Alice smiled a bit at the lofty goals—including the declarations that *No members of this society shall exact more than eight hours of labour, out of every twenty-four.* Such a fanciful idea—but Lovey was clearly excited.

"Please don't give me one of those gently skeptical smiles that you do so well," she said. "I'm serious. I think we can resolve to do things and then make them happen. I'm drawing up a whole list of things and when I'm done, I'm submitting this to *The Lowell Offering*."

"I'm not making fun; I just think that none of this will ever come about."

"They don't take us seriously. All we are to anybody are 'the mill girls,' and I think that should change. Why can't we be daring ladies? Doesn't that sound good? I'd like to be a daring lady. It sounds so brave. Here, listen to this." Lovey picked up a page and cleared her throat: "Resolved: That the wages of females shall be equal to the wages of males, that they may be enabled to maintain proper independence of character."

"Don't you want to be taken seriously?"

"Well, of course." Lovey thought for a moment. "We could be *decorous* daring ladies."

"Well, that sounds good." Alice gave her friend a mock-stern look. "But I think you need to add more."

"I thought you would say that." Lovey sighed, reading aloud as she scribbled. *"And virtuous deportment."* She arched an eyebrow. "I do not guarantee I won't take it out when you're not looking."

Alice remembered the wonderfully grave face Lovey presented at that point. But mostly she remembered what came next: Lovey's burst of cascading laughter. And if there had been something of a hollow edge to it that time, Alice did not catch it.

CHAPTER SEVEN

*T*he carriage came, pulling up in front of the boardinghouse as all the girls stared through the glass of the front parlor. Alice sensed their eyes on her as she walked down the path and prepared to climb in. The driver opened the door and stood back. She pulled her skirts high enough to be above the slushy mud, hoping there would be no stains on her wonderful gown. She retied the strings on Mary-o's bonnet, the loan of which Alice had ruefully accepted, knowing that wearing her beautiful new hat around Daisy would be an intolerable breach of decorum.

She looked around one more time—where was Lovey? She had been alternately lively and sober last night, but Alice had resolved to do no more probing. Lovey would keep her promise; she was sure of that.

Settling into her seat, she gratefully pulled Tilda's borrowed cloak closer and held tight to Jane's bag, a velvet pouch in which the devout Jane usually kept her Bible. "It'll hold your comb and purse," Jane had said somewhat shyly.

"Won't God mind?" Tilda asked teasingly.

"No, I prayed on it." Jane was so earnest, no one giggled.

The coachman closed the door and climbed back into the driver's seat, poised to leave. Alice waved through the window to her friends.

"Wait!"

Lovey was running down the path to the carriage. The hood of her cape had fallen back, exposing her dark curls, whipped now by a slight, icy wind. Breathless, she reached up to the window, handing Alice a tissue-wrapped package.

"A gift for you," she said. Her eyes were tense, but her smile was wide.

Alice unwrapped the tissue and lifted up a beautiful pair of dove-gray leather gloves. For her? Her hands were always gloveless, the knuckles raw and red.

"Lovey, what did you do?" Alice exclaimed. "Are they yours?"

"I'd have them on if they were, wouldn't I? They're for you. How could I allow you to visit the Fiske family without gloves?" Lovey laughed, her typical frothy laugh. "A lady has to have nice gloves. These are yours."

Alice slipped one hand into the soft leather, rotating her fingers slightly, then slowly pushed each one into its proper place. They fit. She flexed her hand, marveling at its sudden languorous elegance. "Where did you get these?" she managed to say.

"The company store. The best they had."

"You spent all your money, you must have—"

Lovey cut her off firmly. "There's no way you're going to Beacon Hill without proper gloves. We are ladies, and we hold our heads up high."

"They're beautiful," Alice said. "Now all I need is a lesson on the proper way to wear them."

"You'll do it naturally, I'm sure of it. Now, do us proud, Alice. I know you can."

Alice nodded. "I'll try. And please"—she paused, groping for the right words—"take care."

"I won't promise," Lovey replied in an oddly jumpy tone. "You know me." She drew a piece of paper from her pocket, hesitated, glanced at it briefly, then shoved it out of sight again.

"Is that something—"

"No, just my usual scribbles. More declarations for the manifesto."

"Lovey?"

"I will tell you everything. I promised, and I keep my promises. And you will be sensible and scold me, and then we'll hug and all will be well." She made such a funny face, Alice laughed.

"Then I'll see you tomorrow," she said.

"Yes, and we'll sit out on the steps and you'll tell me delicious stories about grand living in Boston," Lovey said. Her words tumbled forth so rapidly, they ran together. "I'll have to tug at your nose to bring it out of the air."

Alice laughed again. She heard the smart, crisp crack of a whip, and the carriage began to move.

*I*t was a beautiful, stately city, much grander than Alice had envisioned. Oak trees arched high, touching one another over tidy parks dotted with statues, creating natural cathedrals dappled with evening light. Homes with bowfronts and intricately molded iron banisters were everywhere. The carriage clattered over cobblestones, winding upward into the narrow streets of Beacon Hill, passing by tall houses dotted with glossy black shutters, each one with an iron boot scraper gracing its entrance. Clearly, tracking mud into these homes would not be tolerated.

She felt suddenly inadequate as to what she was supposed to do and be. This was Boston? She had never quite imagined the solid *permanence* of it all. Everywhere, well-swept streets of red brick, with soberly dressed matrons carrying packages wrapped in twine, chatting together as they strolled home. Even the horses seemed calm. It wasn't like Lowell, where people elbowed one another on the streets and rushed about, carrying bags, shouting to each other, and pushing prams. Lowell was raw and unpredictable. Here, everything felt seasoned by time.

The carriage slowed at the peak of Beacon Hill, and Alice gazed at the mansion ahead pointed out by the carriage driver. "That's where you're going, miss!" he shouted.

The horses started up a steep brick driveway lined in stone, straining slowly past a grove of high maple trees gnarled with age. The house rose above all others around it and, bathed in the golden light of a setting winter sun, had a misty wash of unreality. Alice counted: five stories high.

The horses stopped. Alice couldn't take her eyes off the gracefully carved fanlight above the entrance as she lifted her skirts. Feeling quite grand in her borrowed dress, she stepped from the carriage.

Only then did the house door open; Samuel Fiske was standing in the entrance. She hoped her boots weren't caked in mud.

"Welcome," Samuel said. And this time there was no doubt. He was smiling, though somewhat tentatively.

Alice walked into the center hall, shoulders straight, clutching Jane's velvet bag in her gloved hand, trying not to gawk at the immensity of the place. An old Dutch clock was on her left, its silvery chimes marking the hour as she walked inside. A wide, gracefully curved staircase carpeted in red velvet swirled upward from the entrance hall to rooms out of sight. How was such a beautiful staircase built? The walls were covered in a silk floral paper, the likes of which she had never seen. To the right of the stairs hung—among others—an oil portrait of a man staring with haughty demeanor, his likeness encased in an elaborately gilded frame. There was a restraint to it all. Nothing was vulgar, and it all had the muted patina of age.

"My grandfather," Samuel murmured. "He does look as if he might bite, doesn't he?"

She tried to smile.

"This way," Samuel said, beckoning her forward.

She put one foot ahead of the other, intimidated by the marble flooring, looking up only as they entered a large room that took her breath away. A library? Who had libraries like this? Deep-burgundy velvet curtains; walls of books perfectly aligned in glass-fronted cabinets. To read them all, how wonderful that would be, but she must not let herself be dazzled. She needed to pay attention to the people gathered here; they were already looking her up and down with daunting precision.

She focused first on Hiram Fiske and his daughter, Daisy. The family patriarch seemed to have stopped in midpace, hands clasped behind his back as he gave her a brisk nod. Daisy, wearing a silk jacket tossed carelessly over her roller-printed cotton gown, looked as if she had just collapsed into the sofa in which she was lounging. Sitting next to her was an elderly woman with hair as white as Hiram's—perfectly sculpted but thin as spun sugar. A frosty-white lace collar had almost disappeared under the ample folds of her neck. Her cheeks blushed pink, and she seemed to be dozing.

The other woman in the room rose from her chair and faced Alice. Her face was long and narrow, and she wore her dark hair parted in the center. Elaborate sausage-shaped curls bounced when she stood. "How very nice to meet you," she said in a cultivated, thin voice that conveyed the opposite. "Samuel, please introduce this young lady."

"Miss Barrow, this is my mother—Mother, Alice Barrow."

"And this is my grandmother." He nodded in the direction of the woman on the divan, who instantly opened one eye and nodded affably.

"A good-looking girl, Samuel, which I'm sure you already noticed," she said.

Samuel turned scarlet as Daisy laughed, a shrill little tinkle of noise that shattered in the air. "Oh, we're off to a good start, aren't we?" she said.

Hiram Fiske put out a hand to Alice. "Please come sit down,

Miss Barrow. We are delighted to have you visit. Hopefully we can learn from each other."

Alice sat down, tucking her boots underneath her skirt, folding her hands in her lap. A young maid in a white cap eyed her with a chilly expression. Alice's clothes didn't fool her.

"Tea, miss?" she asked.

Alice nodded, feeling the girl's disdain, and reached for a cup.

"Oh my, you drink tea with your gloves on?" Daisy said innocently.

Alice's hand shook slightly as she pulled back. "No, of course not," she said. Slowly she took off her beautiful gloves and folded them carefully in her lap. They would not fit in her bag.

"You are wearing a lovely cameo," she said to Daisy, admiring an intricate piece adorning the other woman's long elegant neck.

"What do you know about cameos?" Daisy asked.

"I liked making them before I came to the mill." At night, by candlelight, she had worked with tiny brushes, enjoying nothing more, even as her father declared making such silly little gewgaws was a waste of time.

"Of *this* quality?"

"Probably not."

"Have you cut from ivory?"

"I have cut only from clay, I'm afraid."

"Hmmmm. I see."

"Where is Jonathan?" Hiram interrupted, turning to his son. "He was supposed to be here."

"I don't know," Samuel replied. Jonathan did whatever he wanted to do and on his own terms, and Father knew it. It didn't matter at the moment. He was more interested in watching Alice Barrow, with stiff grace, fend off his sister's snobbery. The hint of fire in her eyes drew him.

Hiram snorted his annoyance. "Well, we're not waiting for him. Miss Barrow, let's get down to business. You have some complaints, as I understand. Are they shared by others?"

"Yes, they are, Mr. Fiske," she said.

"Are you sure?"

"There are things happening that people are worried about."

"We'll get to that. Let me tell you a little about the history of our company first and why we do things the way we do."

Five minutes later he was still talking. Alice eyed him steadily, trying to nod in the right places, afraid of taking even a sip of her tea.

"I think Miss Barrow is familiar with our background, Father," Samuel said, breaking in finally. He could see the shine of perspiration on Alice's forehead. She shouldn't have to sit here and endure his father's standard lecture.

"That's good, Samuel. Cut him off, he goes on too long all the time." His grandmother was stirring on the divan, her voice surprisingly robust. "Let's hear about the problems the girl is here to tell us about."

Alice took a deep breath. She had written them all down, choosing the proper words; let them help her now. "We are plagued by the heat when all the machines are running," she said. "Cotton fibers float in the air. We breathe them in. If we were able to open windows, we could breathe better."

"My dear, if you opened windows, the cotton would dry out," Hiram said.

"Surely there's a compromise."

"Surely you're not strangled for breath," Daisy broke in. "Nothing so melodramatic as that?"

"Forgive me, I don't consider it melodramatic. The fibers get into our lungs, and we cough up cotton balls."

"Oh, for heaven's sake."

"And those who suck thread through the needles ingest even more. At the mill, they call it the kiss of death."

"Oh, well, here's the melodrama," Daisy pronounced.

Alice flushed, unsure what to say next.

"The girls do seem to have respiratory problems," Samuel said quickly. "We're getting reports."

"Well, why haven't I been told about them?" Hiram looked at his son with irritation.

This wasn't the time or place to remind his father that he preferred to ignore reports of problems at the mill. "I'll inform the overseers to do so more frequently," Samuel said.

"Well, what else, miss?" Hiram's tone was one that had made more than one executive step back.

He was not just trying, he was *expecting* to intimidate her. Her fingers tightened in her lap. She would be forthright and simply say her piece. "Mr. Fiske, there are numerous safety problems."

"Please elaborate."

"Part of our job is to clean the cotton out of our machines at the end of each workday. But the machines sit so high, we can't reach up far enough to clean them thoroughly. And a couple of times, the cotton has ignited. Fire is a true danger."

"Surely there are stools to stand on?" Hiram shot back.

How could he not understand what she was saying? "We've tried; the stools are not high enough," she said. "And we worry greatly about the belts—they come too close to the workers."

"What does that mean?"

"The girls' hair gets caught up in the belts," she explained. "We work very fast, and we get tired and less cautious near the end of a long shift. One girl was almost killed a few weeks ago."

"You young women should keep your hair in tight buns. It's only proper hygiene," Mrs. Fiske interrupted.

Hiram was getting restless. He pulled out his heavy gold pocket watch and checked the time. "It's almost dinnertime, I see. Miss Barrow, any factory has hazards. Do you not think we worry about your safety? Doesn't housing, money in your pockets, and food on the table count?"

"Of course they do, Mr. Fiske. But I'm trying to tell you about working conditions."

"As to those respiratory problems, we'll see what Dr. Stanhope has to say. Now—we've done something for you, and you could do something for the company. Here's my proposal: I would like it if you agreed to be our voice—our interpreter, if you will. If there are concerns, we could explain our mission and goals through you to the other employees."

Alice leaned back in her seat, making sure to hold tight to her gloves, her throat constricting. These people knew nothing. No, that wasn't it. They *wanted* to know nothing. Samuel caught her eye. She wondered first if he understood—there was a bemusement, a separation from all this, in his expression. Or was that only what she hoped to see?

"I wouldn't feel qualified for that, sir. I'm sure you are the best interpreter of your goals. I can only tell you what I think is not working right and ask you to fix it."

Hiram frowned. "You may be passing up a good opportunity, young lady." His eyes glazed over, not exactly cold. No, worse than that: indifferent. He glanced again at his watch and stood, tugging at his waistcoat. "We've spent enough time here. Let us move to the dining room."

Everyone stood quite dutifully and filed through the door to the dining room, with only Samuel holding back. He offered his arm to Alice. With only a second of hesitation, she took it and joined the group.

*T*he dining room was beautiful. Glorious, luminous rose-painted walls, elaborate moldings—and another oil painting of the same formidable ancestor Alice had spied in the entrance hall. Samuel's grandfather seemed to be staring at her, judging her, silently telling her she did not belong.

She looked around, unsure what to do next. A servant pulled out a chair, nodding to her expectantly. She gathered her skirt and sat down—relieved to hide her shoes under the hanging linen cloth—then looked up. The dining table at which she now sat was almost dwarfed by a large chandelier overhead that was ablaze with flickering candles. The effect was breathtaking.

"I do hope you like sweetbreads," Samuel's mother said.

"Of course," she responded, wondering what they were. She hardly heard the conversation at first, which was monopolized by Hiram, leaving her a little time to get her bearings. She stared at the delicate, shimmering silver table setting in front of her. So many forks; so many spoons. But Mrs. Holloway had given her a brisk lesson on the cutlery she would face. She could manage it all, surely.

But when the dinner dishes were brought in by servants, she could not help an audible gasp. Two tureens of soup, one at each end of the table. Then a roast joint on a gleaming china platter rimmed in gold, placed with flourish in front of Hiram. Clearly, he was to dismember it with formidable knives.

A fowl dish was brought in next. Alice thought it was roast duck, but the orange slices, parsley, and other condiments hid its shape, and she wasn't sure. The servant handed her a plate with some strange food. She felt a shiver of alarm. What was this?

"The sweetbreads are delicious," Samuel said, flicking a glance in her direction.

Grateful, she nodded, feeling less vulnerable. She sipped soup, nibbled at the fowl—yes, it was duck—and realized finally that no one was paying attention to her at all. She need not fear scorn. She might as well be a statue in one of Boston's numerous parks. The Fiskes had decided she was invisible.

Only once did Daisy turn to her. "You said you make cameos?"

"I do."

"Do show me your work. If you're skilled enough, I might commission you to make one for me at some point."

Alice started to respond, delighted, but Daisy had turned away without waiting for an answer.

Disaster came with dessert. Even though Alice cut carefully into a cream pastry, it slid from the fragile china plate with dreadful speed and dropped onto the richly hued carpet. She could almost see the heavy cream sinking in, the stain spreading. God, how could she be so clumsy? "I'm sorry," she said, jumping up to find a cleaning cloth.

The young maid who had served her tea was already bent over the stain, cleaning it up. She stood after finishing, casting a triumphant glare at Alice; oh, the message was clear. You are who you are, and no pretensions.

Alice lifted her eyes to the table and began an apology to her hostess. But Mrs. Fiske, a blank look on her face, was chatting with Daisy. Hiram was giving orders to a servant. None of them seemed to notice; not out of politeness but because, to them, she wasn't even there. Was she wrong? Her gaze shifted to Samuel, studying his face. What was it she saw? Chagrin? No, embarrassment. He was embarrassed for his family, not for her. How she knew that, she couldn't say.

He stood. "I want to thank Miss Barrow for coming," he said, cutting into the chatter of his family. "She had the gumption to face us here tonight." He felt a stab of anger, seeing in her eyes the knowledge of her complete invisibility at this table. He wanted to ease this recognition, to allow her a graceful exit. How did he do this without sounding patronizing? "The truth is, we are not easy people to face; I'm sure you'd agree," he said to her.

Alice, surprised, gave him a tentative smile. The others stared at Samuel.

"Miss Barrow, my sincere appreciation. We will follow up on your concerns." He gripped the edge of the table, catching the sympathetic eye of his grandmother, now fully awake—the one anchor in this family he had always been able to count on. "Mary Beth"— he turned to the servant—"will you please show Miss Barrow to her room? The carriage for her trip back will arrive at eight in the morning."

Samuel turned and strode out of the room, surprised at his own sudden anger. What was he doing? He had allowed his self-control to drop. But watching that young woman tiptoe her way through the rituals of a world she obviously knew little about had impressed him, leaving him troubled.

CHAPTER EIGHT

DECEMBER 20, 1832

*T*he ride home was clattery and bumpy; the weather wet and dismal. There was no sun today, just a sky of sullen, gray clouds. It all matched Alice's mood as she stared through the window out onto a wintry terrain.

All this visit had done was make the Fiske family feel better about themselves. They knew nothing about the people who worked for them. She was usually indifferent to that; it was a truth acknowledged with a shrug and a laugh and forgotten on payday. Why had she come? It had been the allure of stepping inside a fantasy; that's what it had been. And she had wanted it, and now she was angry with herself. All they saw was a waif, a supplicant. A woman who knew nothing of the proper etiquette for wearing gloves. She squeezed her hands together, taking comfort from the soft leather of her friend's gift. Lovey would have something wonderfully acerbic to say about the whole experience.

"I hesitate to say this to you, but I do wonder—why did you invite me?" she had asked Samuel just before stepping into the carriage. He was one of them, even after those graceful words at the dinner table; she must be cautious.

"To discuss your concerns," he said.

There were dark circles under his eyes. Could it be that he, too, hadn't slept much last night? "But no one was interested."

Her honesty made him falter. She stood so close, one foot on the lowest step of the carriage. She would vanish in a moment.

"I apologize for my family; I had hoped for something better."

She looked up into his face. "Mr. Fiske, I thank you for your words at the table last night." She took a deep breath. "You have been kind. But I believe I was brought here to feel awed and intimidated, someone to send back to Lowell with a nice story about sipping tea off of fine china, provided by the open-minded Fiske family. Please tell me—am I wrong?"

"Not entirely, and I tell you that in all honesty."

She started to say more but feared she might endanger her job if she did so. Instead, she climbed into the carriage.

He reached through the open window, his hand only an inch or two from hers. "I will be at the mill next weekend," he said, then paused.

His face was so close. She could have reached out and touched him. She waited. What was he asking?

"Perhaps I could show you around and explain how the mill was developed—"

"I'm on the weekend shift."

"Well, then," he said helplessly.

And then the carriage pulled away, hitting, she was convinced, every possible bump in the road on the way back to Lowell.

*U*nsettled, Samuel watched until Alice's carriage vanished from sight. He had given her every courtesy and had been treated rudely. He had every right to be annoyed. It was a train of thought with which he was familiar, but it didn't satisfy, not today.

"Well, after hearing that little exchange, I'd say your flirtation with the Barrow girl didn't quite work out."

He wheeled around to see Jonathan standing in the doorway, looking red eyed, his clothes rumpled.

"Where have you been?"

"What business is that of yours?"

"I couldn't care less, but Father was angry that you didn't show up for dinner last night."

"Oh yes, the 'democracy at work' dinner. Don't you think we're both getting a little too old to be doing his bidding every minute of the day? Maybe you aren't, but I certainly am."

Samuel willed himself not to respond. His brother looked too brittle, not just his usual mocking self. "Where have you been?" he asked again.

"Carousing, of course," Jonathan replied. "And having a good time doing it. A little carousing wouldn't hurt you, Samuel—might loosen you up."

A flash of memory, a twist of melancholy, gave Samuel pause. There had been a time when Jonathan was little, adoring, looking up to his big brother, holding his hand, asking him questions. Still, there was something there in his brother's eyes this morning that reminded Samuel of that younger boy.

"Let's get you some coffee," he said quietly, putting an arm around Jonathan's shoulders. They turned and walked back into the house.

Daisy sat alone in the dining room, picking at a boiled egg in a silver egg holder, flipping through a copy of *The Lady's Book*.

"What do you like so much about that magazine?" Jonathan said as he sank into a chair, yawning.

"Fashion stories, of course," she answered promptly, closing it hastily. "There's nothing else for me to do."

Only Samuel noticed that she had pushed between the pages a

scribbled piece of paper. Once before he had picked up such a slip of paper that had fallen from her magazine and saw a poem written in his sister's hand. It had not been very good; annoyed with himself for having read it, he had said nothing.

"Why were you so unkind to Alice Barrow?" he asked.

"Oh, here we go, I've been expecting another display of indignation from you. Has it occurred to you that *you* were the rude one last night, dismissing your family as badly behaved? You can be so pretentiously noble. I'll wager Father is furious." She hit the egg with her spoon; when a thin spurt of yolk shot upward, she exclaimed in annoyance.

"Sounds like I missed something interesting," Jonathan said as a servant began to pour him a cup of coffee and then rushed instead to Daisy's side, murmuring apologies.

"I want a *six*-minute egg," Daisy complained. "Not a *five*-minute egg, for heaven's sake. Hasn't the cook got that right yet?"

The maid took the egg cup, vanishing into the kitchen. Samuel watched her go, then stared at the morning light dancing over the fresh breakfast cloth, producing prisms of color.

"Daisy, this isn't like you," he began gently.

"Please don't start on all that again," she interrupted. "I'm just not going to try to defend myself to you anymore. I hate my life, and that's all there is to it." There were tears in her eyes as she pushed back from the table, pulling the soft belt of her morning gown close, and left the room.

"Poor Samuel, you really take it on the chin from us, don't you?" Jonathan chuckled as he reached for a slice of buttered toast on the table. "Now of course, with Daisy gone, you can lecture *me*. Go to it, Brother. You'd better hurry. I have things to do today."

Here was that familiar feeling of being weighed down by something ponderous, forced into a role. Samuel stared at his own coffee cup, weary. "No lectures," he said.

The brothers sat in silence.

*I*t felt good to be back. The other girls gathered around Alice, excited, laughing, filled with questions as they all sat down at their crowded table to eat pea soup and boiled corned beef.

What did she eat? What did the silver look like? Describe the dresses. Did you sleep on silk sheets?

She couldn't disappoint them, and so she gave them bits of the fantasy they wanted, describing the chandelier in the dining room, the grand entrance, Daisy's cameo.

"Was it like the pretty one you keep in a box?" Ellie asked.

"How do you know about that?" Alice asked in surprise.

"I'm sorry," Ellie said, aware now all eyes were on her. "I saw a pretty box, and I peeked inside. Please don't get mad; I never touched it."

The child looked so chagrined, Alice felt sorry for her. "It was my mother's," she said. "I made it for her."

"Why don't you wear it?"

Alice smiled. "I don't really know, but it reminds me of a happier time."

The silence at the table was almost tender; all of them could remember other, happier times.

"And you know what? The one I made is prettier than hers."

"Good," Mary-o declared. "I don't like her at all."

The mood was broken, and all were cheery again. But Alice kept glancing toward the door. "Where's Lovey?" she asked.

"I don't know," Tilda said with a shrug. "We all know she's usually here by now. Lovey's not one to miss dinner."

"Except when she's having a bit of fun," said Mrs. Holloway, putting a bowl of turnips and parsnips on the table. "I keep expecting her one of these days to up and go. She's got a restless heart, that one."

"Go?" Alice said, dismayed, putting down her fork. "She wouldn't do that without telling us."

Tilda patted her hand. "But she's been here at this mill before and left without telling anyone and then showed up again. She'll probably pop up in a few hours, it's just her way." Her voice turned wistful. "It does leave a gap when she's not around."

Alice stared at her bowl of soup. Lovey wouldn't do that, even though she had her way of disappearing when she so chose. She might be off somewhere, but she'd be back for work in the morning. Wouldn't she want a full report on the visit to the Fiske mansion?

That night Alice waited on the porch. After all were in bed and the boardinghouse was silent, she continued to wait. Once she thought she saw Lovey's form hurrying toward her, but it was a trick of the shadows.

By five in the morning, still no Lovey. Alice stood, bones and muscles cramped and aching, and went inside. Surely she would be at her loom today, probably with some outlandish story.

No, Lovey was not at the mill. Alice felt her stomach cramping more and more with each passing hour. The others offered sympathy, but after a few jokes about missing Lovey's jauntiness, they lapsed into uneasy silence. Only Delia spoke of her. "I have my little girl because of Lovey," she murmured to Alice as they worked their looms.

All thoughts of Lovey were set aside late in the morning when a spindle cracked off a loom, flew through the air, and punched into a girl's head. The girl, one of the Irish from Newton, was unconscious for five or ten minutes before she came around, and that caused a stir. Mill workers began meeting in little clusters after their shifts, indignantly complaining about old machines and careless overseers.

"And you," said one man in an almost-hostile voice, pointing to Alice as she left work, "what did you find out in Boston? Are the Fiskes going to pay attention and do something?"

"I don't know," she said. "I told them. I can't make them do anything."

"Well, who else can?"

"Talk to Samuel Fiske. I think he'll listen."

"They'll listen when we fight back."

She trudged on home, empty and weary. She wanted her friend. She wanted Lovey.

ON COOPER ISLAND

The morning had dawned sunny and crisp. Just the kind of morning for taking care of such chores as looking for a missing calf, which is what John Durfee had set out to do, heading through the fields of his farm on Cooper Island, a short distance from Lowell. As he herded his animals toward the yard where he kept his winter hay, he noticed a strange shape, what looked first like a bundle of clothes, hanging from a pole that supported the roof of a haystack. He moved forward. What was he seeing?

It couldn't be. But it was.

A woman's body, suspended from a rope around her neck, hung frozen, her knees bent and her toes just above the ground. One hand was pressed against her breast; the other hung stiffly by her side. A rope was looped tightly around her throat.

He turned her slightly, pushed her dark hair back, and gazed at her face. Gently, he let go, ashamed of his immediate relief. No, he didn't know her. He straightened and stared down at the woman, wanting to say some kind of prayer. So young. He looked around, realizing he was alone in this isolated place. Suddenly nervous, he thrashed his way through winter-dry bushes toward his farm to run for help.

CHAPTER NINE

*I*t took two men to lift the frozen body and carry it across the winter-hardened earth and hoist it into the mud-splattered wagon. They had stood self-consciously around the dead girl for a few minutes, charged with another uncomfortable duty. "Take note of everything," the sheriff demanded. "For the inquest."

The woman's cloak was properly fastened, but her shoes, one soiled with mud, had been neatly placed eighteen inches to the right of her stockinged feet. The ribbons of her bonnet were caught under the cord hung tight around her neck. Durfee—with a nod from Hector Borden, the sheriff—then cut the cord and lowered the body to the ground.

Borden directed the loading with as much cool precision as possible. There were four of them, and they worked gently, in a state of embarrassment at their own vaporous grief. A girl, not much more. The morning light made them want to avert their faces; to think of their children, still asleep, left them teetering on the edge of the fear that all parents share.

The reins snapped sharply; the cart lurched forward.

At the farmhouse, three women dressed in fresh white aprons stood in the doorway, watching the wagon bounce over the rocky ground toward them. Nobody spoke much. Not at first.

"Suicide," the sheriff said to one of the women, who happened to be his wife. "Probably destitute."

Clara Borden stared at the rope still tight around the girl's neck. "She hung herself?" she asked.

"I would think so," he said.

"Who is she?"

"Don't know, but she's dressed like a mill girl. We're checking."

His wife pointed toward a man down on knobby knees praying in the vegetable garden, a frown spreading across her well-worn face. "He's doing a good job of flattening my pumpkin vines," she said.

"Don't mind him, Clara. He's a preacher, name of Wilbur Ralston. Started praying as soon as we brought her in. These Methodists, I don't know what to make of the stagy ways of some of them."

"How did he hear so fast?"

"Everyone in town knows by now. Says maybe she was a member of his church."

"Well, if she was, it didn't do her much good, did it," Clara said. She turned and walked into the kitchen, the other two women following dutifully. They had a job to do.

The body was laid out on the bright red-and-white oilcloth covering the kitchen table, which only recently—and hastily—had been cleared of hot oatmeal and pitchers of cream. Clara stared at the girl before them, noting the calluses on her fingers. A mill girl, of course. With a pretty, finely drawn face. The clarity of her young features framed by strands of frost-dampened hair was a bit unnerving; they seemed to still hold the fleeting ghost of animation. She looked like a girl used to smiling and laughing.

"Well, let's get to work," Clara said.

None of them had done this washing before. Each worked gently, as if not wanting to hurt the girl, massaging warm water into the folds of her small, young breasts and between her legs. They stared at her swollen eyes, her belly, her arms; mostly at her neck, darkened with bruises. They could see what appeared to be the indentation of fingers and thumbs. Silently, each put her own hand over the inden-tations; they looked at one another, lips tight. Finally, only Clara could say it out loud. "Suicide?" she said in a troubled tone.

"Maybe murder?" said another.

"Maybe."

"There are no murders here," protested Mariba Ford, the third woman. "We're a peaceable lot."

"Always a first time."

They continued their work, plucking out twigs from the dead girl's hair, brushing away dirt from her arms and legs and cleaning blood from under her fingernails. They stared at the results of their work. A clean, naked girl.

"I'll get my good nightgown, it's white," said Mariba.

"Hurry," said Clara. She pulled a worn comforter over the body, up to the girl's neck. "There will be people here very soon. Poor thing, she deserves some shielding from view."

Her husband cleared his throat from behind her. "The doctor and the coroner are here," he said. "Dr. Stanhope, from Lowell. Doing his rounds up here; we got him as he was leaving."

"No good he can do," his wife responded.

"We need confirmation of death."

Clara looked at the tall older man standing, hat in one hand, a cane in the other, next to her husband. She had little confidence in his skills, but she had little confidence in any medical skills. At least he didn't pretend to be important. She stepped aside.

Benjamin Stanhope looked down at the girl, the color draining slowly from his face. Silently he handed his cane to Hector Borden. With a slight tremor in his hands, he turned her head. The rope around her neck was imbedded a good half-inch into her flesh. He did not pull down the comforter; instead, he stepped back.

"You know her?"

He nodded.

"A mill girl?"

He nodded again. "Lovey Cornell, a patient of mine," he said heavily.

"What do you know about her?" John Durfee pressed. "Mr. Hicks here"—he nodded at an elderly man squinting over glasses—"is the coroner. Needs a little observational help, I feel free to say."

"She was with child," the doctor managed. His face was stiff as he lifted his hat to his head and turned away. "I'll notify the Fiske family."

Gasps from the women. "Poor thing," Mariba finally managed.

"Pregnant?" The clergyman from the garden had followed the coroner inside. He looked horrified. "She's not one of ours, then."

"What do you mean?" snapped Clara.

"We take no one of low virtue."

"You and your kind. Just leave my house," Clara said.

Elihu Hicks, the elderly coroner, stepped forward next, peering shortsightedly at the body; his examination was brief. He studied the blackened bruises on Lovey's arms and legs. He examined her swollen lower lip where she had bit down, probably as the rope went taut. He probed her belly. An autopsy would be performed before burial to confirm her pregnancy, but all seemed in order. In silence, he scribbled out his verdict in a worn black leather notebook, nodded, and walked out.

That evening, Benjamin Stanhope stepped slowly up onto the porch of Boott Boardinghouse 52. He took his hat off, clutching it tightly, and knocked on the door.

Alice had seen him through the window, noticed the slump of his shoulders and the way he clawed at his hat, and knew. Right then, as she took in a deep breath, Alice inhaled for the first time the smell of her own grief. It would be the moment she would remember most vividly: the darkened sky, the crisp air, the sharp corners of the chipped glass doorknob cutting into her hand, the sound of Benjamin Stanhope's boots shuffling reluctantly up the steps. A page of Mary-o's songbook had come loose and been blown into a corner of the porch by an errant wind.

She opened the door.

"I bring sad news," he began. His words had been carefully rehearsed, but it didn't matter. Alice slumped against the door, banging the wood with her fists as he delivered the news.

She didn't want to believe it. No, not Lovey.

One by one, tiptoeing silently, arms crossed tightly in front of their chests, the girls in the boardinghouse gathered in the parlor. Pressing themselves almost self-protectively to the walls, they leaned against one another. No whisperings or questions. The sight of the company doctor in their midst told them all they needed to know. The warnings and scoldings of disapproving relatives when they came here, the brazen daring of pulling on aprons and walking into a factory for the first time, excited and free, eager to pocket pay and stay respectable—all of it was jumbled together in this room as they waited for the doctor to confirm their fears.

Benjamin Stanhope recited the facts. Alice rocked back and forth in one of the chairs, pulling her knees to her chest as she listened, holding them tight.

"Are you saying this was suicide?" Mary-o asked, tears trickling down her cheeks.

"That's what the coroner says," Stanhope replied.

"No," Alice said forcefully. "Lovey would never commit suicide, never."

"There was a particular circumstance," he began, and then stopped.

No one spoke. But instant understanding swept the room, the kind that comes without language, that sends a fist into the gut.

"Dear Lord, the same old story," Mrs. Holloway said. Her voice held a deep, sad weariness. She stood in the doorway, still in her dinner apron, arms folded in front of her.

Stanhope started to speak, then paused, obviously hoping Mrs. Holloway would save him the trouble. She did.

"The girl was pregnant, of course," she said.

There were moans around the room.

"You knew?" asked Stanhope.

"No. But why else? I've seen it many times before, poor girl."

Benjamin Stanhope cleared his throat, vaguely unsettled now at losing the center of attention. "That is correct," he said.

"How do you know?"

"She came to see me. I asked her symptoms and confirmed it for her."

"Oh, God, we would have helped her." It was Jane, pious, disapproving Jane, wringing her hands. "We would have done something."

The room went silent as they thought of what that might be, of what it could not be, of their own helplessness. "She couldn't tell anybody, I know how it works," Delia said. "One whisper, and you lose your job. I know."

"No," Alice said. It was as if she hadn't heard any of them. "She didn't kill herself. It didn't happen that way."

Benjamin Stanhope was now in a hurry to leave. He put his hat on his head and stood, reaching for his cane, edging toward the door. "My condolences to her family," he muttered.

"There is none that we know of," Alice said.

The girls stared at one another in confusion, realizing how little they knew about Lovey.

"She has at least a mother, I think in Fall River," Alice went on. "They were not on good terms."

"Where will she be buried?" Tilda, always the practical one, asked.

"On the farm where she was found. After the inquest."

"No church service?"

Again, Stanhope cleared his throat. "They called in a preacher who said first she might be a member of his church, but when he heard she was pregnant, he refused to do a service."

"Odious worm," spat out Mrs. Holloway.

"They're not going to dig a hole and throw her in. That's not what's going to happen, I won't let it." Even Mrs. Holloway paused at the ferocity of Alice's declaration.

"Doctor, what else can you tell us?" Mary-o asked.

Benjamin Stanhope tugged at his collar, looking desperately uncomfortable. He shoved one hand into his pocket and pulled out a key. "This was in her pocket," he said.

"For her storage case, I suspect," said Mrs. Holloway, stepping forward and taking the key.

"She will not be tossed in a hole," Alice repeated. Her resolve steadied her. She searched Stanhope's face, trying to find an entry point; a weak spot. Something more, something that would make all this untrue.

"I must go," he said. "Please do brace yourselves for a deluge of reporters and the like. People are upset. I understand one of the Fiske sons is coming to offer his family's condolences. You certainly have mine." He turned and pulled open the front door and exited, head hunched forward, heavily burdened by the sadness and pain he had introduced into the Boott Boardinghouse, number 52.

After a bleak, barely touched dinner, Lovey's roommates crowded together around Lovey's bed. Mrs. Holloway got down on her hands and knees and pulled out a battered trunk, its leather straps worn thin; mute acknowledgment of the gypsy nature of Lovey's life.

Alice knelt down next to her, inserted the key, and paused before turning it. The act felt intrusive, almost a violation. None of them had a right to paw through Lovey's possessions. Alice wanted no such task, but she knew already, without the words fully formed, that Lovey's privacy no longer existed. It would be as piteously exposed as her body must have been on the sheriff's kitchen table. She turned the key, acknowledging also that she shared with the other girls something else: a reluctance to know.

The lid was heavy, the hinges rusty, protesting as Alice pushed it open. She peered inside.

There was very little there. A few trinkets, including a brooch with glittering green and yellow stones that Lovey had bought on their last trip into the Lowell store. "Who needs diamonds?" She had laughed, pinning it to her shirtwaist. "They're so ostentatious. Isn't that a wonderful word? I read it somewhere and just found out what it means."

A Bible was tucked into a corner, the one from which Lovey had torn out pages, shocking more than a few of the girls in the mill. Next to it were the carefully stacked sheets of poetry that had adorned her loom. What else? A doll she had bought and tucked away as a surprise for Ellie's birthday. Two shirtwaists. A bright purple off-the-shoulder dress with flared short sleeves that had horrified Mrs. Holloway when Lovey wore it to church. Not much more. There were no explanations here.

"What about that?" Mary-o said, pointing to a small bundle of tied papers tucked into a corner of the trunk. Alice reached down and pulled out the package, untying the string that held it together. In her hands were three pieces of paper, each containing a scrawled note—one on plain white paper and two more, written on yellow and on pink stationery. She peered into the trunk, seeing what the papers had hidden: a glass vial filled with liquid and wrapped in newsprint.

Alice opened one note and read it out loud. It was dated December 8.

I will be here on the 20th if pleasant at the place named at 6 o'clock.
If not pleasant the next Monday eve. Say nothing.

"It's unsigned," Alice said. The others stared at her in silence as she opened the pink one, again a note about a planned meeting. And finally the yellow one:

No word to anyone. Bring the letters I sent to our meeting.

"It isn't Lovey's handwriting," Alice said, showing the notes to the others. "Clearly she was meeting someone."

Mrs. Holloway nodded. "There's no other possible explanation," she said.

Delia held up the glass vial, squinting at it. "It has a yellowish fluid in it," she said. "Medicine, perhaps?" They looked at each other with uncertainty.

"We'll get these to the sheriff in the morning," Mrs. Holloway said.

As Alice prepared to close the trunk lid, she spied a scrap of paper caught under a bottom slat. A wrinkled piece, torn raggedly from a notebook. The carelessly scribbled words were instantly recognizable. No question, this was Lovey's handwriting. For a strange second, she could almost see Lovey chewing on the end of her pencil as she wrote, the way she did when she copied poems or worked on her manifesto. She could see the pencil scrawling out her message, even feel the haste with which Lovey must have written it. She reached down and picked up the piece of paper, which lay crumpled and gray in the palm of her hand, and read it aloud.

If I should be missing enquire of the Rev. Mr. Avery of Bristol. He will know where I am.

Dec. 20th. SM Cornell

A memory flashed: the piece of paper Lovey had pulled from her pocket when she stood by Alice's Boston-bound carriage.

"Who is the Reverend Avery?" Alice asked out loud.

The girls looked at one another, puzzled. Except for Mary-o, who turned pale and covered her face.

"Do you know who he is?" Alice asked.

Silence first. When she spoke, Mary-o's voice was toneless, almost resigned. "Yes," she said. Her eyes were watering. She stared at Alice across the sparsely filled, almost-forlorn trunk yawning open between them. There wasn't a sound in the room. It was so still, Alice could hear the clattering of dinner dishes and pots being put away in the kitchen.

"Tell me."

Mary-o's chin was trembling. "I can't tell you, I have to show you."

"Well, then, show me."

"You have to come somewhere with me. Tonight."

Alice said nothing, just walked to the hook where her coat hung and took it down, pulling it on and buttoning up. "I'm ready," she said.

They trudged for at least half an hour on a rock-littered path, with Mary-o leading and saying very little. Alice followed, pushing away branches that hung over the path, wary after being slapped in the face by one of them. Their shared sadness clung to every step. Finally Alice spied a clearing ahead, a broad circular space surrounded by tall trees as straight and forbidding as sentinels. The air was sharp with the scent of smoking campfires.

They emerged from the trees and stood on a small embankment that gave Alice a full view of the clearing. There was activity everywhere, almost as if they had stumbled on some kind of village. Dozens of small shabby tents dotted the landscape, with women standing over washtubs in front of them, scrubbing clothes and shouting to small children. In the center of the clearing was a raised platform built of rough wood painted crudely in white. A stream of men and women was emerging from the tents and making its way toward the platform, some singing, some appearing to pray.

"This is the revivalist campground," Alice said. It wasn't a question.

Mary-o nodded. "Don't move too much," she cautioned. "We don't want to be noticed."

Alice caught sight of a man who was striding toward a raised platform, his back to them. He was tall and walked with the graceful, confident fluidity of a person who expects to be known and respected. His frame was broad and powerful as he moved with ease past the tents, patting a child's head here, conversing with the women.

Curious, Alice turned to Mary-o to ask who he was. But her friend was focused on what was happening closer to the platform—which was clearly a stage. Alice could hear music, an instrument she could not place, until she realized it was a merging of voices, with no instrument at all. People gathering at the stage were swaying and chanting, arms overhead, at first gently, then louder and louder.

"What are they doing?" she asked Mary-o. They did not move from the edge of the clearing.

"Praying to be saved," Mary-o said sadly. "I was with them before. But I felt foolish when I didn't have any more money to give them. They didn't seem to care about my salvation after that."

"What have you brought me here to see?"

"Look," Mary-o whispered urgently, grabbing her arm. "There he is."

The man she had seen—clad now in a long white robe—had mounted the podium, moving gracefully, slowly raising his arms toward the sky. "Welcome, brothers and sisters," he said in a rich, warm voice that carried through the clearing. "Come all ye sinful and sorrowful, come to Jesus."

A wave of yearning sound rose from the crowd, a sound as full as that of a roaring wind. "Glory, glory!" shouted a husky man with scars on his face. His words were borne into the air, mixing, echoing with the other voices, producing a haunting refrain the likes of which Alice had never heard.

"Know this," the man in white said. "God accepts all sinners, if your penitence is real. There will be no hell, no ocean of liquid burning brimstone, for those who confess and pray." Murmurs through the crowd. "Come, prostrate yourselves before God," he coaxed, beckoning. "Come, come. Don't hold back."

A woman walked forward, head bowed, arms folded across her chest. She threw herself to the ground; a man followed suit. Then another.

The preacher looked down at their prone figures. "God welcomes you," he thundered. "Tonight brings you salvation." He turned to the larger crowd and began clapping his hands. "Shall we salute these reformed sinners?" he cried. With a sharp pivot, he signaled to a band of assistants poised below the stage. They ran forward, each one holding a large bucket. With practiced speed, they began wending their way through the singing crowd.

Through it all, the soothing drumbeat of the preacher's voice never stopped. "Support us, my friends, and know this—we are your pathway to God. Join us, and we will stand with each other through eternity."

"Yes, yes!" came cries from the crowd as more people surged forward, tossing money now into the buckets. The clapping began again. With tears streaming down their faces, men and women continued to prostrate themselves before the stage. The man in white stepped down to walk in their midst, speaking all the while, soothing them with the rhythm of his deep and powerful voice.

"Do you see, do you understand?" Mary-o murmured. Her eyes were shining with tears, and she seemed to be forcing herself not to step forward.

"Lovey wasn't part of this," Alice said. Her own heart was pumping faster, caught in the manipulative emotion of the scene. That frightened her.

"I thought I could convert her at first. But she saw things so clearly. She didn't mock and poke fun; she didn't do that to me. But she stood here and watched it all. I remember, she said, 'Who counts the money?' And I found myself watching through her eyes."

Riveted, Alice couldn't look away.

"He's coming this way." Mary-o stepped back. "Don't let him see you."

Too late. The man in the white robe was moving through the crowd with contained grace, in no hurry, offering blessings as he went. He stopped suddenly and looked up, directly at them. As if he had known they were there all along. He stared at them through round, green-tinted glasses that magnified the size of his eyes. His lips—full and soft—curved into something of a smile, except it wasn't quite a smile.

Alice found herself unable to move, held by the magnetic pull of his still, ordered face. She felt paralyzed for a moment. She thought of Lovey.

"Who is he?"

"The Reverend Ephraim Kingsbury Avery." Mary-o said his name slowly, almost fearfully, drawing out each vowel. "And once I knelt before him, too. Once I felt transported."

"Did you have reason to suspect—"

"She didn't treat him with reverence, not like the rest of us. She didn't pray. She liked the fact that he was smart. He noticed her."

"Then what—"

"Remember that time she and I first came in late?"

Alice nodded, recalling the flushed, excited look on Lovey's face when the two of them finally came home that night.

"I had gone to a final prayer session. Lovey said something about finding God in her own way. Jokingly—you know how she is." Mary-o's voice was shaky. "We were supposed to meet here, on this hill; she was so bold, she wanted to talk to him, face-to-face. To tease, to challenge? I never knew with Lovey. So I waited. It was a long time before she joined me. And she looked—you know, that reckless spark she would get in her eye; something had happened. I didn't know what to think."

Alice's eyes were still locked on the preacher named Avery. She couldn't let go. Then with one sudden, whipsaw movement that set his white robe swirling, he turned and strode away. Not with authority, as before. No, he looked like a man ready to run. Or perhaps that was wishful thinking.

*I*t was close to midnight when she and Mary-o returned to the boardinghouse. Mrs. Holloway was waiting in silence for them; no reprimands. Mary-o said nothing, just headed into the dormitory. But Alice did not take off her coat, asking Mrs. Holloway for Lovey's note.

"I have more questions for the doctor," she said. "And they can't wait."

"No, it's too late to go out again."

"It's important. I owe it to Lovey."

A moment of hesitation before Mrs. Holloway sighed and turned away. "I'll leave the latch off," she said. "Please be careful."

Alice half ran, half walked into town, a thin layer of ice crackling under her feet. When she reached Stanhope's office, she pounded hard on the door. There was no answer. She leaned down, picked up chunks of ice, and threw them at the second-floor windows. He was there; she knew he was.

He opened the door, dry metal hinges complaining shrilly.

"My goodness, do you know the hour?" he said, blinking sleepily.

"I'm sorry, but I must talk to you."

"Come in, Miss—"

"Barrow."

"Yes, Miss Barrow?"

"I've found a note Lovey wrote." She thrust it into his palms. "And three others in another hand, unsigned."

He read, then stared at the floor. He locked his hands, flexing the fingers up and down, his face weary with more than age. In the silence, Alice could hear an unseen wall clock ticking steadily.

"When she came to see me, Miss Cornell hoped what she suspected was untrue. But it was my unhappy duty to tell her she was wrong. I expected weeping and wailing, but she stayed under control. She even laughed, made a small joke. Strange."

Not strange; that was Lovey. Give her hard news, and she would find a way to toss her head, to mock, to challenge. Yet how terrible it must have been for her to sit here and have her fears confirmed.

"I tried to counsel her," Stanhope continued. "I told her the man who did this to her must be held accountable. That she needed to confront him and demand either marriage or money. She said that avenue was closed. Quite matter-of-factly." He looked at Alice, as if waiting for a reaction. She said nothing.

"Well, then I urged her to demand money or threaten to expose him. God help me, I did that." He paused, mopping his brow with a sturdy white handkerchief.

So all of this had burdened Lovey, all held inside, in the darkest places where secrets grow. Each secret demands more: another avoidance, another lie. The fact that she knew quite precisely how this worked was unnerving.

"Did she tell you who he was?"

"She said he was a prominent figure in the community."

"Nothing more?"

"No."

The face of that strangely mesmerizing man at the campground hovered in her memory. "Did she say he knew she was with child?"

Stanhope nodded. "He promised to help her. She was hoping he would give her money to go away and have the baby. She seemed determined to keep the child if she could."

Alice flashed back to Lovey's announcement that she was going to "learn about love." Was this what she had meant? "But he didn't."

"No, no. Instead he gave her a medicine to induce miscarriage. She was a clever woman, and she brought it to me first, to ask what it was. When I saw what he gave her, I was absolutely appalled." He stopped, took off his glasses, and pulled the same white handkerchief from his pocket, proceeding to scrub the spectacles vigorously.

"What was it?"

"I must be careful here, I'm not accusing anybody—"

He made her impatient. "Just tell me, please."

"It was oil of tansy—a poison. In large doses, it dissolves the intestines. He urged her to take thirty drops." He shook his head back and forth.

"That's too much?"

"Four drops is considered a large dose. If she had taken it, her internal organs would rot. It would have killed both her and the baby."

Alice drew her breath in sharply. "Was it in a small glass vial? A yellowish substance?"

"Yes," he said. "You mean she kept it?"

"It was in her trunk with letters that were obviously from him. That man wanted to kill her. . . ." Now, certain as she was, she could hardly swallow.

Stanhope raised his hand in a flutterly, feathery gesture of caution. "He may have said *three* drops, of course."

"Yes, well, the words do sound alike," she said evenly, holding back her impatience. She briefly closed her eyes, imagining how such news would affect Lovey. Had she truly expected help from that false man of God?

"How did she react?"

"She just sat there, in the chair you are in now, stunned, I think. I waited for her to understand the obvious. But then she laughed." He shook his head in disbelief. "She actually laughed. She said, 'Well, that makes me something of a fool, I suppose.' I know, that sounds strange."

"Not to me. I knew her. What else did she say?"

"She said he wasn't going to get away with it. She would expose him if he didn't help her."

They both fell silent.

"Why didn't you tell us all this at the house?" Alice finally said.

Stanhope leaned forward slightly, spreading his large, tapered hands wide, planting one on each thigh. The clock chimed, a thin, brittle sound.

"Miss . . . Barrow . . . more important, why didn't I stop her? I fear I sent her to her death." He paused, slowly straightening his glasses, which had slipped down over his narrow, almost spindly nose. "I know you all see me as someone afraid of my own shadow. But I thought I was, at least, capable of taking care of my patients."

She felt a need to offer something, but it could only be the half-truth that consoles or comforts and comes with a price. "You were trying to help," she said.

He didn't seem to hear her words.

"And I am left to wonder, what kind of doctor am I?" he said, staring now without focus.

She stood slowly. "I'm giving all the notes and the vial to the sheriff first thing in the morning," she said. Surely there was enough evidence to charge Avery with murder. "I wish you had told all this to the coroner, but now you must come forward."

Stanhope seemed to shrink in size as he looked away. "I can't be sure of what she said; I may be wrong."

She looked at him in disbelief. "You told me she said it was someone important in the community. Well, I think it was a revivalist preacher named Ephraim Avery. He had the opportunity and the motive."

"The inquest will uphold the coroner. And then who am I, possibly implicating an innocent man?"

He was dodging the obvious truth of his own words. "Are you afraid of something?" she asked, bewildered.

He cleared his throat and refused to look directly at her. Instead of answering, he said, "It's too late."

"What do you mean?"

"If this man Avery had anything to do with this, I'm sure he's fled already."

"And you would give up?" she sputtered.

"It's too late, I said. As the Bible says, 'The wicked flee when no man pursueth.'"

"Then perhaps someone should pursueth."

He smiled faintly and stood. "I wish I could help you, Miss Barrow. It is past midnight, and I have a full day tomorrow. I fear I have babbled on too much, and I regret that. Maybe your evidence will be useful to the authorities; I hope so."

"I'm giving the note to the sheriff in the morning. You could go with me and tell your story."

He shook his head vigorously. "I have a very busy day," he repeated.

"Dr. Stanhope, let me know when you decide to stand up for what you believe is true," she managed to say.

He replied with an unexpectedly strong voice. "Miss Barrow, you judge me quickly. Perhaps you at times feel uncertainty, but I will tell you only this—I am swallowed by it."

"Perhaps you mean paralyzed by fear," she said stiffly, and then turned to go.

*I*t was mid-afternoon the next day when Hiram Fiske deposited his valise on the floor of the entrance hall of the family's rooms at the Lowell Inn, his joints stiffer than usual from the hurried journey up from Boston. News of the mill girl's death had moved through town after town with incredible speed, and Lowell was in turmoil. You could feel it pulsating out from the clusters of agitated people talking at street corners. One of the mill girls had brought a note to the sheriff she found in the dead woman's trunk that implicated some itinerant preacher. So now the coroner was vacillating over his verdict of suicide. The old coot had better hurry and make up his mind, or the preacher would vanish, if he hadn't already.

Hiram sat down abruptly, unbuttoning his jacket while he talked about all this with Samuel, who had followed him into the room.

"We're not going to let this damage us," Hiram said. "If it's suicide, we'll do plenty of handholding to calm things down. If it's murder, we'll hire the best lawyers in the state and get a conviction as fast as possible. Nothing is going to cast a shadow over how well we take care of those girls and keep them safe. I won't allow it." He rubbed one fist into the other, straightening up. His energy was coming back.

"We'll have to do more than that," Samuel said.

"Obviously you have something to say."

"The agitators intend to turn this in their favor. If they can get people to believe the girls who work here aren't properly protected, they strengthen their hand. We'll face criticism on every front, especially safety."

"Slander, stupidity." Hiram slumped again, staring at nothing.

Samuel walked over to the sideboard in the dining room and picked up a crystal decanter filled with bourbon. He held a glass in the other hand and poured. Silently, he handed it to his father.

Hiram's face wrinkled into something of a smile as he reached for the glass. "Thank you," he said.

"I'm thinking of visiting the boardinghouse where the dead girl lived," Samuel said.

"Good, that's wise. Give them our regrets. Find out about her family so we can send condolences." Hiram stopped and eyed his son shrewdly. "Does that pretty little girl we had to dinner live there?"

"Yes. She's the one who found the note."

"I see. Don't get yourself too involved."

"I'm not sure what that means."

"I believe you do."

CHAPTER TEN

Samuel Fiske approached the porch of Boott Boardinghouse, number 52, with some diffidence. He noted its sturdy structure with an automatically calculating eye. Built decently and safely, the dormitories in Lowell were a matter of particular pride to his father. The mill workers had made small attempts here and there to give this one some distinction, such as lining up plants in clay pots along the railing. No sign of any blooms coming from them at the moment, but they looked well tended. There was a fresh coat of paint on the front door, something of an orange shade, brighter than he would have expected. He tried to concentrate on such small particulars as he ascended the steps but lost focus when he saw a slender hand pull back the lace curtains and a blurred face staring at him. The curtains were quickly closed again.

He knocked firmly.

Mrs. Holloway opened the door. He could hear in the background the chatter and clatter of dishes that signified dinnertime. What he hadn't prepared for was the utter devastation registered in this woman's face.

"Yes, Mr. Fiske?" she asked. In other circumstances, she would have smiled and bobbed her head and invited him in with flustered courtesy. This was new to both of them.

"I understand this was the home of Sarah Cornell, and I'm here to convey my family's condolences," he began. The proper thing to say, and yet it rang sour in his ears.

"Sarah?" Mrs. Holloway blinked, gazing at him. A dawning recognition came. "We know her as Lovey."

"May I come in?" he asked.

Mrs. Holloway seemed in some unexpected way to be thinking it over before she opened the door wider and nodded him in. "It's not a happy time," she said. She gestured back to the dining room, where he could see women sitting at the nearest table. A few of them had turned and registered his presence. Their talk diminished. A different sort of murmur threaded through the room; some faces were astonished; others just stared. He could smell fish chowder.

A familiar figure, seeing him, rose to her feet. Her face was drained and pale, her eyes slightly wild, her demeanor one of grief.

"Miss Barrow—," he began.

"Mr. Fiske, thank you for coming, but I have a favor to ask," she said without preamble. "Please do not allow Lovey to be dumped in the ground without a proper burial. It dishonors her, and we ask you to disallow it."

The table went silent.

"I didn't know that was being contemplated."

"We have been told that is the plan. Please change it; can we count on you?" She worked to keep her voice strong, reminding herself: Stay resolute.

To Samuel, her voice rang so clearly, so calmly. Very different from the light, mannered hints and requests of the women he knew in Boston.

"I will make sure that doesn't happen," he said. He was rewarded with a collective sigh of relief from the crowded table.

"Will you join us for dinner, Mr. Fiske?"

Alice Barrow, to Samuel's disappointment, did not offer the invitation; Mrs. Holloway did.

He cleared his throat, gazing again at Alice. "I would be de-lighted," he said.

Samuel sat at the table for the better part of an hour, tackling a bowl of fish chowder put in front of him, faintly surprised that it was tasty. It was awkward at first, but he was determined to coax out conversation.

"Tell me about Miss Cornell," he said.

"She was a respectable woman," Jane said in a strong voice, a pinched look on her perpetually worried face. "And you mustn't believe anyone who says otherwise. She—she—I think she was, un-derneath it all, a believer in God."

Alice reached out and gently touched her hand. "It's all right, Jane, we don't have to make her out to be someone she was not." She turned to Samuel. "Lovey was no saint. But she was brave and lively and a good friend to us all. She made us laugh."

"And sometimes cry," Jane said, remembering the britches on her bed.

"She saved my child," Delia volunteered. "I would have done anything for her."

"She could do more looms at a time than I could," Tilda said softly. "We had something of a game between us, a challenge. She made the long hours go by faster."

"She never laughed at me," Mary-o said, after a pause. "Some do, here. I may not be so quick or smart as others, but Lovey never made me feel she was laughing at me behind my back. She would sing when I played the piano. She had a lovely voice."

"She was not the obedient type, if that's what you want to know," Alice said. "We're not claiming that. She was clear-eyed about the compromises of working at the mill."

"I should like to know more about those compromises."

"They are the ones I told you and your family about in Boston."

"You're talking about health dangers in the mill, isn't that right?"

"Yes," she said.

Samuel took time to place his spoon at a careful angle on the chowder bowl. "Your concerns will be addressed," he said. "I promise that. And I keep my promises." He stood, prepared to leave.

"Alice, would you be so kind as to walk Mr. Fiske out?" From somewhere, Mrs. Holloway had brought forth remembered grace notes of an earlier time.

Alice pushed back her chair and stood as Samuel donned his coat. She walked with him onto the porch, the door clicking closed behind them.

"I'm not just here as a representative of the Fiske family," he said. "I am truly sorry that you lost your friend."

"Thank you." She looked up at him, surprised at his directness. She had been wrong to assign him an attitude before letting him establish his own. "You were kind to come," she managed.

"There will be a proper funeral, I promise," he said. "It will be here in Lowell, her true home, from what I can see."

"Thank you." Where were her words?

"I will be there," he said. "My entire family will be." Was there anything he could do to extend this conversation? Samuel stood on the top step, taking as much time as possible to button his coat. But he could think of nothing that would give true voice to what he wanted to say.

"Good night, Miss Barrow," he said.

"Good night, Mr. Fiske." Alice turned and went back into the boardinghouse, but not without an unexpected and unexplainable quickening of her heart.

The funeral was to be at Saint Anne's. With Hiram Fiske in town, the message was clear: all of Lowell's respectable citizens were expected to present themselves. There were no murders in this

peaceful part of the country; who could remember the last one?
With so many reporters crawling through town, clustering around
any shop clerk or mill employee with something to say, the violent
death of this lowly mill girl had quickly become cause for horror and
indignation.

Their fevered attention turned to the industrialists who had cre-
ated the town. Wasn't the cotton mill of Lowell supposed to be the
shining example of how industrialism could benefit both owner and
worker? Wasn't protection of these farm girls flocking to Lowell of
paramount importance?

Then more news. John Durfee, the man who had found the body
of the poor girl, stepped forward and told reporters he was convinced
now a murder had been committed. The coroner had made a terrible
mistake.

"I'm not an educated man," he said to a crowd clustered around
the county courthouse. "But I know how to tell the difference
between a hanging suicide and a hanging murder, and I'll talk only
to the sheriff."

Well, some said, the governor was coming; maybe he would put
pressure on the old coroner to change his hasty verdict. Surely, people murmured, it was just a matter of time.

*W*hat?" Alice could hardly believe her ears when the message was
delivered to the boardinghouse.

"I'll say it again. Foreman Briggs is not excusing anyone from
her shift for the funeral." It was Mrs. Holloway's duty to deliver the
news, and her voice went clipped and hard.

"How can he not let us go?" Alice was dumbfounded. "That's
so—"

"Cruel," Tilda finished.

They were all sitting at the table, staring at one another and the
platters of meat and cheese in front of them.

"Lovey was right. When they wanted to parade us around for the president, they gave us green parasols, and we marched for our supper." Tilda, who was never resentful, was seething now. "The fact that she was one of us holds no weight with the Fiskes."

Mrs. Holloway shook her head. "I don't see how they can make Lovey's funeral a lavish show of how they want to protect you if you aren't there."

Silence fell. One by one, the girls arose from the table and disappeared out the door, leaving the slabs of beef and mashed potatoes to grow cold and congeal. Alice was last, sitting there and staring at the uneaten food.

What had happened to that compassion she had sensed in Samuel Fiske? Surely he knew she and the others were being denied time to attend the funeral. If he did, he was no better than the rest of them.

On Wednesday morning the girls from Boott Boardinghouse 52 trudged across the bridge to the mill in almost-total silence. Mrs. Holloway had protested, but there was no appeal. The mill cannot afford to have so many looms shut down, this is a competitive business, and they should know it, the foreman said. If you want your money, you work.

There was little talk as the morning hours passed by. All Alice could think of was Lovey frowning and laughing as she memorized poems and read her Bible pages, working her looms more expertly than any of them. She couldn't be dead; it left a hole in everything. Alice felt dead herself; right now all that was alive inside was her anger.

Her fingers flew across the looms, weaving the fibers deftly, hardly seeing the product of her work. Briggs knew he had no moral right to deny Lovey's friends a chance to say good-bye. None at all. The mill girls weren't slaves, they were free women, and that was what it came down to. But he was blustering about, pretending he hadn't been pressured to keep them on the job.

So what finally moved her hand up to the controlling switch? A question Alice couldn't answer, but there she was, reaching up and clicking it off. It was without prior thought, just a decision that seemed completely right. First one of her looms, then another. The bleak winter sun filtered through the closed windows as she wiped the sweat from her forehead and stood still.

Jane was next. She looked frightened, but she, too, turned off her looms. Timid, pious Jane.

"A turnout?" Mary-o whispered in sudden fear. There had been no talk of challenge among them, nothing. With a steady hand she reached up and turned her looms off, amazed at herself.

Delia and Tilda were next. One by one, the five women from Boott Boardinghouse 52 stopped the roaring power of the machines that left their ears ringing for thirteen hours a day. The shrieking noise they lived with morning and night subsided. They stood in place, momentarily stunned at what they had done.

"What's going on here?" Jonah Briggs was standing in the door-way, arms crossed. His hoarse voice sounded even louder than usual in the relative silence.

No one answered.

"Turn those looms back on."

No one moved.

"Turn them on. *Now.*"

Carefully, Alice wiped cotton threads off her hands and stepped away from the looms. Without a word, she pushed past the red-faced Briggs straight to the coatrack by the exit. She removed her apron and pulled on her coat. The others did the same. Workers were whispering and staring. Still without a word exchanged, they walked out of the mill and down the path that took them to town. A soft shower of snow had begun drifting and swirling around their feet.

Mrs. Holloway was waiting at the main gate. "I thought you might be here," she said. "I'll walk with you." Her face was very pale, and her lips pulled tight. Alice smiled gratefully. Of all of them, Mrs. Holloway perhaps had the most to lose. She was old; if they fired her, there was nowhere to go. But if bravery was doing what you fear to do, Mrs. Holloway was brave. The thought calmed her; she was able to take deep breaths now and walk with a bit more of a stride.

"Where are we going?" Jane asked, speaking not much above a whisper.

"To Saint Anne's, of course," Alice replied.

They were passing Boott Hall when suddenly Alice stopped. "Wait," she said. "I have to get something." She disappeared into the house, reemerging a moment later carrying a small package.

"Let us go."

*T*he church was jammed with people crowded together, coughing and murmuring discreetly as they waited for the funeral to begin. The acrid smell of their damp wool coats mingled with the heavy scent of hothouse flowers lining the altar—an aromatic mix, but no one headed for fresh air.

Samuel's father leaned over to him, a faint smile of satisfaction on his face. "No one will be able to say the Fiske family didn't handle this tragedy properly," he said. Samuel nodded noncommittally. The entire family was there, of course. His mother, looking sternly proper, sat next to her husband. His grandmother's head bobbed sleepily next to her, while Daisy kept looking around, delighted with reporting the prominent names mingled throughout the congregation. Jonathan seemed unusually subdued.

Samuel glanced past Lovey's coffin of ebony and gilt, which rested on a flower-laden platform at the foot of the altar, surrounded by tall black candles in brass candlesticks. Where were her friends? He turned, puzzled, and scanned the church. There were no mill girls there.

"What's wrong?" his father asked.

"Where are the mill girls seated?"

"Briggs agreed, we couldn't spare them. They understood."

"That's the craziest thing I've ever heard." The words flew from his mouth in astonishment. Could his shrewd father have actually made such an error?

"Don't call me crazy, Samuel." Hiram's eyes narrowed to slits as the organ music from the loft of the church grew louder, signaling the funeral would soon begin.

Samuel started to reply when he heard stirrings in the crowd. Heads were turning to the back of the church. He whirled around.

There they were, seven of them. Six women and a child, obviously coming directly from the mill. Standing in front was Alice Barrow, her shabby work apron still on, staring straight ahead at the coffin. There were no seats available, but she began walking up the aisle, followed by the others.

Samuel stepped out into the aisle, facing her. She moved with fluid grace, each foot firmly stepping ahead of the other; her face showed a resolve that drew his eye and would not let him go. To the contrary, it held him fast.

He had no need to think through what he was going to do, no need to clear it first with his father.

"Please join us," he said, gesturing the group into the family pew. "My family welcomes you." His eyes never left Alice's face as the others climbed in and the Fiske family scrambled to move over and make room. One muttered oath from a surprised Jonathan was the only protest.

"We regret being late," Alice said.

She held back, still staring at the coffin. Inside was her friend:

lying motionless, without breath, without voice, without laughter. This is what it all came down to, and this absurdly gilded box was hollow grandeur in the face of death. It should be plain. Pine, with the nailheads showing, that's what Lovey would have wanted, not this pretension. Enough, enough. Slowly she opened the package in her hands and took out the gray leather gloves Lovey had given her, smoothing her hand one last time over their buttery softness, remembering how Lovey had looked at them. She placed the gloves gently on top of the coffin.

Samuel watched, riveted by the sight of Alice's slender fingers. As she turned back to him, he folded one hand around hers and led her into the box next to him. He was at first surprised by his reluctance to let go, but he let himself experience what was happening without stiffening or questioning or caring about what was proper. He felt amazingly calm.

*T*hat worked out very well," Hiram said. The funeral was over, and their carriage led a long procession heading for the cemetery just outside of town. "I don't think any of the reporters realized those girls were intruders, of a sort. You were right, Samuel. Ridiculous call, that was. But don't you ever use the word 'crazy' around me again."

Samuel nodded, barely hearing his father. He was still picturing Alice's pale, calm face as she firmly rejected his offer to transport the girls to the cemetery, informing him that putting Lovey into the ground was too much to watch. "I do not want to see shovelfuls of earth tossed down on her," she had said as they left the church.

"May I come by to see how you are all doing tonight?" Samuel asked. To walk away, to climb into a carriage without her nearby, felt just about impossible at the moment.

It took Alice long seconds to reply. The coffin was being loaded into the hearse, but the gloves she had laid down as her gift to her friend were gone. Someone had plucked them out of the flowers; a contemptible act, stealing from the dead.

She looked up at him, eyes steady. "Yes, you may," she said. Alice had seen his expression as she and the others walked into the church, had seen the welcome in his eyes. She knew instinctively he had not played a part in barring them from Lovey's funeral.

*T*hat night, Alice crouched as low as she could into the old rocking chair in the parlor after supper, wishing only to crawl into her bed and sleep. To shut out the world. She must have dozed, for the next thing she heard was Samuel's voice. Her eyes flew open. And there he was, looking down at her. For just a few seconds, there seemed to be nothing separating them. He spoke, breaking the spell.

"I won't stay long," he said. "I just wanted to make sure you were all right." He seemed momentarily at a loss. "Miss Barrow—" he said, and stopped.

"I'm fine," she said automatically, sitting up straight. She sensed rather than saw several pairs of eyes on the two of them and worked to keep her voice steady. "I think I'm very tired, I'm afraid," she said. "Thank you for coming to console us."

Samuel drew back. He gave her a small bow and let his eyes travel the room. "I will keep all of you informed on the investigation," he said to the others. "We'll find a way to bring justice to bear."

*T*ension was high in the following weeks. The girl was already buried. Why hadn't the formal inquest produced a verdict yet? Any minute now, went the rumors drifting out from the courthouse chambers. Soon.

The announcement finally came one morning as the mill girls were streaming into the factory, and it shocked them all.

Suicide. Sarah Cornell had killed herself, the three-man jury declared. Lovey's note casting suspicion on Avery? It was written by "a woman of dubious character" and therefore had to be rejected as evidence, along with any testimonials to their relationship. The judges made a point of pronouncing the Reverend Ephraim Kingsbury Avery to be a man known for the "purity of his moral, Christian, and ministerial character," while Lovey Cornell was scorned as a woman "addicted to almost every vice." They saw no need to question the many convenient character witnesses the Methodists brought forward to denounce a young woman they had never met. Instead they quickly confirmed the elderly coroner's initial verdict. The young woman with loose morals, this Lovey Cornell, had taken her own life. Case dismissed.

The verdict was greeted with relief by the Methodists. After all, an attack on a minister of their own—even if he was part of the ragtag, somewhat-dubious evangelical fringes—was an attack on them. They had mustered resources to defend the preacher, and now his exoneration meant theirs as well. Yes, a great relief.

But the town of Lowell was in an uproar.

"They've made a stupid mistake," Hiram announced to the family gathered at breakfast in Boston, glancing up from the document announcing the verdict brought to him by a rider from Lowell. "Nobody believes that girl committed suicide."

"It's a convenient ruling for those who wish to cast a shadow over us," Jonathan said.

"The revivalists, of course. That bunch of zealots with their illiterate preachers hates anybody with money. They can go about now whispering that we exploit the mill girls so harshly, this one took her own life." Hiram let out a derisive grunt. "Exploitation? Why, they exploit *everybody* at those camp meetings of theirs."

He settled into his seat and reached for the teapot. "I'm not going to let this matter rest," he said. "I've worked hard to build a good environment for my employees, and I'm proud of it."

"What can you do?" asked Jonathan.

Hiram cradled the warm cup now in his hand, gazing at his sons, one at a time. "I intend to be the person who gets justice for that girl," he said. There was a glint in his eye. "I've got the power to make things happen."

Samuel felt a familiar comfort, hearing his father's words. They had been true all his life, and he was proud to be Hiram Fiske's son.

Jonathan seemed lost in thought. He said nothing, staring at the rasher of bacon on his plate with distaste. Daisy sat, as usual, poking at an egg that was never cooked the way she wanted. The girl was always listless, which made Hiram impatient. "Daisy, can't you muster up some interest in this?" he snapped in his daughter's direction. "We're going to get this fellow for murder."

"The minister? Oh, I'm reading about him," she said quickly. "He was notorious for seducing women. It's quite a scandal, all my friends are talking about it."

"Good, good, the more outrage the better," Hiram said with satisfaction. He stood, tucking his morning newspaper under his arm. "I'm not letting this preacher get away with his crime." He gave his watch a quick glance and left the room.

Daisy let out a long, dramatic sigh. "Now we can get down to important things." She arched an eyebrow, casting Samuel a cool glance. "You've taken quite a fancy to that girl Alice. I saw how you looked at her at the funeral. Watch out, you know Father isn't going to let it happen."

Samuel took a bite of his buttered toast and a sip of coffee before replying, trying to contain a flare of anger. He couldn't. "I think you need something to do with your time," he said to his sister. "I don't think you are quite as vapid as you try to appear. But perhaps I am wrong."

He rose to leave, but not before seeing the stricken look in Daisy's eyes.

Jonathan's voice, a lazy drawl, followed him out the door. "Do you see, Sister dear? It's as I told you. He's getting to be just like Father."

*T*hat evening Daisy sat alone in the drawing room, which was rapidly darkening in the gathering shadows. She stared into a smoldering fire, a copy of *The Lady's Book* in her lap, unread.

Samuel stepped through the doorway and cleared his throat. "Daisy, I'm sorry," he said.

"You were right, you know." She smiled up at him, almost wistfully.

He walked over to the hearth, picked up a poker, and stirred the embers until a healthy flame shot up, engulfing the stacked logs. He wondered if Daisy ever felt the pressures of family he lived with every day. At times he envied her ability to remain unencumbered with expectations. "I was harsh, not right," he said.

"I hear myself sometimes, as if from a long way away. I get so very bored, listening."

She spoke so solemnly, Samuel was tempted to smile, but a glance into her eyes told him to respond seriously. "Perhaps you need some challenging interests," he said.

"I write poetry." She reddened. "Very badly, I'm sure. And I like painting. Well, I don't seem to stay with anything very long. Everything ends up boring me."

"Maybe you don't try hard enough to get better," Samuel said. He didn't really know how to talk with his sister, but he wanted to help.

"The thing is, nobody expects much of me anyway."

"You could go back to school. You could read more."

She pursed her lips and nodded. "I'm going to do something. Soon." She sighed deeply. "I see why you're taken with the mill girl. She came marching into that church with her head high, not caring that someone might throw her and her friends out at any minute.

She's so"—Daisy searched for a word—"*certain* of herself. Not like me."

Samuel sat down and put his arm around his sister. "None of us is all that certain," he said.

"But we have to pretend to be."

He thought of Alice walking up the church aisle, her eyes focused on her friend's casket. "Sometimes we do," he said.

They sat together in companionable silence, watching the flames of the fire.

CHAPTER ELEVEN

"*H*ow could they be so blind?" Tilda asked. The question wasn't directed toward anyone, just offered into the air, unanswerable and without even the strength of anger.

"They aren't blind; they know what they're doing," Delia said wearily. "We think we're rising in the world, working in the mills. But there are those here who want to sweep us all away, like trash."

Alice once again sat in the rocking chair, gripping the arms tightly, feeling some visceral need to anchor herself. The smug cruelty of the coroner's jury had been unbelievable. Lovey, "addicted to almost every vice"? Depicting the adulterous Avery as a man of high moral character?

"Alice, this note came for you earlier." Mrs. Holloway dived into the copious pocket of her apron and pulled out an envelope, handing it to her. "It is certainly addressed in a forceful hand," she said with a twinge of curiosity.

Alice opened the letter, her eyes traveling to the signature: *Samuel Fiske*. The sight of it made her hand tremble slightly.

> *Dear Miss Barrow,*
> *I know the news you are absorbing is shocking, and I swear to*

you, we will not let this verdict stand. It is outrageous. This was not a suicide, I know it, my father knows it. This so-called man of the cloth has been in trouble for seducing women before. The judges ignored that. They also ignored the evidence piling up that proves Avery is guilty. We have a ferryman who has come forward and placed him near the scene of the crime. I promise you, we will get this overturned. I will not rest until it is done.

Yours faithfully,
Samuel Fiske

Alice read it twice, first, with surprise; then, eagerly, gratefully. She could almost hear this man's voice. It was confident; it spoke to them. It spoke to her. She read the note to the others. "He's going to fight for us," she said.

"All very well." Delia grimaced. "But Avery has fled. Why would an innocent man run from the law? That's what those pompous judges have done. They've given a guilty man a chance to escape."

"Why is Mr. Fiske writing you and not everybody?" Ellie asked Alice unexpectedly.

Alice flushed, but Delia spoke first.

"Hush, child, he is a friend to all of us," she said immediately. "He made sure we were protected from Mr. Briggs's wrath after the funeral."

*T*here was another accident at the mill late the next day. Just more carelessness, said Briggs with a shrug. He spoke loudly as the day shift walked past him, weary and ready for home. Not a terrible one—no one's hand was caught in the machinery, no woman yanked up by the hair and left dangling. No, just a small fire, overheating; singed the eyebrows of one of the new workers handling a bale of raw cotton; nothing terrible.

"There are too many damn things happening," spoke up one of the men as he shuffled through the door.

"There wouldn't be if you heeded the warnings I give you every day," shot back Briggs. He was bossier than ever since getting lectured for barring the mill girls from attending the funeral. Alice was quite sure he was casting about for a way of regaining stature, and they would have to tread carefully. With the others, she trudged out of the mill and started across the bridge, noting with some startlement that it was warmer tonight than usual. A lone blue jay was singing—a jaunty trill, nothing indifferent. Her spirits lifted slightly. Maybe spring was going to come early after all.

$\mathcal{M}$rs. Holloway strode into the dining hall at breakfast and slapped a copy of the town newspaper, still damp with ink from the press, down on the oilcloth. "They've thrown out the verdict," she announced, her voice filled with excitement.

Somebody choked. Someone else cheered. Chairs were scraped back from the table as the girls scrambled up and bunched together around the paper, peering at the headline, touching it, heedless of ink transferring to their fingers.

It was true. The attorney general had voided the verdict on the grounds that the coroner's jury had delivered a ruling in the wrong jurisdiction, a puzzling technicality—but welcome all the same.

"It's this easy? This is how they can do it?"

"But"—Alice could barely get the question out—"isn't it too late? Hasn't Avery vanished?"

"They found him last night, hiding out somewhere in Rhode Island. Oh my, they moved fast—he's in jail already, and he's being formally charged tomorrow."

They all stared at one another, stunned. There would be a murder trial after all.

Mary-o let out a laugh, the first laugh heard in Boott Hall in many days. Soon everyone was talking at once.

"Alice"—Mrs. Holloway pulled her aside, lowering her voice—"the Fiskes are sending a carriage for you. You might have to be a witness, and they want you deposed in Boston."

"What does that mean?"

"The lawyers on both sides question you. It's in case they need your testimony at the trial. They'll do Mary-o, too, but they want to start with you."

"They have to get Dr. Stanhope, he's the most important," Alice said.

"Well, tell them that tomorrow morning when you get there." Mrs. Holloway gently patted her on the shoulder. "You might want to get some rest. The carriage won't be here until around three in the morning. You'll be traveling at a dreadful time, but they want to start early."

Tilda stepped to her side. "You can borrow my cloak again," she said.

"And my bonnet," Mary-o chimed in.

For a moment they all stood in silence, remembering the excitement when they first sent Alice off to Boston. That already-long-ago pinch of time, when they could fantasize that a beautiful dress might be a magical ticket to a larger world.

"Thank you," Alice said gratefully. No, it didn't matter anymore. There was no need to strain for respectability. She looked down at her work dress, hardly interested. There was a stain on the bodice, but that mattered not a whit. Her mind told her a more complicated truth—she was going back to Samuel Fiske's home territory, and that thought made her pulse run faster.

"Take the cloak," Tilda said gently. "You need it to keep warm."

———

*T*here was one more thing. On impulse, Alice went into the dormitory and opened the box holding her mother's cameo. She cradled it in her hand and studied the careful lines of the silhouette she had carved so long ago, remembering her mother's smile when she had opened her gift. Why should she not wear it? What was the use of having something precious if it was kept hidden away? She held it another minute, indecisive, then opened the clasp and pinned the brooch to the throat of her dress. She would wear it proudly.

*O*nce again, this time in the dark, Alice found herself heading off for Boston in a clattering carriage. She tried to doze, curled up under Tilda's cloak, but it was a cold night, and she couldn't warm her feet or hands. Outside the carriage window, she could see the moon. And it was a full moon, just as it had been some nights when she and Lovey sat together on the porch steps. She stared at it, squinting. A dark, starless night, that round serene globe above—it should rest her spirit. But try as she would, she could see neither the man nor the woman, only the cold curvatures of some mysterious, unknown terrain. It was all just imagination, a fairy tale, and she mustn't allow fanciful dreams to intrude on harsh reality.

Somewhere along the route, worn out, she closed her eyes and gave in to sleep.

*M*iss Barrow?"

She opened her eyes to a cold, gray morning, only belatedly realizing the carriage was in the driveway of the Fiske home. The door was opening. And there, lifting up his hands to help her down, his face gentle, was Samuel Fiske. This was the second time he had awakened her, and her defenses were not fully in place. She reached out, he lifted her, and then she was on the ground, pulling herself upright and clutching her cloak tightly, wishing there had been some time to arrange her hair or straighten her dress. Only then did she see Daisy standing in back of Samuel.

"Daisy will help you refresh," Samuel said. The sight of Alice, rumpled and sleepy, stirred him.

Alice was more conscious now of Daisy's critical eyes than she was of Samuel. But when she looked straight at Samuel's sister, she saw in her face more of a woman's practical assessment of another.

"You need to be wide awake for that deposition," Daisy said. "Come with me."

Alice followed Daisy past the richly gilded paintings and up the red-carpeted stairs, still barely awake. To be here a second time was to yearn again for something she couldn't have, and she must quell that feeling. They had two hours, Samuel had said. Two hours until the attorney general would be here; two hours until she had to face his questioning. She wanted to use the time to defend Lovey and sweep away the coroner's jury's harsh proclamation. To stand up for herself, for all the girls—she clung to the smoothly polished railing, gripping it tight, resisting the pull of being once again enveloped by these opulent surroundings.

"Would you like to bathe?" Daisy asked.

Nothing would be more soothing now. At least she could admit that to herself. She nodded.

Daisy tugged at her hand and drew her through a door. They walked into a spacious room with a marble floor, its walls painted a cool, peaceful blue. In the middle of the room, dominating every-thing, was a massive claw-footed tub made of burnished copper. With a nod from Daisy, a servant carrying a pail of steaming water poured its contents into the tub. She turned and, to Alice's astonish-ment, released a faucet, allowing running water to pour forward into a ceramic sink.

"We have an attic cistern," Daisy said, seeing her surprise. "It fills with rainwater, which gives us running water through the whole house." She sighed. "Father was very fussy about that, thank goodness." The servant—the same girl who had served dinner the last time—cast a slightly wicked glance at Alice. "I think it's hot enough now, ma'am."

Alice stared at the inviting tub. How wonderful it must be to bathe like this all the time. And without a moment of hesitation nor waiting for permission, she unbuttoned her wrinkled, stained dress and let it fall to the floor. Her drawers were next. She stood naked, and she didn't care. And then she stepped into the tub, slid down in the blessedly warm water, and closed her eyes. Oh, it was bliss.

Daisy eyed her discarded clothes dubiously. "I see I'm going to have to find something for you to wear," she said, an edge of annoyance in her voice.

Alice sat up as straight as she could in the curved tub. "I can wear my own clothes, thank you," she said.

"Mary Beth, bring her into the guest room when she's finished." Daisy was not ready to give up her annoyance quite yet. She was doing this for Samuel, not for the girl named Alice.

*H*ere, I think this should fit."

Alice, wrapped in a towel, looked around the room first. She caught her breath. This was a far cry from the sparely furnished servant room she had slept in before. The wallpaper was dazzling—languorous boat scenes of women holding parasols of blue and gold rippled and flowed from wall to wall, and she felt as if she floated with them on a blue sea. She had to restrain herself from touching them. Over by a floor-to-ceiling window sat a writing desk on delicately bowed legs. Was this a French design? She saw an open velvet jewelry box on the desk, purple beads tossed carelessly next to it. Her gaze moved to the bed, a four-poster, covered in tufted white silk.

She blinked, then focused on the dress. It was of plain homespun, green with a bit of lace at the collar.

"Thank you," she said.

"It isn't mine, obviously," Daisy said. "It's Mary Beth's. It's to be returned, of course. The laundress will wash your clothes and have them ready when you leave."

Alice looked swiftly at the servant standing now with her arms folded and a satisfied smile on her face. No, a smirk. Does she really believe I care, Alice wondered. "I appreciate your kindness," she said directly to Mary Beth. The smile on the girl's face faded slightly, and she turned to leave.

"When you are ready, join us in the drawing room," Daisy said. "You remember where it is, I presume? The room beyond the library?"

Alice paused before answering, seeing something in the other woman's face. Something fragile. The way she held her chin thrust forward, the wary way she hugged herself. They were both about the same age, she guessed. But Daisy had, in this glorious home, a place of privacy and peace. And yet Alice suspected the tiny furrow carved into her forehead never quite went away.

It mattered little that Alice had never been in the drawing room. "Yes, I do," she said.

CHAPTER TWELVE

*A*lice walked slowly down the curved staircase, pausing midway on the landing to gaze at the muted elegance of her surroundings. A weak morning sun had begun to flow through the leaded-glass window, sending dancing shafts of red and gold light onto the huge crystal chandelier suspended from the ceiling. Hundreds of tiny crystals shivered slightly as she moved beneath it, creating an even-more-beautiful display of color. She could hear the murmur of voices, but there was no one in the entry hall. She was, for the moment, in this alien space, alone.

An easy step, then, to float into her imagination. Yes, of course, let's pretend. Ah, she came down these stairs every morning, thinking about breakfast, and then a stroll in the garden—she would plant flowers everywhere—and then perhaps visiting a millinery shop and buying a new bonnet, maybe two. It would be a sunny day; every day would be sunny; oh, this invitation to dream.

She drew a deep breath and pulled at the scratchy, slightly too-short cuffs of her borrowed dress. Her pace quickened as she descended, turning left at the foot of the stairs.

She was once again in the library. The books that surrounded her were as inviting and unreachable as ever, their charm shrouded this time in semidarkness by the heavy velvet curtains. She continued walking, following the sound of voices, and entered the drawing room.

It was immense, with Oriental carpets scattered throughout, anchoring sofas and chairs. Through open windows, a slight breeze puffed at the creamy white silk curtains, sending them softly billowing into the room.

"So, our pretty emissary has come back." Hiram rose from a large tufted chair and greeted her with an expansive smile, taking her hand and brushing it with his lips.

"Thank you, my dear, for understanding the urgency and coming so quickly."

She nodded, imagination fading, her mind back in charge. She had been given no choice. Nor was she his emissary.

"I want you to meet our trusted friend, Albert Greene. Mr. Greene is, of course, the attorney general of the state and will be in charge of the prosecution."

The man who rose and gave her a quick, crisp bow had glistening black hair and a rock-solid body shaped like a milk jug. He wore pantaloons tucked into high riding boots and a cutaway jacket, and his dauntingly watchful eyes bore in, giving the impression he rarely blinked.

"So you're the young lady who found the note written by the unfortunate Sarah Cornell," he said.

"Yes." She hurried to correct him. "Her name is Lovey."

He lifted his shoulders in a slight movement that could have been a shrug.

"Surely it implicates this preacher?" she said.

"Not necessarily, Miss Barrow. The defense will try to get it thrown out as hearsay."

"What about the other letters? The ones where he acknowledged they were to meet? That made it clear he knew why?"

"Who is this 'he'?"

She stared at him, uncomprehending.

"Those letters aren't signed," he said almost gently.

A flush began moving up her neck into her face. "Are you saying none of those letters—or Lovey's note—can convict him?"

"There are no guarantees. It's the way of the law, Miss Barrow."

He looked so smug, she could not stay still. "Then the way of the law is flawed, Mr. Greene."

He seemed to like her answer. "We intend to mount a meticulous case built on witnesses at every step of this crime," he said soothingly. "Put your mind at ease, Miss Barrow. This venal preacher will not escape." His tone grew brisk. "Now, to the job at hand: I'm not putting you on our witness list, but I want you on the record. That's why you are here."

"I do hope you have talked with Dr. Stanhope. Lovey as much as told him Avery was—"

He waved his hand, a small movement, more a flick of the wrist. "Yes, the father of her child. The defense will try to have it dismissed as hearsay, too. But he will testify under subpoena, no question about that."

"Dismiss *that*? How outrageous!"

Greene offered a small smile. "My dear, the law covers obscure terrain that often surprises; just leave it in our hands."

"Make sure he tells you about the poison—"

"I said leave it in our hands."

She swallowed the admonition. What choice did she have?

Then a familiar voice: "Don't worry, Miss Barrow, this isn't all on your shoulders. We want justice done as much as you do."

It was Samuel speaking, standing behind his father's chair. She hadn't even noticed his presence. His face was tense, quite business-like.

She started to reply but stopped at the sound of a loud knocking at the front door. A servant hurried to answer.

Greene turned to Hiram and said, "Well, they're here. She doesn't have an attorney, does she?"

"She doesn't need one," Hiram replied. He nodded at Samuel. "My son studied the law, and I'm quite knowledgeable, as you know."

This time Greene addressed himself to Alice. "I hope your stamina level is high, Miss Barrow. The gentlemen just arrived are the attorneys for the Reverend Avery. We'll begin momentarily."

"She needs something to eat first," Samuel interrupted quickly, annoyed. "Tell them to sit and wait." There should have been time to prepare this young woman for the coming ordeal, but the defense lawyers had arrived too early. She looked dazed but also resolute. How could he help her? "Come with me." He offered his arm.

"What do they want from me?" she whispered as they sat together over a basket of rolls and berry muffins and a silver pot of coffee. She was very hungry and grateful for his intervention and moved quickly to apply a generous slice of butter to one of the muffins.

"Just the truth, you will be under oath," he said. He couldn't help noticing the soft beads of sweat above her lips; he wished he could wipe them away and calm her fears. "Just what you know. But they'll ask you maddening, repetitive questions that will sometimes seem absurd, and the defense lawyers will try to cast doubt on everything you say."

"All I did was find Lovey's note and the ones Avery sent," she protested.

He put his hand over hers, not caring if the servant behind him noticed or not. "Alice—may I call you by your name?" he said, then paused.

She managed a smile and nodded.

"They will probe away to get any information they can about your friend's character."

"She's not on trial," Alice said, her eyes widening.

He cleared his throat. "In a certain way, she is. You must be prepared."

"Will you be there?" The words had just spilled out.

"If you want me to be, of course."

Yes. Yes, that was what she wanted. "I do," she said. And for the first time, she let vulnerability show in her eyes as she smiled.

*W*ithout that warning, she couldn't have made it through the barely concealed contempt exhibited by the defense lawyers. Especially the one named Jeremiah Mason. Her first impression upon seeing him was that of a slightly stooped man with gray hair and fleshy pink lips, not unlike Avery's. His smile was affable, but his eyes never quite focused as he asked question after tedious question. They looked oddly blank, turned in on themselves.

It was he, as the afternoon shadows grew long, who finally slammed down his folder on the table, and shot out, "You have an admirable desire to deny the true character of this Sarah Cornell, whom I understand you knew for less than a year. But of course we all know she was nothing but a prostitute. That is true, is it not, Miss Barrow?"

"No, it isn't." She wanted to scream. How many times and in how many ways this afternoon had he tried to get her to say that?

"Come, come, you are under oath. Don't tell me she was a woman of virtue." He laughed deep from the belly.

"That's enough," Samuel interjected impatiently. "You've got your answer, sir."

Attorney General Greene stood up and cast a theatrically disgusted glance at Jeremiah Mason. "Yes, that is enough," he said. "This girl needs no more bullying by the defense. Your client is in serious trouble, Mason, and we've got the evidence."

"Not on the basis of the deposition she's given."

"My dear colleague, you are due for a few surprises."

"You and I know what this trial is really about, Greene. We know the true adversaries."

"There's no question about that. Give your Methodist clients my best regards."

The two lawyers stared at each other briefly. Mason broke eye contact first. "We'll match you step for step," he said softly, his pink lips parting in a smile as he gathered his files and stood to go.

*I*t was too late in the day to send Alice back to Lowell, Hiram declared. Daisy was to take charge of making her comfortable for the night. No one questioned him, least of all Alice. She was caught up in something larger than she understood, and her energy had drained away. All she wanted to do was sleep.

There was dinner first. She didn't care this time which fork or spoon was right; even what she was eating. She thought of the girls back at the boardinghouse, of how their muscles must ache right now, how the usual complaints would be mixed with gossip and singing and joking . . . well, the way it used to be. She picked at the peach ambrosia in front of her.

"Your dress is laundered and ready for you tomorrow," Daisy said. "We'll need the one you're wearing tonight."

"For what?" Samuel said, startled.

"Mary Beth wants her dress back," his sister replied, lifting her eyebrows in mock exasperation. "That's certainly not unreasonable, now, is it?"

Samuel put his fork carefully down on his plate, restraining himself from the desire to publicly reprove his sister. Was she not able to hear herself? He looked around the table, his eyes resting briefly on each member of his family. His father, the brilliant, awe-inspiring linchpin. His mother, hair arranged just so, always prim; never one for conversation beyond the weather and other banalities. Jonathan, slouching in his seat, looking bored.

But there was his grandmother at the far end of the table, rarely included in any conversation. She knew what he was thinking—

those vivid blue eyes knew everything. He had always been able to count on intelligence and understanding from her. She had known more about him than he knew about himself since the time he was a small boy. When he told her with eighteen-year-old braggadocio that he had been admitted to Harvard, she had given him never-to-be-forgotten advice. "Samuel, that place has its share of windbags, and don't ever forget it. And don't believe everything you're told, especially how important you are." His lips twitched at the memory. She caught it and was smiling back.

His family. He was seeing them again tonight, even himself, through the eyes of this one young woman, this outsider. Except for Grandmother, at this moment they did not make him proud.

Enough. This girl took him to dark places. He rose from the table and excused himself, casting a quick glance at Alice before leaving the room. She did not look up.

*F*or all her exhaustion, Alice couldn't sleep that night. She walked out onto the second-floor landing, clad in a nightgown borrowed from Mary Beth, and listened, counting the strikes from the grandfather clock in the front entry. Midnight already. She walked down the hall from her room, stopping to gaze out the window at the sleeping city of Boston below. She stood there, hardly aware of the cold as she pulled the gown close around her. No moon tonight, just a milky sky of clouds and the lights of this alien town.

"Alice?"

She turned. Samuel was at the top of the stairs at the other end of the hall.

"Are you unable to sleep?" he asked with some diffidence.

"It's been a strange day for me."

"You did very well. May I ask—"

"What?"

"Are you comfortable here?"

Maybe it was because she was tired, but she didn't feel surprised by his question. Or maybe it was because staring out at the calm sky, wondering about many things, she didn't feel afraid of being honest. "It was a hard life, living on the farm," she said slowly. "But the rules were simple. They aren't so simple here."

"I found myself at dinner wondering—"

"Mr. Fiske—"

"Don't, please. I am Samuel."

"Samuel." She said it quietly, tasting the syllables. "How do I answer your question? And I wonder about—losing your interest if our goals do not coincide with yours."

"Not if I have anything to say about it." His voice was firm but tired. "This will sound forward, but could we talk a bit? I'll stay here by the stairs."

She thought fleetingly of her night clothing; it was not proper, of course not. But he was leaning against the banister; in the moonlight she could see the way he smiled—how his lips turned gentle around the edges. His eyes, set deep, were calm. He seemed almost to have shed his Fiske identity for the moment, dropping it like a tight-fitting jacket. The thought occurred to her, not for the first time, that perhaps even he could be locked into an identity. She felt a strange intimacy. She remembered the warmth of his hands.

"That will be all right, I think," she said.

Samuel sat down heavily on the top landing, gazing at her. She looked ethereal, almost floating inside her nightgown, as if unanchored from flesh and bone. He wished he could put out his hands and lift her high, even float with her. He rubbed his forehead savagely. Such absurdity.

"I admire you for today," he said.

"I thank you for your help. I couldn't have done it without your support." Perhaps it was where they were, the darkness, the quietness, but Alice found herself ready to risk asking questions. "You seem different from the rest of your family," she ventured. "Are you?"

"If I am, it's because of my grandmother," he said. "She likes to talk about working in a saloon, but she had all these causes when I was a boy—everything from the need to build more almshouses for the poor to making sure all children could read and write. She would bundle me up and take me to rallies and meetings from the time I was nine years old." He laughed quietly, shaking his head. "I remember one day in particular—we were down on the Common listening to a man named William Garrison firing up a crowd over abolition when a gang of thugs began beating people, including the women. She got me out of there fast, and even though Father was furious, I've never forgotten what I saw and what it taught me."

"What was that?" she asked.

"If you want change, you have to push for it."

"My mother taught me that."

"How?"

"She faced down the county schoolmaster to make him let me attend school," Alice said. "I was six. She dressed me in a pinafore, braided my hair tight, and demanded a seat in the classroom. Oh, she was fierce. She said poor people had rights, too. And I could read better than most of them, as it turned out. I went through secondary school, got my certificate of completion." It felt important to add that.

"You should be proud," he said.

"It's not like going to college."

"College isn't everything. Those rallies with my grandmother balanced out the smugness of Harvard."

"You went to Harvard?" she asked shyly.

"Yes."

"Some of the other girls are saving to send their brothers to college."

"That's—quite ambitious, isn't it?"

She had anticipated his question. "We all save money—well, many of us do. For different things."

"You do, I know. For any particular reason?"

"Independence," she said, curling her toes tight, hugging her bended knees, absorbed now in telling this quiet man something about herself. "I want to decide how to live my own life, and not have it all decided for me."

"What would that life be like?" Samuel asked cautiously, thinking of his sister.

She smiled faintly. "I don't know, but not knowing is what I relish."

"That is most admirable," he said. He wondered if his father had any idea of what his model for Lowell had opened up. Listening to this young woman, he saw no reason that they should not come true.

"Alice—" He hesitated. "How did you and Lovey become friends? You seem very different."

"We understood each other," she said. "From the very first night we sat on the steps and talked. I wish I could explain how brave she was. She would have been a reformer, maybe like your grandmother, with half a chance." Her voice was wavering; her eyes tearing.

"Please, don't cry." He didn't even realize he was standing and walking toward her, and then he was reaching out, touching her cheek, smoothing away the tears in her eyes.

Surprised, Alice twisted from his touch and pushed him away. "Would you be so eager to smear my reputation the same way it was done to Lovey?" she burst out.

She couldn't see his face as he recoiled.

"I'm sorry, I'm an idiot, please forgive me," he blurted, then turned and strode away, head down.

Her spirits sank. What was wrong with her? He had only meant to be kind, hadn't he? But how dare he be so presumptuous; she, in a nightdress. She could only imagine how his family would react. She must be careful, she couldn't *want*, certainly not the barely formed fairy tale in her head right now. But then, could she at least savor the remembered sound of his voice as he sat on the stairs, asking her questions and listening to her answers?

CHAPTER THIRTEEN

*T*here was no true sleep; every now and then, a few seconds of dozing, then just hours of staring at the ceiling. No, she wouldn't think of Samuel. Instead she tried in the stillness of the night to re-create the sound of Lovey's laughter, the humor and fun that she produced so naturally. She couldn't. The sound was gone.

Somewhere in the early morning Alice drifted into sleep. At seven o'clock, she awoke with a start; she never slept this late. She rose and dressed herself in her own clothes, which had mysteriously appeared, laid out over a chair at the end of the bed. Mary Beth must have somehow tiptoed in and left them there. She was probably already scrubbing the clothes Alice had contaminated by the simple act of wearing them.

She stared into the mirror by the side of the bed. Her eyes were glazed by lack of sleep, and her hair was hopelessly tangled. She feared Mrs. Holloway had not packed her a comb; her fingers would have to do. That wasn't her main concern. What mattered was arranging her face in such a way as to erase as much expression as possible. Her feelings had hardened over the sleepless night. She was just a mill girl; he was a rich man who could have any woman he wanted, and she would let him know she was not going to be some kind of casual dalliance.

But her reflected image was too mobile, too revealing, even when she pulled her lips into a straight, firm line, tightening her jaw. Soon she had to descend those stairs again and make her way to the dining room. For him, probably, last night could be shrugged off. He would be at the spotlessly clad white linen table, dressed in his usual proper fashion, drinking coffee, talking soberly to his father. He would probably pull out that ponderous-looking watch of his, checking the time, eager to pack her into a coach for the trip back to Lowell.

It helped to fantasize such coldness from him. She felt entangled in the intimacy of their talk last night, still hearing the quiet reflectiveness in his voice, but she could not let herself be fooled. She had endangered herself by staying there, talking, in her nightdress; that was the fact of it. She would not think, could not think, about the gentleness with which he had touched her face.

She groped in her handbag, looking for her mother's cameo, and slowly took in that it was not there. And in that sickening moment when one knows something is truly lost, she realized she had forgotten to remove it from her dress last night. She gasped aloud. How could she have done such an idiotic thing? Frantically, on her hands and knees, she searched the floor. It must have rolled under the bed surely. No, it wasn't there. Had it gone into the washing tub with her dress? Had it been ruined or even stolen?

She was crying now. Just sitting on the floor, a stupid girl, out of her depth, wishing only to be somewhere else. But only for a minute or two. No more tears, she told herself, straightening her shoulders and pulling herself up to a standing position. She would find the cameo. She would search. Alice forced herself to breathe deeply.

The dining room, on first glance, seemed deserted. Where was the family? But there, at the end of the long table with a large silver coffee pot before her, sat Samuel's grandmother. She had a wide linen napkin tucked under her chin. Her white hair had been shaped into small corkscrew curls, a fashion of another age, but it softened her face. She looked up at Alice with eyes both alert and strikingly blue.

"Good morning, my dear," she said, smiling. "Have we been properly introduced?"

"I am Alice Barrow, I work in the mill—," Alice began.

The older woman flapped her napkin impatiently. "No, no, I know who *you* are. But I'm quite sure you don't know who I am, because none of my family ever bothers to call me by name. I'm just Grandma."

"Well, may I ask—"

"Gertrude Fiske, that's my name. Call me Gertrude; the one who needs the deference of being called Mrs. Fiske is my daughter-in-law. Hiram is my son. Sit down."

Obediently, Alice sat down. There were no servants hovering, no one else but the two of them. The emptiness made the room feel less elegant today—actually rather drafty and hollow.

"I must ask—"

Gertrude held up a hand, silencing her. She took a healthy sip of coffee, white curls bobbing, patted her lips with the napkin, and leaned back. "There's been a bad accident at the mill," she said. "One of the workers unloading cotton, I've been told. He slipped and got caught in some machinery."

"Oh, my goodness—" Alice knew none of those quiet, grunting men with bulging shoulders, but she had watched them heave the heavy bags of cotton out of the wagons and onto the loading dock of the mill.

"I'm sorry to tell you this so bluntly, dear, but I'm afraid it has affected your travel plans home. The messenger got here very early this morning with the news, and Hiram and Samuel left for Lowell many hours ago. They asked you to wait another day until things calm down."

"Calm down?"

"There was a bit of an uproar last night after the accident. An unruly crowd. Samuel convinced Hiram they should go there to show their concern and make sure the man had adequate treatment." Gertrude looked at her kindly. "Not a good environment for the moment, but I am delighted to have your company for a little longer."

"But the other girls will have to work my looms another day, and that is a burden on them. I have to get back," Alice protested. "I can't stay here. And what if they were harmed—"

Gertrude calmly picked away at a small dish of stewed apples. "Samuel said to tell you he would make sure they are safe," she said. "He is a man of his word. And he promised to be back this evening. Truly, that new train service between here and Lowell is going to change everything."

Suddenly, confusingly, Alice felt relieved, then alarmed. "Still, I—"

"Can we talk facts, my dear? My grandson can't look at you without dissolving; you realize that, don't you?" Gertrude Fiske's spoon paused, suspended halfway between the dish of apples and her mouth. She put it down. "He's a good man. I've known him since he stomped around as a little boy and complained that the servants shouldn't have to eat downstairs."

"I—"

"Oh, never mind. I can't put you in a position where you have to answer that. But don't make the mistake of thinking he's like the rest of them just because Daisy wants to take borrowed clothes off your back as fast as she can. Except for Samuel, none of them wants to remember that I sang in my father's saloon when I met their grandfather." Her tone turning more reflective. "Perhaps you're too young yet to see how the tides go in and out. For all the wealth and luxury in this house, there's nothing magical about it. One generation toils away so they can wear fine clothes and eat off silver dishes. The next drifts along, barely bothering to paddle the boat. And then it is up or down. My dear Samuel has responsibility, but not much relish. . . . I don't know what comes next." Gertrude dipped her spoon again into the apple dish. "Well, *that* was an excessively long speech," she said with a laugh. "I'm not saying I don't love them all, but I see them with a clear eye. Would you pass that nice corn mush, please?" She swallowed a sip of coffee and pointed to a silver bowl farther down the long table.

Silently Alice passed the steaming bowl of hominy, then regained her voice. "You are a singer?" she ventured.

"Not on the respectable stage, I assure you." The older woman chuckled deep in her throat. "I love the expression on poor Hiram's face when I drop it into a conversation every now and then. He's a dutiful son, but somewhere he lost his sense of humor." She sighed. "Actually, they all have."

"Samuel said you were a social reformer," Alice said shyly. "That was very brave of you."

A shadow fell over Gertrude Fiske's face. "Not really, my dear. I made noise and all, but I didn't follow through. Too comfortable to make the effort, I suppose."

"Your grandson is very proud of you," Alice ventured.

"He sees more than is there. I wish I had tried harder," she said.

She seemed to be fading, so Alice spoke with haste. "Mrs. Fiske—"

"Gertrude."

"I have lost my mother's cameo. It was on my dress yesterday, I must find it. It's not valuable, but it matters greatly—"

"Well, you already have."

Alice whirled around at the new voice. Daisy stood behind her, holding out her hand. She was dressed in a fine-textured cream linen dress; in her palm was the cameo.

"Mary Beth gave it to me this morning," she said, gazing at

it critically. "Quite acceptable work, I must say. For using clay, of course."

Alice resisted snatching it from her hand. "Thank you," she said.

"My dear Daisy, how can you be so good at making a compliment sound like a criticism?" Again, that chuckle from Gertrude.

Daisy flushed. Quickly she handed the cameo to Alice, walked around the table, and sat down a few seats away from her grandmother. She frowned down at some invisible wrinkles in her skirt, taking time to smooth them out. Her hands, Alice noted, were of such thin bone they looked as if they could snap.

"I heard all the fuss this morning," she said finally. "I hope Father and Samuel are careful. I don't see why they had to rush up to Lowell anyway."

"Even though someone who works for them was badly injured?" Alice said. She tightened her fingers, cradling the cameo under the edge of the tablecloth.

Daisy looked at her as if she were a child who had spoken up inappropriately. "That's rather a rude thing to say," she said. She swiveled slightly as a servant hurried in, carrying a glass of cider, which he put in front of her. "I want toast this morning, lightly buttered," she ordered. The servant nodded, then disappeared.

"Daisy, where are your manners? What about coffee and toast for Miss Barrow?" Gertrude picked up a tiny bell from the table and jingled it. Immediately the servant reappeared and began pouring coffee for Alice. She declined the novelty of toasted bread.

Daisy stared at her grandmother and blinked. "I assumed she was leaving soon," she said.

"Well, she isn't; your father's orders. So dismount from your high horse and be polite."

Daisy seemed to wilt at this astonishing acerbity from her grandmother. "I'm not impolite," she began, then gave up.

"I would prefer to go now," Alice said. She couldn't bear this house for another minute, nor the people in it.

"Samuel predicted you would say that," Gertrude said with a sigh. "You are not chained here, Alice. But I could see that it wasn't just safety he had in mind. He wanted very much to see you again today. Perhaps there is a particular reason?"

"Oh, for heaven's sake," Daisy mumbled, rolling her eyes.

Alice paused, mute, her mind flashing back to the encounter on the stairs.

"Again, you don't have to answer. I will send for a coach if you insist."

Finally Alice found her voice. "I will stay," she said.

"I'm greatly relieved," Gertrude said, patting her lips to conceal a yawn. "Now it's time for my morning nap."

And right there, in her seat, Gertrude dozed off, her chin resting comfortably on her abundant bosom.

"I like your grandmother," Alice said to Daisy. She picked up a spoon for the apple dish that had mysteriously appeared before her.

"She's something of a busybody," Daisy answered, then quickly amended herself. "Sometimes."

"I'm relieved that you found my cameo."

"Where is your mother?"

"She died."

"Oh. Well—I'm sorry." A pause. "I'd like you to make one for me."

"I would, but I don't have the brushes and tools here."

"I've got those things upstairs. And clay for molds."

"You do?" Alice's eyes widened in surprise.

"I tried making one once. But I have no talent whatsoever and botched the job." Daisy took a swallow of juice, not looking at Alice.

"Why do you want one?" Alice couldn't help but be baffled. "You have a gorgeous cameo. I've never worked with seashells, let alone precious stones, and yours is far better than anything I can make."

"But you could draw my face and shape it in clay, couldn't you? And then maybe later do it in ivory?"

"I may not be skilled enough, but I would love to work in ivory."

"Good. Can we start after breakfast?"

Alice studied Daisy's face. It would, in profile, be quite striking. "I'll do the carving and shaping," she said. "Perhaps I can teach you how to do the finish work."

"Well, perhaps. Please."

The two women sipped coffee silently to the sound of Gertrude's gentle snoring—but, to Alice's surprise, not unpeaceably.

The sun was sending a glow of fresh morning light through Daisy's bedroom as they made their way upstairs. It was a beautiful room, even more beautiful than the one in which Alice had spent the night. A massive, deeply carved bed took up one wall, framed by burgundy-red drapings at the head, and it was covered in the most striking woven tapestry coverlet that Alice had ever seen. She had to stop herself from running a finger over the intricate weaving of white, gold, and red threads creating such an impressive bedcover. How was it done?

"I hide the pots of paint and brushes tucked away in my dressing room," Daisy said, pointing to an adjoining doorway. Alice peered in. The dressing room, walls covered in gold brocade, was almost as large as a dormitory for six at Boott Hall. At least ten gowns, all crisply arranged by color, hung suspended from poles along the walls.

Daisy was on her knees, pulling out a heavy box hidden behind the hanging clothes. "I've got everything in here." She was flushed and seemed excited.

"Why do you hide them?" Alice asked.

"So the servants don't laugh at me. I told you, I can't do anything well."

Together, they hauled out the box and deposited it on a chair near an expansive desk by the window. Daisy opened the box, and Alice gazed at its contents. It was all here, more than she had ever had herself. Wonderful little pots of paint, all the brushes and carving tools needed, molds, fabric. Everything. She felt her fingers itch as she opened a tightly closed container. Good, the clay was moldable. She sat down at the desk and began rolling some clay into a small ball, then flattened it out. She picked up a pencil, looking at Daisy critically. "Sit down," she said, "and turn sideways."

*I*t took three tries. Even though the sun climbed higher, Daisy insisted on inspecting each profile drawing, objecting to something—her nose wasn't that long, surely. And her hair—could Alice raise the curls higher in front? Finally she was satisfied. Alice reached for a carving tool, squinted, and began her work. "Don't talk," she ordered, vaguely aware that she had given Daisy Fiske three orders in a very short period of time.

The carving took several hours. Alice sank into the pleasure of her work, easing for the first time the sadness that had enveloped her since Lovey's death. She forgot Daisy's hovering presence. She forgot everything. She chose clay the color of cream for Daisy's profile; for the background, a deep brown, wishing she had ivory beading to burnish the design. How many times had she imagined working on shells or semiprecious stones? Maybe someday she could work in better materials, but this felt good.

"I like this," Daisy said, gently touching the newly carved profile. "Are my lips really that thin?"

"You compress them a bit tightly," Alice said. "It's not done, of course."

Daisy cast her a cautious look. "I won't be able to finish it, I'm too clumsy. As long as you're here all day . . ."

With angers soothed, embarrassment gone, and the joy of creating once more in her hands, Alice had no hesitancy. "Yes," she said simply.

Impulsively, Daisy reached into her box of supplies and pulled out a still-sealed box of clay. "Here, this is for you to take when you leave. For practice, perhaps?"

Alice smiled and reached for it. "Thank you—for practice."

CHAPTER FOURTEEN

*I*s she here?"

Gertrude looked up from her embroidery and smiled at the sight of her grandson's tense face as he walked through the entrance parlor, peeling off his coat, looking right and left.

"You can relax, dear. Yes, she stayed," she said.

Feeling a wave of relief, Samuel sank into a chair next to Gertrude. It would have served him right if Alice had insisted on leaving after his behavior of the night before.

"Where is she?"

"She's been up with Daisy carving a cameo for most of the day; I would suspect she heard your carriage arrive. You look exhausted."

"I'm glad we went. The man wasn't that badly injured, but we've got to deal with this, it is happening too often." He couldn't help himself; he kept glancing at the stairs to the second floor.

"Check the post while you're waiting for her," Gertrude said, nodding toward a neat stack of letters resting on the mantel. Her voice took on something of an artless quality; she slapped herself lightly on the forehead. "My goodness, you know what's up there? The family Handel and Haydn Society tickets for tonight's oratorio."

Distractedly, Samuel shuffled through the letters, still glancing at the staircase. "Yes, well, Father won't be back until very late."

"And your mother is off to some dinner event. Daisy, of course, never goes. Pity. They count on our support."

He cast a swift glance at her. "What are you saying?"

"Samuel?"

He looked upward. Alice was descending the staircase, a careful, tentative expression in place.

"Are my friends all right?" she asked.

"They are, and they look forward to your return."

The two of them paused, eyes fixed on each other. He told her the details of the mill accident, hoping all the while she understood the unspoken apology beneath his words.

Gertrude broke in. "Daisy," she said to her granddaughter, now standing on the stairs behind Alice. "Will you use the oratorio tickets tonight? The Fiskes need to be represented for this one, your mother insists. It's the final fund-raiser for finishing the Bunker Hill Monument."

Daisy made a face. "I think the monument design is ugly," she said. "What's on the program?"

"Messiah."

"Oh, that tedious thing. I've heard it, haven't we all?" Daisy flounced past Alice and collapsed into a chair. "No, I don't want to go."

Gertrude clucked, shaking her head, somehow not looking distressed at all.

"Pity," she said again.

Samuel stared at his grandmother, noting her hint of a smile. He saw the challenge in her eyes. This was what he loved about her.

He turned back to Alice, a determined spark in his own. "Miss Barrow, will you allow me to escort you to the concert tonight?" he asked.

An instant of total silence.

"Samuel, really!" a shocked Daisy sputtered, sitting upright.

"Why, I think that's a marvelous idea," Gertrude said, her face pink and smiling.

Daisy turned furiously on her grandmother. "You know what Father and Mother would say. I can't believe—" She stopped, casting an uneasy glance at Alice.

But Alice had not heard her, only Samuel. He was actually inviting her to join him for an evening at some fine musical event. There were no rules for how to respond, because this did not happen. She looked into his determined, upturned face and felt instinctively that he would treat her with respect. And she could respond in kind. She reached toward his outstretched hand and let his fingers close around hers.

"I would enjoy that," she said. Four words, perhaps the most daring of her life.

The shadows of night were gathering as Samuel and she—once again in a quickly borrowed dress, this one from a resentful Daisy—drew up in his carriage to Boylston Hall. Alice nervously smoothed the somewhat-wrinkled silk skirt of pale lavender and tugged as discreetly as possible at the low bodice of Daisy's gown, remembering Gertrude's whispered words as they had left the Fiske home. "Just stand straight and be proud," she had said. Alice willed herself to stop fussing, lowering her hand, allowing her bosom its fashionable freedom.

The redbrick building, on the edge of Boston's town center, loomed imposingly above the cobblestones. She peered up at its graceful belfry, which was topped by a spire of polished copper that surely would glint as much in moonlight as in sun. Samuel had told her the first floor of the building was for Boylston Market, which she realized on swift observation of its elegant corridors was hardly like any market she had known.

What, she asked timidly, was the Handel and Haydn Society? A group of Bostonians intent on promoting a love of good music, Samuel replied.

"Some are a bit stuffy," he said, "but anyone who enjoys music has benefited from their productions." He glanced out at the concert-goers making their way up the stairs, realizing how alien a scene it must be to Alice. "Don't be intimidated," he added gently. "Tonight will be a treat—*Messiah* with full orchestra."

She smiled nervously. Was there a way—how could she ask him, what was this music called *Messiah*?

Too late. The carriage had stopped; the doors were opening.

Samuel stepped out first, raising a hand to Alice. Her cape flut-tered open as she stepped out, caught by a small gust of wind. She gasped as the wind licked at her exposed throat, resisting an instinct to cover herself up, even when she saw Samuel's eyes rest on her bosom. His gaze flickered; he looked away.

Cradling her arm in his, he guided her to the stairs. As they mounted the steps, a clear, almost-piercing female voice sang out:

"Why, Samuel Fiske, how delightful to see you here! It's been far too long, hasn't it?"

Alice turned her head and saw a young woman with arched eye-brows and very rosy lips reach out a slender hand to Samuel. She saw the glitter of emeralds at the woman's throat. Her wrap was of some floaty, white fur. It was obvious to Alice, suddenly, that Daisy had made sure she was not properly dressed for the occasion.

"And who is this?" the woman caroled again, her eyes traversing Alice in one swift zigzag cutting glance.

Alice began to step back, but Samuel drew her forward. "Lydia, may I introduce Miss Alice Barrow?" he said in his most formal voice. "Alice, Lydia Corland and I are old childhood chums."

"A little more than that?" the woman teased. "Samuel, you are such an upright sort." Her eyelashes fluttered. "And where are you from, Miss Barrow?"

"I am from Lowell," Alice said. She mustn't panic. But she saw the sudden curiosity in Lydia Corland's gaze, the darting glance at Samuel; the faint smile that tugged at the woman's lips.

More people were approaching, greeting Samuel with lavish attention while casting curious glances at her. The men were clean and crisp in dress coats and white ties, the women in gowns that rippled and flowed beneath furs and velvet wraps. One wore a tiara in her abundant hair that looked, to Alice, truly fit for a queen.

"Have you heard *Messiah* with full orchestra?" the woman named Lydia asked her as they reached the third-floor music hall.

"No, I haven't," she managed.

"My dear, you are so wise to dress sensibly for these events," Lydia continued, taking on a confidential tone as she stared at Alice's simple silk dress. "I really wonder why we get so fancied up to be with our own kind."

She said something else, but Alice wasn't listening; she was absorbing the dimensions of the splendid hall. Such a sweep of space! Rows of chairs, all covered in thick green velvet, rising upward, offering unimpeded views of a deep, massive stage.

Samuel guided her to seats in the front row, nodding and murmuring to friends, introducing her when people seemed to expect it, hoping she was comfortable under this scrutiny, hoping this hadn't been a brash impulse to bring her. He glanced at her face, which was quite pale. But how beautiful she looked—her lovely eyes, her calm demeanor—there was no one, no one, he would rather have by his side tonight.

Their seats, Alice found with uneasy heart, were next to Lydia Corland and her parents.

A ripple of clapping surged through the hall. A choir of more than a hundred men in black robes was filing onto the stage, arranging themselves in bleachers. Then came the musicians, each carrying an instrument. How grave they looked as they studied the papers on racks arranged before them.

"Can I point out the instruments?" Samuel asked gently.

"Please. I've never been to a concert," she confessed as quietly as she could.

Samuel had to resist the impulse to hold her tight as he pointed out the flutes, the first violins, the clarinets. Sitting now so close to her, he could feel her breathing. Something was passing between them; he was sure of it. It was all he could do to keep his mind on the orchestra.

The oratorio began. Alice was almost immediately swept into the glory of Handel's masterwork—such sound, sound she had never heard before. It swelled and filled the room as it filled her heart. The singing, the music—then the voice of a single, pure soprano singing an aria that brought her to tears. As the aria ended, Alice clapped as vigorously as she could, only to realize suddenly no one else was joining in.

Lydia Corland leaned past Samuel, her voice carrying just enough to reach the ears of the nearest audience members. "My dear," she said to Alice, "in Boston, we wait to clap until the conductor raises his hands at the end of the performance. They do it differently in Lowell, I presume?"

Samuel took Alice's hand, holding it tight. "It's a stodgy rule and it's changing," he said evenly.

"Of course," Lydia said soothingly, leaning back into her seat.

Alice held herself as stiffly as she could for the rest of the performance, forcing herself to think only of the music. She would not let this be spoiled, she would not. Gently, she pulled her hand from Samuel's embrace. She did not belong with these people, and Samuel's protectiveness was a thin shield against those who identified interlopers in their midst. She closed her eyes, claiming the music for herself.

---

*H*iram Fiske and his wife were waiting in the foyer when she and Samuel arrived back at the mansion.

"Samuel, how could you?" his mother said. Her eyes were red.

"How could I *what*?" Samuel said, taken aback. He had spent the entire ride home trying to get through the protective shell behind which Alice had retreated. He had wanted to kiss her hands and tell her no snob would hurt her again, not if he had anything to say about it. There was no way in. So they had talked about violins and piccolos, and that was that.

"I want to talk to you in the library," Hiram said to his son. He turned his attention to Alice. "Miss Barrow, thank you for coming. Your coach will be here at seven in the morning, and I hope you have a comfortable trip back to Lowell. Samuel, please come."

Mrs. Fiske nodded at Alice and stepped onto the stairs. "I'll escort you up," she said in a faint voice.

The situation was clear to Alice. "Thank you for a lovely evening," she said to Samuel. "It is indeed time for me to go home." She turned and followed Mrs. Fiske up the stairs, holding her body straight, her head high.

*W*hat is this absurd treatment?" Samuel demanded angrily as the library doors closed behind him and his father. "I will not—"

"You have exposed that poor girl to humiliation," Hiram said. "Not to say your parents. I understand from Daisy my mother was creating a little mischief. But did you not see you put us in a compromised position taking her to the oratorio? What were you thinking?"

"I see no reason why I couldn't do exactly what I did."

"Well, listen closely. I know you gravitate to these new freedoms that are rampant these days, but yanking this poor woman into your own social circle goes too far."

"I'm a grown man, Father. I will do as I please."

"Then you're a fool," Hiram said. "Do what you want with her in private; that doesn't concern me. But let there be no repeat of this behavior tonight." He wheeled and walked out of the room, slamming the door behind him.

*D*reams were just that, dreams. Nonsense. As the carriage clattered homeward the next morning, Alice dissected hers, punctured the night before. Samuel's gesture inviting her to the concert was generous, but just that—a quick walk through his world, and nothing more. It was all right; she told herself she didn't care.

She had kept repeating that to herself as she exited the front hall of the Fiske home, noting that Samuel—there to say good-bye— looked quite haggard. That pleased her, oddly.

"I'm sorry," he said as she stepped into the carriage.

"Why? The evening was lovely," she replied coolly.

No, she wouldn't think of him. Instead she did her best to replay Handel's music in her mind for the entire ride home. That was an experience no one could take from her. It had opened a place in her soul she did not know was there. Who knew music could do that?

Yet something more than exhaustion began creeping through her as she walked the final steps to the boardinghouse. A new morsel of wisdom. She shouldn't have accepted Samuel's impulsive invitation. She, too, had stepped over a line, and it mustn't happen again.

Wearily, she pulled open the door.

"Well, hello, there."

A girl about her own age was sitting at the piano, listlessly poking at a few keys. An unfamiliar face. Her skin had the sallow appearance of someone rarely outside, which was unusual, since most of the mill girls in Boott Hall came from farms. Her frame, hunched over the piano, seemed all sharp angles.

"You must be Alice," she said, glancing up. "I've already heard quite a bit about you." She said it with a slight edge to her voice; not quite the warmest of greetings.

"And who are you?" Alice asked, trying to be cordial.

"You've got an opening here, and I've been assigned to it. Just my luck, getting a dead girl's bed. I'm Hattie Button."

Only then did Alice spot Ellie peeking around the corner at the new girl. Her eyes were wary.

"Hello, Ellie," Alice said, holding out her hand. "Have you met Hattie?"

Ellie nodded, reaching out, while casting Alice something of a desperate glance. "Mrs. Holloway told her I'm Delia's little sister, and I'm a very good bobbin girl," she said rapidly.

Alice smiled to reassure Ellie that her warning had been heard. With a stranger coming in, Mrs. Holloway knew better than to presume Delia and Ellie were safe.

Hattie barely glanced at the child; she just kept poking at the keys. "I didn't want to come here, it's bad luck," she said sullenly.

"There's nothing wrong here, we have a good house," Alice objected.

"Well, I don't want to sleep on the same mattress of somebody who is dead, and I'm not going to."

"You can have my bed," Alice replied.

"You're the one all the way in the back, that's too far. I want a closer one."

"Well, you can't have it," Ellie said stoutly.

Hattie ignored her. "Too many odd things going on here. Plus you've got somebody sick, and I don't want to be around sick people."

Alice turned to Ellie, alarmed. "Who's sick?" she asked.

"It's Tilda," Ellie whispered. "She was coughing so bad last night, she almost couldn't breathe. We took her to the doctor."

"That's another thing." Hattie was warming to her grievances.

"Those Fiskes keep thinking if they show up and pretend to be concerned when people get sick or hurt, that's all they have to do. They should spend more time talking to the crowds at the mill. There's been talk about a turnout, a big one. Lucky for them that mill worker who got hurt is going to survive."

"Where is Tilda now?" Alice asked Ellie. She had had quite enough of the new girl.

"At the doctor's. He's giving her medicine."

$\mathcal{A}$lice hurried down the steps of the boardinghouse and turned toward town. Her head throbbed. She needed rest. She almost tripped and fell as she came within sight of the flapping sign announcing the presence of Benjamin Stanhope's surgery. This time he came immediately to the door when she knocked.

"She's finally sleeping," he said without preamble as he moved aside to let her in. He then led the way to a small room off of his office. Tilda, her small form still, was lying on a cot. Her skin was tinged with gray, a ghostly hue devoid of light.

"What have you been able to do for her?" Alice asked as she moved to the side of the cot and took Tilda's limp hand into her own.

"I bled her. There is not much else I can do," Stanhope said.

"Is she going to get better?"

"I think so, but she's quite weak." He seemed calmer and less uncertain than the last time she saw him. "I've put in a request for some potassium carbonate, and I'm going to press my case with Samuel Fiske. He listens better than the others."

"Will you be testifying at the trial?"

He stirred in his seat, uneasily. "Yes," he said. "I've been subpoenaed."

"And how do you feel about that?"

"Nervous, I'm afraid. But it's the only right thing."

"I was afraid you would resist," she said with relief.

A flush spread upward from his neck. "I'm a timid man, Miss . . . Miss—"

"Barrow."

"Of course. I've asked you that too many times, haven't I?"

"Yes. And you've described yourself as timid before, too." She softened the tartness of her reply with a small smile. She then leaned forward to stroke Tilda's hair, gently pushing it away from her face. "Will she sleep through the night?"

"If the morphine works, which I think it shall. That gives her time to build her strength. I'll take care of her, Miss Barrow. Do you know what Samuel Fiske said when he was here?"

"No."

"He told us he was going to get those, ah, these were his words"—Stanhope cleared his throat—"those 'damn windows' at the mill open tomorrow. I raised the question," he added somewhat diffidently.

So Samuel was who she wanted him to be, who his grandmother said he was. But somewhere inside, she already knew that.

"Thank you for speaking up," she said to the doctor.

For just an instant, she saw a flash of pride in his eyes.

By the time she got back to the boardinghouse, everyone was in bed. And yes, there at the end, in her cot, she could see the lumpy shape of the new girl, Hattie. She had accepted her offer after all. Alice undressed quietly, reaching across her friends for her nightdress, which was hanging on a hook just past Lovey's bed. She slipped it on, shivering a bit; it was wet. A pitcher was very close; some water must have been splashed on the gown. No matter. She crawled into Lovey's bed and pulled up the blanket, remembering how Lovey would yank it so hard it would come undone, and everyone would groan and complain and Lovey would laugh and crawl down to tuck it in again, tickling somebody's toes in the process. She buried her face in Lovey's pillow and let the tears trickle down, licking the salty taste from her lips. Her friend was no more. And her night at the oratorio, experiencing another world, seemed a lifetime away.

*T*hey're doing this questioning thing today; tell me what to do. Samuel Fiske is back in town and escorting me to a law office. Odd, isn't it, that he would come for the likes of me and not send a worker? He's a fine man. I've never been in a law office." Mary-o's voice was tense as she sat down next to Alice at breakfast a few days later. She was wearing her Sunday church dress and had combed her hair into a proper bun. Her hands were trembling as she spooned out oatmeal into her bowl.

So he was here. A sudden guilty thought: she could at least breathe the air of Lowell today and know he breathed it, too. "Just answer their questions, but talk slowly and don't get upset if Avery's lawyers try to say terrible things about Lovey. Especially the one named Mason," she said.

There was a knock on the door. Alice rose and went to open it. And there he was, once again only a step or two away. "Good morning, Mr. Fiske," she said, trying to reclaim the hard-won protection of distance.

Samuel's expression showed nothing. He tipped his hat and bowed slightly. "Good morning, Miss Barrow," he said.

Neither was quite sure what to say next.

At that moment Hattie brushed by Alice, bobbing her head respectfully toward Samuel, even as she darted a curious glance at them both. Alice didn't like her arch, knowing look.

"Excuse me, Mr. Fiske, sir, we're heading for our shifts at the mill, nice to see you visit us. Coming, Alice?"

Samuel quickly moved to the side, clearing the doorway. "I'm here to pick up Mary Dodd for her deposition," he said, now looking past Alice. His voice was quite formal.

Alice pulled her coat off the rack and quickly put it on, not looking at him, then followed Hattie and the others out the door.

*H*er head was pounding, her ears ringing. It was bothering her more today than usual. The endless motion of the machines reverberated through her body—not just in her ears but in her stomach and down to her burning, aching feet. She would soak them tonight, try some of those salts Lovey always used. Alice wiped the perspiration from her brow and looked around. This was home now, strange as that seemed. And for all the rigors of the mill, all the dangers, the place had taken up residence in her bones. As had her friends. Lovey was gone. Tilda hovered somewhere between health and illness. But there was Jane, so solemn and earnest, mouthing her prayers as she worked, trying frantically to keep Tilda's looms going as well as her own; Delia, a scarf tightly tied around her hair, frowning intently, casting protective glances every now and then toward Ellie as the child hustled back and forth with filled bobbins. Perhaps this is what motherhood would have been like for Lovey. It could have worked.

*D*inner that night was quiet. Mary-o, her plump face solemn, seemed overwhelmed with the experience of having faced all the important men of law who actually *listened* to her, but all their questions had made her feel guilty of something. "I'm not sure of *what*," she whispered to Alice at the dinner table.

"They try to make you feel that way," Alice said.

The shadows had already descended when Alice went out alone after dinner to sit on the steps, rubbing her aching fingers. Yesterday she had been carving a cameo; today, working her looms. She still felt the pounding, pulsating noise of the machines. If she turned her head too quickly her ears would ring, but there was nothing new about that. She sat as still as possible, hoping she wouldn't be missed by the others.

Mary-o, limp from her grueling day, had gone to bed. Hattie, the new girl, was arguing about something; Alice could hear her voice from the parlor. She didn't like the girl. And yet, in truth, she would probably be hostile to anyone who took Lovey's place.

"Alice."

She looked up and saw a shadowy figure at the end of the walk, under the branches of a large oak tree. She could not see him clearly. But she knew the voice.

"I will leave immediately if you so wish," he offered.

"I don't want you to go." Those first words stumbled forth, unscreened, but were quickly followed by common sense. "This isn't right. For either of us."

"I don't share my father's rigidities," he said. He heard himself; he sounded like a prig. What did you say when there was no pattern to follow, no convivial exchange of ritual formalities?

"Will you take a short walk with me?" he asked.

"I think it's quite late," she said.

"I'm sorry for putting you in such an unfamiliar position the other night, and I ask your forgiveness."

It might have been the tone of his voice or the simple way he reached out his hand to her, but she found it easy to tell him the truth. "You don't have to apologize," she said. "I loved the oratorio, it was magical."

"But the night before—"

"I overreacted." She pushed a strand of hair back from her face, hardly able to shift her eyes from his handsome, earnest face. "Please understand. My friends and I have been tainted by the lies about Lovey, do you see that? We have to avoid even the appearance of liberties being taken."

So she could be blunt as well as brave and honest; finally, a window to her had opened. "Alice, Alice. Please walk with me," he said.

She didn't consciously make a decision. She simply found herself standing and taking his outreached hand as he, with gentle pressure, drew her to his side. They walked together down the path, slowly.

"I was proud to take you to the oratorio," he said. "You were the most dignified, beautiful woman there. And I would never hurt or alarm you—for anything."

The timbre of his voice was both hesitant and tender, and the sound of it steadied her. To be standing close to him, alone under the shadowed trees of Lowell, was so different.

"Alice—" He stopped.

Wordless, she realized neither of them knew what to say.

His arm was encircling her, gently pulling her closer. She turned her face to his chest and felt the soft wool of his jacket brush her cheek.

"I admire you, that's the true word for it," he said.

"I find you warm and kind," she said.

"We have a start, then?" His voice was husky.

"I need to go back," she whispered. Yet she didn't move away, and he held her tighter, one hand moving upward, gently cradling her head. She breathed in and somehow did not breathe out, but then her body relaxed, and there was nothing to think about other than being held in his arms. There was no war to fight, not now.

They had only reached the oak tree a few yards past Boott Hall.

He lifted his head, listening. "Do you hear the music?" he asked.

She listened. The notes of a waltz were floating out from the boardinghouse into the quiet night. Someone was playing, someone quite talented—was it Jane?

Samuel reached one arm behind her waist and took her hand with his. "I'm not very good at this," he said diffidently. "But may I have this dance? If I'm not being too forward again."

She smiled. "Yes," she said.

There was no space between their bodies now; no pretending. For a few short moments, they danced amid the brambles and twigs, he, stumbling a few times. It was she who had the ease here, in her world. The music was rich and melodious, warming the cool air. She tipped her head back, feeling the brush of his lips against her cheeks, and wished not to think of anything but this.

He found her lips. His kiss was first tentative, then less so, then intense and full. No thought or worry or grief, for past or for future. She wrapped her arms around him, kissing him back, pulse beating fast. She would worry later, but right now, she wanted to be nowhere else but here.

The music faded away. Still they stood, entwined, unwilling either of them to let go.

Then a faint noise, a rustle. Alice looked toward the porch and saw Hattie Button standing there, staring at them with an oddly feral expression. Before Alice could do anything, Hattie retreated, disappearing into the house as quietly as she had stepped out onto the porch.

*W*here have you been? It's late, and I've been waiting to talk to you. Sit down."

Hiram Fiske looked up from the desk in his office at the hotel, peering at his elder son over the top of narrow spectacles that couldn't hide the strain in his eyes.

Wary, Samuel sat down. If his father intended to wax indignant again about class propriety, he would have none of it. "I thought we were done for the day," he said.

When Hiram spoke again, his words seemed carefully chosen. "Son, I have to tell you something, and you're not going to like it." He stared down at the ledger of figures lying before him on the desk. "I've got to cut wages for the mill workers, across the board."

"What? When they're making such poor wages now? You can't do that."

"Do you have any idea what's happening in the mill business?" Hiram said, his voice tight. "Greed, that's what happening. We brought in a new economic model, and now anybody with money is buying all the land facing streams or rivers and building their own mills. We already have four companies out to get us in Massachusetts alone. Profits are falling, and it's going to get worse. I'm not the only one with everything at stake here—my partners agree this is the only solution."

"Shortchanging the workers who make the cotton mill possible?" Even as he said the words, an incredulous Samuel knew his father wouldn't listen. "They'll turn on us. If they aren't paid a living wage, they'll walk off the job, don't you see that?"

"We can quiet the troublemakers by getting that preacher convicted," Hiram said. "Everybody in this town—including all the mill workers—want justice, and we'll be the ones to make it happen. A lot of them don't like those revivalist camp meetings any more than we do, and they'll rally around us. And may I point out, you have twice now questioned my judgment. That's intolerable."

Samuel started to answer, then decided against it. His father looked drained, not ferocious. He bought himself a little time by slowly taking off his coat and folding it over the back of his chair. "I apologize," he said finally. "But a wage cut at this time? Many of them don't make decent money as it is. And with the accidents—"

Hiram cut him off. "You realize ordering the foremen to open the windows at the mill is going to dry out the cotton, don't you? Did you think no one would report that to me?"

Samuel stiffened. "Right now there's a sick girl from one of the boardinghouses at the surgery who inhaled so much cotton, she may not live. I see firsthand what we're doing, and we can't keep pretending it isn't happening."

"You're too close to this, and it's because of that mill girl you've taken a fancy to. I'm the one who gives orders around here. And don't you forget it."

"If you question my motives, there's not much I can say. But this has nothing to do with Alice Barrow."

This time the silence stretched long. Hiram finally broke it, swiveling his chair around, turning his back on his son. "You can leave," he said. "I'm going to bed."

Samuel stood again on the balcony, gazing down at the town of Lowell, working to swallow his frustration. Over to the left, he could see the boardinghouses where the mill girls lived, and if he counted carefully, he could identify Boott Boardinghouse, number 52.

Count back, just two hours ago: he had held that proud, beautiful young mill girl in his arms. What he had fantasized sitting next to her at the oratorio had come true under the trees. She came from a farm, no Boston pedigree. He could hear his family, his friends, cautioning in his ear: Be sensible. But she was a woman of intelligence and grace, and he could not get her out of his mind.

He breathed deeply, as steadily as he could. He couldn't bring himself to go back inside, not yet. He stared at the stars, but, almost as if pulled by a magnet, his gaze returned to the boardinghouse. He imagined smoothing his fingers across Alice's brow, tracing the curve of her cheeks. If he concentrated—and not too hard—he could almost feel the softness of her skin. She was here, inside him. How had that happened? A moan escaped his lips.

This was idiotic. Samuel gave himself a shake, turned, and walked back into his room, firmly closing the balcony door.

He would talk to his father when he was in a calmer mood. There was a better solution to the deteriorating business climate than what he was proposing; there had to be. Otherwise the people who did the hard, dangerous work at the mill that allowed his family to live in luxury would surely rebel. It was already happening in England. There were these new worker cooperatives, maybe that was something—it was an idea that seemed to work for hatmakers and bakers.

He threw himself into a chair, head throbbing. The trial loomed over everything else right now. He and Father would find a better solution for the mill, but there would be no sensible talks until it was over.

After that, maybe, he could allow himself to think about Alice.

I saw you."

Alice froze in the act of climbing into bed.

"I guess I see how you get special favors around here."

"That's ridiculous," Alice said.

"Of course you think so. Am I surprised?" Hattie let out a loud yawn and turned to the wall. "Sweet dreams, Alice."

Alice crawled into Lovey's bed, lay on her back, and stared at the ceiling. Not even Hattie could mar the memory of those short, sweet moments with Samuel Fiske. They belonged to her, no matter the repercussions.

But there it was, just as she slipped into sleep: a tremor of fear.

CHAPTER FIFTEEN

SPRING 1833

*T*ime drifted for Alice through the long weeks before the trial that followed, and her thoughts wandered along vague paths.

Then Mrs. Holloway would be there, leaning across the table, pressing a letter into her hand. By tacit consent, neither spoke of whom it was from.

Alice came to know his handwriting. The minute she saw it, she would fold the note tight, retreat to a corner of the parlor, and read. The letters were always proper. But she could read inside the loops and flourishes, imagine the heartbeat of the man writing innocuous words, asking after her health, giving her small details about the progress of the case, and, yes, there was the weather to discuss. . . .

Twice she had the courage to answer. Can you read me, she thought, can you hear beyond these words?

And through it all, the hammering, pulsating noise of the looms, the stifling humidity, the cotton fibers floating—the world she lived in, so different from his.

And always, she was aware of Hattie Button's sharp eyes.

$\mathcal{T}$he trial was finally beginning. Alice walked slowly over the rough cobblestones of the main road from the dormitory to the county courthouse, dubiously eyeing her destination. It was a somber, forbidding place, even with the flowers planted in front of its grim façade. But they were blooming—purple azaleas, even grape hyacinths, struggling out of the soil, reaching up to the bright morning. So there was still grace and beauty in the world.

Alice climbed the steps, glancing around at the busy, officious-looking men hustling ahead of her, many of them carrying large, stuffed briefcases. Others, clutching notebooks, stood at the entrance, scanning those ascending with quick, darting eyes. These were the reporters, hungry-looking men. Everywhere, there was tension; a hum of lowered voices as the crowds streamed into the building.

Stepping inside, Alice was confronted with a dank smell of old wood and stale tobacco juice that filled her nostrils. A male place, acrid, harsh. All those spittoons shoved up against the heavy walls were infrequently emptied, she guessed.

At the far end of the courtroom was the towering desk where the chief justice and two assistant judges would sit. Her eye traveled to the witness chair—a heavy, ponderous hulk of carved wood surely designed to intimidate witnesses. Suddenly she spied Hiram and Samuel Fiske at the front of the room, and it was as if a fist squeezed her heart tight. There he was, the man with the handwriting she would now know anywhere. She hadn't seen him in such a long time. He looked so strong and grave, shaking hands with important-looking men and listening intently to murmured conversation. As the news of the Fiske family presence rippled back through the crowd, people nodded their approval. She scanned the packed courtroom, wondering where she was supposed to sit. His presence was unnerving. Had she really kissed him?

*T*he mill will let one girl each day attend the trial," Mrs. Holloway had announced last night with a satisfied smile. "They've learned their lesson, it seems. Alice, you are first. Each of you, pay good attention. You will be our source of information, other than rumors, which will abound. And you'll still get your pay."

"What do I do when they call me to testify?" Mary-o said anxiously. "I don't want to be alone."

"You won't be. If you testify, either Alice or I will be there to support you in the courtroom. Mr. Fiske insisted."

"We know which Mr. Fiske, I'll wager," said Hattie with an arch glance at Alice.

Alice was saved from a too-hasty answer by Tilda, sitting wrapped in blankets in the parlor, looking dreadfully wan. "We certainly do, and we thank him for standing up for us," Tilda said. Her voice was scratchy. She coughed, and they all fell silent. When Tilda coughed, her whole body shook, and no one could fail to see it.

A somber Stanhope had said she could come back to the boarding-house, but not to the mill. "Not quite yet," he had amended. "We'll see how she does this week."

*H*ello, Miss Barrow," said a brusque voice, cutting through Alice's thoughts. Startled, she looked up into the face of the unsmiling attorney general, Albert Greene. His black hair was slick with pomade today, his jowls more pronounced than she remembered. "I suspect you are looking for a seat?"

"Yes," she said.

Greene turned to a large man wearing a buttoned jacket that strained to cover his midsection, his face red from a too-tight collar, who had draped himself across a bench in the middle of the courtroom. "Make room, please, for the lady," he said. The man looked up, startled, then glanced at Alice. Surely, Alice thought, she didn't meet his definition of a "lady." Grudgingly, he moved over, and she slipped into the seat.

"Thank you," she said.

Greene gave her a curt bow of the head and moved away.

A stir now as three policemen surrounding a fourth man marched from a side room and led their charge to a seat at a long table. It was Ephraim Avery. His eyes looked like flat black stones. And after weeks in prison the flesh of his face had drooped markedly, carving out dark hollows in his cheeks. No more hiding out for this coward. No white robes anymore, just a shabby frock coat, with an ill-fitting black vest and pantaloons. Alice willed him to be a pathetic, evil figure to all in the courtroom, willed as hard as she could.

Yet Avery appeared almost bored as his gaze wandered lazily around the courtroom. It was as if he were saying, I have to put up with this hysteria for a while longer, but none here can touch me.

Look at me, she thought, clenching her fists.

As if he had heard, his gaze shifted and fixed on her.

She felt abruptly swallowed by ice. Such strange eyes, peering out from behind those green-tinted spectacles, eerie in their calmness. The instinct to flinch and lower her gaze was almost too powerful to resist, but she would not give him that.

"The court will come to order," bellowed a clerk.

Only then did Avery turn toward the bench. From the left side of the room, Chief Justice Samuel Eddy and the assistant judges strode in, their black robes curling and swishing around their feet, taking their places and facing the courtroom. Avery bowed to each of them in turn, an action on the edge of a mocking flourish, then took his seat. His lawyers clustered quickly around him, vigilant as crows. Three men dressed in the black garb of Methodist ministers leaned forward from the first row, jaws set, close enough to almost be part of the defense table. They were reputed to be honorable men and were certainly hard put to hide their distaste for the defendant. But they had opened the church coffers and dug deep to pay for his lawyers, convinced the only way to protect their church's reputation was to fight for Avery's exoneration.

Judge Eddy tapped his gavel on the desk, sending a sharp sound of authority through the room. The crowd went silent. "Stand, Mr. Avery," ordered the chief justice. "The clerk will read your indictment."

Avery stood, stiff as a soldier, betraying no emotion.

Until this moment, it had not felt quite real. But now the words that filled the courtroom made it all true.

"Upon being moved and seduced by the instigation of the devil," intoned the clerk, "you, Ephraim Kingsbury Avery, are charged with beating, strangling, and hanging one Sarah Cornell, a mill employee in Lowell, Massachusetts, causing her instant death."

"How do you plead, Mr. Avery?" asked the chief justice in a strong baritone.

"Not guilty, Your Honor." Avery's voice rang defiantly through the courtroom.

Alice closed her eyes. She was hearing the arrogant voice of the preacher at the campground, the man who had clutched the lives of all those vulnerable people in his hands. And this was the last voice Lovey had heard before she died.

*P*resenting much more of a bedraggled appearance than the judges, the jurors chosen over the past few days then filed in and took their seats. "Can you believe it? Over one hundred challenges," a voice behind Alice whispered. "It was very hard to find any who don't believe Avery is guilty."

Alice studied the faces of those chosen, trying to remember what each juror looked like; how each one acted. Her friends at the boardinghouse would want to know. She wished she had brought paper and pencil; all she could do today was draw them in her mind. She had seen most of them around town. There was a moonfaced barber with kindly eyes and a legal clerk whose chin quivered each time he moved his head. The owner of a local grocery store sat in the back row, frequently clearing his throat. The foreman, Eleazer Trevett, had some deep scars on his cheeks, perhaps the result of a bout with the pox.

Finally all were seated. They looked expectantly at the judge.

He nodded and turned to the attorney general. "Mr. Greene, proceed."

The murmur swirling through the crowd subsided. The trial had begun.

Albert C. Greene stood and thundered forth: "Gentlemen of the jury, we are here to avenge the cruel death of a young woman that has shocked us all. We will prove a murder took place. And we will prove who did it—and why." He pointed a finger at Avery. "This man, under a hypocritical cloak of piety, violated and murdered Sarah Cornell, known to her friends as Lovey. Some have tried to protest that she took her own life. She did not. Others have protested that there is no evidence linking her to Ephraim Avery at all. Yes, my friends, there is."

He paused to pick up a heavy stack of documents before him on the table and hold it aloft, then let his voice ring out through the room, leaving no observer needing to cup an ear to hear his words. "Tragically, the prisoner is a minister of the Gospel." He nodded at the stiff black-clad Methodists behind the defense table, his voice softening. "So it is understandable that these fine men of God want to defend one of their own. But, gentlemen, I must inform you—evil has wormed its way into your midst, and we intend to convince you of its presence."

It was an impressive performance, Alice thought. Surely it would influence the jury.

Greene wasn't through. He pointed again to Avery, his voice

soaked in contempt. "This man has brought shame to the thousands of Methodists who have listened to his words and tried to live upright lives. Our town, this state—we all want our citizens to be safe from the depravity of a cowardly hypocrite. The honorable young women who work in the mills are crying out for justice—and we will bring it to them."

A spurt of applause erupted, stopped by the judge banging his gavel. "There will be no disruptions, and if there are any more, I will clear the court."

The crowd collectively held its breath as Greene turned to the bench. "Your Honor, I would like to call Mr. John Durfee as our first witness."

The farmer who had first found Lovey's body stood up and walked toward the witness chair, his eyes flitting back and forth between the judges' bench and Greene. He took his seat, clutching a well-worn cap darkened with perspiration. He looked lost, somewhat frightened. He raised his hand and was sworn in.

"Mr. Durfee, tell us how you found the body of Sarah Lovey Cornell."

"Well, sir, I was looking for my calf when I saw her hanging there, poor dead young girl. Awful shame, a murder like that."

"Objection," snapped Jeremiah Mason from the defense table. "Witness is drawing a conclusion."

"Sustained."

Durfee looked bewildered.

"It's all right, Mr. Durfee," Greene said gently. "Just tell us what you saw and did."

Haltingly, Durfee told the story of carrying the girl back to the sheriff's house and finding out from the Lowell doctor that she was pregnant. How the sheriff and the coroner immediately thought, in her despair, that she had committed suicide. How he thought that couldn't possibly be true, but he wasn't the law like they were.

"And why couldn't that be true?"

"Sir, the rope around her neck was tied with a clove hitch." Durfee stopped, as if that explained it all.

"Will you explain what that means for those of us who don't know what a clove hitch is?"

"See, a clove hitch is used on sailing ships, and it can't be pulled tight with the ends of the rope parallel."

"And what does that mean?"

"It means that the weight of that poor woman's body couldn't have tightened the knot around her neck," Durfee said.

"And how do you know that?"

"Sir, I'm a retired sailor. I know a clove hitch. I'll demonstrate if you like."

"That won't be necessary," said the chief justice. "I do some sailing myself, and you're right."

Jeremiah Mason rose for his cross-examination, understandably flustered after the judge's words. "No questions," he said curtly.

*B*y noon, Alice was holding herself so still and tight, her shoulders were aching. The defense could no longer claim Lovey committed suicide, that was clear to her—but she was bewildered. The defense obviously was conceding nothing. When Mr. Hicks, the elderly coroner, tried to explain why his verdict was changed from suicide to murder, he stayed stubborn under Mason's scornful questions as to what "new" evidence produced such an abrupt about-face.

"We just changed our minds, me and the jurors," he said.

"No prejudices?" sneered Mason.

"Don't know, Mr. Mason, we just changed our minds."

Before Mason could explode, Greene moved swiftly to the jury box, arms spread wide, as if to embrace them all. "Gentlemen of the jury," he said, "Mr. Hicks was brave enough to reassess the evidence and establish the truth. *This was murder.* From here, we will show you how that truth leads directly to the Reverend Avery."

"What a travesty this is," spat out Mason. "Total lies!"

The chief justice banged the gavel again. "Enough, gentlemen. We will reconvene at two o'clock for afternoon testimony."

*A*lice stepped outside the courthouse doors, looking for a quiet corner away from the chattering crowds. She hoped not to be noticed. But she saw disapproving glances with just a hint of wary curiosity, as if some invisible brand were etched into her forehead. For all the initial indignation in town over Lovey's fate, she and the other mill girls were still outsiders. She mustn't embrace too totally the idea of Lowell as her town. In truth, her identity drifted somewhere in the shadows.

She saw Samuel making his way through the crowd toward her. His face lit up when their eyes met, and her heartbeat quickened. He was moving sideways, shoulder first, working without effort, exchanging nods. It was as if a respectful sea was parting. He had held her close, had kissed her. She mustered a tentative smile.

"Hello," he said quietly. "I'm glad to see you."

"And I, you," she managed. Where to go from there, she had no idea.

"The trial is going fine," he said. "Mason is posturing. Greene has his strategy worked out."

"I didn't expect it to be so—so cadenced." She tried to say it better. "It seems deliberately theatrical."

"A trial can be like that," he said. "All that matters in the end is what the jury believes. And they will believe us."

He was standing almost as close now as when he had embraced her, and she felt a gravitational pull forward. But the entire town of Lowell crowded around them, what was she thinking? There was some anonymity in Boston, but none here. She took a quick step back.

He looked puzzled for an instant; then his face relaxed. Almost playfully, he reached up and tipped his hat. "Good to see you here, Miss Barrow," he said formally. "We'll talk again?"

"Yes," she said.

He turned and blended back into the crowd. Eager hands reached out to shake his. He was disappearing back into his true life, and no amount of her pretending could change that.

At a quarter of two, the crowd began making its way back into the courthouse. Many of them were too full of their heavy midday meal to move other than sluggishly, but the chief justice's impatient gavel warned them to hurry. Alice looked to the front of the courtroom and saw that she was none too soon. Greene's afternoon witness was just now easing himself into the chair, looking out with evident misery at the crowded room.

She inhaled sharply. It was Benjamin Stanhope.

$\mathcal{A}$lice could endure the next round of questioning only by holding her hands clasped tightly and staring at the floor. Tell yourself it isn't about Lovey, she thought. Just tell yourself that.

And yet it was. Question after question about the state of Lovey's body, spelled out so graphically she wanted to weep. The rope around her neck, pulled so tight it had cut as much as two inches deep into the flesh. The bruises on her face. Her poor body, laid out on a stranger's kitchen table, naked, for examination.

Benjamin Stanhope's voice was reedier than usual, the cords of his neck bulging prominently as he talked, and his eyes seemed somehow those of a man held behind prison bars. But even though he sat uneasily in the witness chair, he held himself with dignity. He told of his initial examination, then of a hasty autopsy he was delegated to perform. Of finding the fetus, a fetus deprived of all chance of life. He tried to tell the court about the lethal vial of medicine

Avery had given Lovey, but was shouted down by Mason. Hearsay, hearsay. Through it all he held himself straight, hands clutching his knees. Alice could see he was suffering. How strange he was. She was fueled by her anger, not defeated; clearly, for him, anger was an enemy.

$\mathscr{A}$lice trudged home slowly that afternoon, aching, not from hard work, but from the tension of holding herself still for this entire long day. Samuel had made no further attempt at conversation, which was obviously sensible, given where they were. But it was with a sudden longing for comfort that she once again climbed the steps of Boott Boardinghouse, number 52, opened the door, and was greeted with the rattle of pots and pans and shouts and general noise of the dinner hour from the adjoining dining room. She stretched out her arms, sweeping Mrs. Holloway—who looked a bit surprised—into a fervent hug. It was good to be here.

I think you should be the one going every day," Jane said at dinner. She spoke into the confused silence that fell after Alice had recounted the day's events. "I cannot imagine sitting there in such a crowd listening to lawyers shout about things I don't understand."

"No, we all need to bear witness," Alice objected.

"Do they care?" demanded Jane. "It sounds as if they're more interested in playing games than convicting Lovey's murderer."

"I don't think I've explained it right," Alice began.

"Yes, you have," interrupted Mrs. Holloway. "Girls, do any of you want to spend time at the courthouse?"

"I wouldn't mind getting away from the bloody looms," Hattie said. There was something about the harshness of her voice that made her words sound mocking.

"You didn't know her, Hattie. I'm sorry, but I think it should be one of her friends." Mrs. Holloway said it gently, but there was no doubt of the firmness of her words.

"Well, I can't," said Mary-o. "I think I'm going to have to testify, since I was with her at the camp meetings." She poked at her meat listlessly with her fork.

"I don't want to be away from Ellie for that long of a stretch at a time," confessed Delia.

Tilda cleared her throat to say something, but stopped when she began to cough. "Not me," she finally said with weariness. "We all know that."

Again, a silence.

"All right," Alice said. "I'll do it."

"Nobody will look out better for Lovey's interests than you," Tilda said quietly.

And what did that mean? To somehow be an advocate for Lovey in that strange world of legal posturing at the Lowell courthouse? A fury was building inside her. Lovey, Lovey, what were you doing? Why did you have relations with that preacher? Why, why, why jeopardize everything? She waited for some vestige of inner calm to return before speaking. "I'll bring paper and pencil tomorrow," she said to the others. "And I'll go earlier, so no one can deny me a seat."

*I*t was ten o'clock, and Alice sat alone on the porch steps, still shaken. She wanted to be laughing; reading stories; picking flowers instead of staring at them. Strolling to town on Saturday, admiring shiny leather boots in the window of Lowell's general store. What would Lovey have said if she were sitting here right now? And the answer was there: Fight for me, but don't drown; don't let all this engulf you.

Behind her, the front door banged open. She did not turn around.

"You're quite the loner, aren't you?" a voice said.

"I like a bit of privacy every now and then."

"So your gentleman friend is back in town. But he isn't showing up tonight."

Alice turned and stared at Hattie. "I'll ask you to stay out of my business," she said.

"Don't you want to know why he isn't coming?"

"I don't want to hear anything from you."

A quiet, self-satisfied chuckle. "Well, Miss Nose-in-the-Air, you will."

"What are you saying?"

"Maybe there are things you don't know about that he does. You so sure you know everything?"

Alice looked full at her, puzzled. "What are you trying to say?"

A snort from Hattie. "You people make me tired," she said. She turned and went back into the house, letting the door bang again behind her.

Samuel turned the knob of the door to the Fiske rooms in the Lowell Inn and saw, to his surprise, Daisy sitting in a chair, hands clasped together, a troubled frown on her face.

"What's wrong?" he asked.

"I need to talk to you about something," she said.

He looked at her questioningly.

"I've been hearing rumors. . . ." She paused. "It seems ridiculous, of course."

He felt a stir of irritation. This was Daisy, all uncertainty, hints, innuendos—what was it this time?

"Just say it, my dear sister," he said.

"I'm bringing this up because it is so preposterous, but on the other hand, he was out all that night—"

"Who are you talking about?"

Daisy, uncharacteristically, took time to choose her words. "You probably don't remember, but when I hear these rumors, I—I feel worried. I'm talking about Jonathan."

Samuel went still.

"He was gone all night when that girl from Lowell died."

Samuel nodded slowly.

"He knew her. He'd been flirting with her the week before, he told me so."

"I know. He flirts with all the girls. What are you saying?"

"I don't know. He's been so tense. He didn't want to go to the funeral; Father insisted." She looked at him with a flicker of uncertainty in her eyes. "I love him and I know you do, too. But I feel something's not quite right, and I don't know what it is."

"Why would his not wanting to go the funeral be something"— Samuel groped for the right word—"disturbing?"

"People here at the inn keep whispering and then stopping when I come close. There's talk going around, and I think it's about Jonathan, and I'm afraid."

"Daisy, what *are* the rumors?"

"I've just been hearing snatches of conversations, but some people are saying he was with the mill girl on the day she was murdered." Daisy was visibly trembling.

"Why did you wait so long to tell me this?" Samuel tried to control the harsh astonishment in his voice, but he saw his sister cringe.

"I didn't quite put it together myself, but I'm telling you now. Please don't get angry."

He saw her distress and squeezed her shoulder. "I'm sure there's nothing wrong," he said. There was no way his brother could be involved. These were just the types of vicious rumors that accompanied any high-profile trial. Yet he felt his heart hammering.

"There was this funny, sharp-looking girl in the lobby tonight talking in a corner with some man who looked like a lawyer, and when she saw me, she turned away."

"Maybe she is a witness."

Daisy looked unconvinced. "Are you going to tell Father?" she asked.

He hesitated. There was nothing here, just wisps of gossip; nothing tangible. "No. At least, not unless I find out there is anything to be concerned about. I'll talk to Jonathan first."

CHAPTER SIXTEEN

The next morning was cold and gray, dulling the colors of the vibrant bed of flowers outside the courthouse. The crowd of men in heavy coats and women in billowing capes was as big as yesterday's, but there was a different mood, a buoyancy to their shouts and chatter. While yesterday there had been frowns and shaking heads—a murder trial was of great rarity, after all—today there seemed to be an expectation of entertainment.

Alice looked around slowly; yes, it was in the air. Lovey as a flesh-and-blood person was already fading from thought. Transferred to the courtroom, she was tinder for the lawyers; transferred to the pages of the newspapers, she was a creation of paper and ink. The reporters were part of the general cheerfulness, leaning against the stone walls of the courthouse, hats tipped forward, trading jokes and banter.

"It always happens, Alice. Don't let it discourage you."

She jumped. Samuel was standing next to her.

"How do they forget so fast?" she said. Just having him standing so close made her voice quiver.

"It's human nature, I suppose."

But it bothered him, too; she could see that.

"This will be a difficult day," he said. "The women who prepared Lovey's body are testifying. It will be more"—he seemed to be searching for the right word—"more graphic than yesterday."

"I'm prepared for that," she said promptly. He lived in a world of propriety, where women were shielded from the rawness of life and death. He quite surely knew no other woman who had birthed calves, slaughtered chickens, and cleaned out a pigsty.

In some strange way, that knowledge seemed there in his smile. "I suspect you are," he said.

Alice noted nervously that people were again glancing sideways at them.

"Is there anything happening I don't know about?" she asked quickly. Hattie's gibe from last night was still digging into her mind.

"Why do you ask?" he parried.

"There's a new girl in our boardinghouse, and she's hinting that there's more to this case than I know."

"Damn rumormongers." It burst out of him. "Alice—"

The doors of the courthouse had opened, and the crowd was surging forward. She was about to be swept inside with the others. Heedless of glances, she grabbed his wrist. "You would tell me if something else were happening, wouldn't you?" she said.

"Yes," he said.

She released him, an uncertain expression on her face, and hurried inside.

Samuel watched Alice go, uneasy in his mind. She was vanishing into the courthouse—he could call her back, say something. But what it could be, he wasn't sure.

Damn, he had to talk to Jonathan first. Immediately. He owed it to his brother.

———

*A*lice had to scramble again for a seat, but she no longer held back from pushing herself forward. She would not be ignored and shoved aside—not now, not ever again.

The crowd hushed as proceedings began. Avery slouched deep into his chair, looking sullen, picking at his teeth with a toothpick. A quick whisper from Mason; Avery straightened, assuming a posture of prayer—hands folded, bowing his head slightly—a trick for the jury. Could anyone not see through this man, Alice wondered. There was an arrogance to him, an aura of scornfulness, as if he was here only to endure the fools who had so stupidly insisted on his presence.

First on the stand, called one by one, were the men who had helped load the body into Durfee's cart, all solemnly swearing they did their best to observe as many details as possible at the scene of the murder.

A laborer named Benjamin Manchester started off, corroborating John Durfee's testimony about the knotted rope that had been wound around Lovey's neck. It was indeed a clove hitch, he said. "We use it for killing calves, passing the cord twice round the neck, pulling it horizontally. It couldn't be tightened by someone hanging themselves."

"What else did you notice, Mr. Manchester?" asked Attorney General Greene.

"I found a piece of a woman's hair comb about twenty yards away from her body," he said. "It was lying in the weeds."

Greene held a piece of a tortoiseshell comb aloft. "Is this the fragment you discovered?"

Manchester peered at it closely and nodded his head. "That's it," he said.

Greene then held another piece of a comb up, facing the jury. "Gentlemen, this piece of comb found in Miss Cornell's tangled hair fits perfectly with the piece discovered by our witness here. I would ask that the two pieces of this comb be introduced as our next piece of evidence. As you can see, it is one entity. Something happened that snapped the comb." He slowly brought the pieces together, and they were indeed a perfect match. "They would not be found so far removed from each other if there wasn't a struggle."

"Is there anything else?"

"Yes, sir." Manchester paused and rubbed his hands together nervously. "It seemed strange that her bonnet was tied nice and tidy, because her hair underneath was a mess, with bits of leaves and twigs in it."

"Yes, strange indeed." Greene looked toward the jury. "Can anyone believe she tied that bonnet back on herself?" He cleared his throat. "And what do these facts mean, you might ask? I will repeat, they provide evidence that there was a struggle, that someone was there with Sarah Cornell, someone who set out to kill her. This young woman fought for her life—and lost."

Mason rose. "All of this assumes a murder, which has not been proved," he said. "This young woman, probably in despair at her own reckless behavior, killed herself. We will have our say in good time." This last, with a cheerful nod, to the jury.

The sun had broken through the gloom outside, and it was obviously close to noon. After a few more exchanges with the lawyers, the judge declared court dismissed, to be continued that afternoon.

Samuel was nowhere to be seen in the crowd outside the courthouse. Alice strolled around the building as slowly as she could, hoping to catch a glimpse of him. It gave her at least an aura of purpose, when in truth she had none at the moment. Sitting through this trial was akin to being trapped in a cage. There was nowhere to go; no room to show rage or even tears.

The courthouse sat on a slight rise, and Alice, from the steps, could see down the main street as far as the Lowell Bank. It seemed a long time ago, that day when Lovey grabbed her hand and pulled her up the stairs to meet the Fiske brothers. A long time since she had exchanged her first stiff, embarrassed words with Samuel.

Alice turned away from the view of Lowell and continued walking around the courthouse. People were already pushing their way back inside. Enough of this, he wasn't here. Why did she search? She mounted the steps, holding up her skirt, forcing herself to be oblivious to all.

*T*hree women sat wedged together at the prosecution's table. Each sat perfectly still, staring straight ahead. They were the women who had stood around Lovey's dead body, laid out on a kitchen table. The last people to see her as a human being. Did they cry, Alice wondered. She hoped that one of the women, at least, might have felt so inclined.

The first woman called settled her ample figure into the witness chair and faced Albert Greene as if he were an executioner.

"Mrs. Borden, we regret deeply having to call on you and these other honorable ladies to give what we know will be distasteful testimony," he began. "It is not standard procedure to question women on such personal issues as these, but we are forced to do it today."

Clara nodded and tightened her clutched hands.

"You are the wife of the sheriff of the county?"

"Yes," she said. "And they laid her out on my kitchen table."

"Will you describe, in as much detail as you can remember, the state of this girl's body?"

"There were green marks on her knees," she began. "Like she was forced to kneel in the grass."

"What else?"

"Her poor body was beaten up in the belly area, and there were bruises all around her neck. Like thumb marks."

"What else, Mrs. Borden?"

Mrs. Borden began to respond when a man in the front of the courtroom let out a raspy yawn. She stiffened. "We saw she had been dreadfully abused, and she was young and pretty and didn't deserve this, and we did our best to clean her up," she said. "This was on my own kitchen table, and I see that girl's body there every day. There's nothing to yawn about." She lifted her chin and glared at the offender. A slight titter shook its way through the crowded courtroom.

"Fine, thank you." Greene said, looking toward Mason, who shook his head firmly. No cross-examination here.

*H*our after hour was filled with testimony from a string of witnesses reaffirming the prosecution's claim that this death was murder, not suicide. Proving that Ephraim Avery had intimate relations with Sarah Cornell and had reason to want her silenced was taking longer.

Hardest to bear for Alice was listening to people who might have possibly saved her—but for a reluctance to intervene.

"The factory bell was ringing when I heard screeches, and we had two cords of wood to split up," said a shop owner named Eleanor Owen, who appeared in a hurry to say her piece and leave. "I told the boy to open the door to hear more distinctly, but I did not hear the screams again."

"So you did nothing?"

"There was nothing to do," the shop owner said with a thread of indignation in her voice. "I had enough work on my plate."

"I heard screeches and then stifled groans," testified her husband. "I thought it was a woman and someone was beating her."

"Could you locate the source of these cries?" asked Greene.

"They were in the direction of the stack where she was found.

I heard the sounds for three or four minutes and started to go up there."

"Why did you change your mind?"

The witness shrugged his shoulders, appearing a bit abashed. "Well, the screeches stopped."

The entire courtroom went silent. The jurors, to a man, looked stricken. Greene said nothing, nor did the defense. It was a good thirty seconds before Greene spoke, and then it was with great weariness. "You may step down," he said.

The chief justice banged down his gavel. "Court is dismissed until tomorrow morning at nine," he announced. He and the other judges stood, their black robes again swirling in unison, and filed out of the courtroom.

Alice watched them go, wondering, what were they feeling now? Were they capable of closing their eyes and imagining the sound of a poor woman screaming for help, when no help was to come? Or did they truly have the dry and dusty hearts of men of the law?

*A*lice looked around one final time. No Samuel. She had seen Hiram at the prosecutor's table, but Samuel hadn't been in the courthouse since the morning. She felt—what? Strangely lonely. Yet waiting for something—and it was an uneasy feeling.

*T*hat night, the corner of the dining hall where they gathered to eat was subdued. Alice read from her notes and answered questions as well as she could, her voice shaking slightly as they talked about Clara Borden's dignified reaction to the man who yawned.

Delia clutched at Ellie and pulled her onto her lap as they talked, her fingers squeezing so tightly into the child's shoulders, the girl protested. She kissed her quickly. No one teased; everyone knew Delia saw threats everywhere.

Mrs. Holloway let out a sigh and put down the heavy platter she was carrying. It hit so heavily, juice from the meat oozed over the side and onto her carefully scrubbed oilcloth. Uncharacteristically, she made no attempt to clean it up.

"I should have been more charitable to Lovey, I could've been. Maybe if I hadn't fussed at her so much she would still be alive." Amazingly, tears were inching their way down Mrs. Holloway's dry, crepey cheeks.

Mary-o rose swiftly and put her arms around the woman. "Lovey didn't mind. You make this place home for us," she said. "Maybe we should stop complaining about the food and tell you that sometimes."

"Oh my, this is all so sticky sweet," Hattie said. "How did I get sent to this happy place?" She poked at the stew, moving it around on the plate. "I think the food here is usually awful, so I'm the fly in the ointment, I guess." She gave a mirthless giggle. "Or in the overcooked stew."

"Hattie, we know very little about you," said Delia, still holding onto Ellie. "Where are you from?"

"A farm up in Maine," Hattie said. "Don't think I chose to come here."

"Is that why you're always so cranky?" Ellie piped up.

"It's the company that does it," Hattie fired back. The table fell silent as she pushed her chair back and stood. Her hair was braided so tightly it pulled the skin on her face taut, giving her a strangely doll-like appearance. "I don't have to sit here and be insulted," she said before marching out of the room.

Alice jumped up and followed her into the outside corridor. "What were you hinting at before?" she demanded.

Hattie whirled around and faced her. "I wasn't hinting at anything, I was *telling* you that someone pretty important is involved in all this, that's what I've heard. And you're mixed up in it, too."

"Who is it?"

Hattie appeared to be struggling with herself. But to hold a delicious morsel of information back clearly was not her style. "It's Jonathan Fiske," she said. "Now aren't you surprised by *that*?"

"Jonathan?" Alice reached for the door frame, steadying herself. "What are you saying?"

"I'm hearing he was right near where the so-called murder was committed that night, but because he's a Fiske, nobody who knows will speak up. Instead the whole county has gone after the Reverend Avery. They'd condemn an innocent man, they would." Her eyes were burning now.

"What are you trying to say?"

"If Lovey was murdered, why couldn't it have been Jonathan Fiske? He'd romance any tramp. That's what my preacher says."

The truth dawned on Alice. "You're a revivalist, aren't you—one of Avery's converts. You're saying this out of spite."

"Oh, so the upright Samuel hasn't told you about his brother?"

Alice opened her mouth to respond, but could bring no words out.

"You listen to me. Reverend Avery is a great man, being slaughtered by the likes of you and that whore who probably killed herself," Hattie spat out.

Suddenly Mary-o emerged from the dining room, moving swiftly toward Hattie, her hand raised. With full purpose, she slapped Hattie across the face. "Lovey was *not* a whore, and you will never say anything like that around here again," she said fiercely.

Hattie stepped back, eyes narrowing. "Mary, you're the one who brought that woman to our meetings. You should be ashamed of yourself."

"And do you not remember the attention Reverend Avery gave to her? Did you not sniff out any hypocrisy then? Or are you one of those who not only would gladly prostrate herself in front of him, but turn over on your back as well?"

Alice could hardly believe what she was hearing from the gentle, mild-mannered Mary-o. She put out a hand to steady her furious friend as the others, open-mouthed, clustered in the hallway door and listened.

Hattie had recovered, standing straight again, eyes hot as smoking cinders. "I'll not forget those words, Mary," she said. "And you will pay for them." She looked around at the others. "I came here because it was my duty, and I've learned what I think is true, so I'll not spend another night in this infernal house. You think you're respectable—well you're not, the people who run the mill just let you think you are. And you—" She turned to Alice. "I know what's going on. And I know some people who will be very interested. You'd be wise to protect yourself."

"What is she talking about?" Ellie piped up.

Mrs. Holloway pushed forward, standing now between Hattie and the others. "Get your things together," she said. Her voice was firm. "I'll arrange for a new place for you in one of the other boardinghouses tonight."

The girls watched silently as Hattie exited the house, carrying her battered bandbox in one hand and a soiled looking pillow in the other—her own, she announced, and let no one accuse her of stealing from this godless place. She left with her chin up, her bony shoulders pulled back, looking oddly vulnerable.

"She wants to hurt us, too," Jane said, watching her go.

"I thought she looked familiar," Mary-o said with a quiver. "I couldn't place her, it was always dark at the camp meetings—I should have known."

None pressed Alice about Hattie's accusations, for which she was grateful. Yet there were glances, some puzzled looks. As Hattie's figure vanished into the night, Alice lowered herself into the parlor rocker, worn in mind and spirit. Could Jonathan be involved in this? No, no—Samuel would have told her. Wouldn't he? She knew in her bones who had murdered Lovey, they all did. But there had not been surprise among the others at the mention of Jonathan's name. Rumors must be going around, rumors she hadn't heard. For almost an hour, she rocked, eyes closed, before rising to go in and join the others in the bedroom.

*A*lice?"

It was Mary-o, her voice gently cutting into the darkness.

"I have to testify tomorrow, and so does Mrs. Holloway, and I'm frightened."

Alice managed a small smile in the darkness. "After confronting Hattie tonight? You don't have to be frightened of anything."

"Not even judges and lawyers?"

Alice laid her head on her pillow and closed her eyes. "Not even judges and lawyers," she said, and started to drift off to sleep.

"Oh, I wish that were true."

Alice turned on her back and stared up at the heavily shrouded ceiling. "So do I," she whispered.

*W*here have you been?" Samuel slammed the door behind him as he strode into the parlor of the family's rooms at the Lowell Inn and stared at his younger brother, slouched deep in a chair by the fireplace. "I've been hunting for you. You've been doing a vanishing act again."

"I'm making an appearance, aren't I? I don't have to tell you where I am every minute."

"This isn't the time for some fancy smirking response," Samuel said, eyes narrowing. "I'm hearing rumors about you, Jonathan, and I'm worried. I need to ask you some questions."

"I'm always supposed to be in trouble," Jonathan tried with a ghost of his usual insouciance.

"Where were you the day Lovey Cornell was killed?"

"Out trying to enjoy myself."

Samuel couldn't hold the anger back, not anymore. No sensible sternness, no knuckle-rapping. He grabbed his brother by the collar and pulled him to his feet.

"Don't you fool with me. I've got to know. There's a man on trial for murder, and whatever happened, you can't hide behind the family. I need to know."

Jonathan wrenched away, but his mouth was quivering slightly. "Some brother you are, where is your loyalty?" he managed.

Samuel stared at him, set back by his petulant, aggrieved tone. A time frame had slipped; this boy was not yet a man. Or was this the man he was to become?

"I need to know the whole truth," he said. "Everything that happened."

"Will you stand by me?" There was fear in Jonathan's eyes.

The question gave him pause. He did not believe his brother had done harm to anyone, certainly not to Lovey Cornell. No matter how he obsessed, how he walked around the possibility that he might be wrong, he never could believe it. So it would be an act of faith, his reply.

"I will," Samuel said. "But I won't hide the truth."

Jonathan lowered himself slowly back into his chair and folded his hands in front of him. He lifted a sober face, a face aged in a minute with the first recognition of what couldn't be dodged or shrugged away. "Fair enough," he said. "But no one will believe me."

"I'm listening." Samuel pulled up a chair, sat down, and waited.

CHAPTER SEVENTEEN

*A*lice firmly settled the lunch basket Mrs. Holloway had packed onto the empty space next to her in the courtroom. It was late, almost time for the day's testimony to begin. It had been difficult to elbow her way past Avery's supporters passing out pamphlets proclaiming his innocence. They were growing more aggressive, pushing face-to-face, chins jutting, insisting on acceptance of their message.

Alice craned her head above the crowd, looking for Samuel at the prosecutor's table. Again, he wasn't there—but she recognized instantly the hat on a woman's head in the row just behind the table. The woman turned, and her profile left no room for error—it was indeed Daisy Fiske.

The judges were filing in. Was it her imagination, or did they look impatient and cross? No matter. The day's testimony had begun.

*M*r. William Pierce, you are a ferryman, is that right?"

The first witness, a short, stout man with muscular arms, nodded. "I do the Cooper Island Ferry run, sir. Have now for years."

"And you know Ephraim Avery?"

"Yes, sir, I've ferried him over at that spot several times."

"Did you take him over on the day before the murdered girl was found?"

"Objection," snapped Mason. "No—"

"I know, you still are calling this, laughably, a suicide," Greene rejoined.

This time, a cackle from one of the jury members, quickly suppressed. It was Eleazer Trevett, the man with the pox scars serving as foreman. Greene gave him a jaunty grin, then turned back to his witness. "Just eliminate the word 'murdered,' sir. The question is the same."

"Yes, I took him over to the island. Thought it was strange he wore no cloak." The ferryman resolutely avoided looking at Avery.

"He says he never left the mainland that day."

"Well, I'm sorry, sir, but he was on the ferry to the island," said William Pierce firmly.

Avery let out a snort. Alice heard the sound of the pencil in his hand snapping in two. His fingers grabbed at a sheet of paper, crunching it into a tight ball as his lawyer leaned over with a whispered warning. Avery said something sharp and settled back in his seat.

"Which takes a passenger directly to the town of Clayville, near the farm where the girl was found?"

"Yes."

Greene looked triumphant, and Alice was thrilled. Now they needed eyewitnesses in Clayville. But surely the jury would note that Avery had been caught in a lie.

One by one, Greene called witnesses to the stand who could help establish Avery's presence near where Lovey had been found. The keeper of the Bridge Tavern in Clayville said he saw Avery in town, dressed in a box coat and hat, but no cloak, walking very fast, perhaps to ward off the cold. "Somebody said, 'There goes that Avery preacher again,'" he said.

"And this is a positive identification?" Greene's eyes were hopeful.

The tavern owner hesitated. After a long pause, he said, "I do not swear positively that he is the man, but I say he very nearly resembles him."

Greene pulled at his collar, sweating in his jacket, though the courthouse was drafty and cool. He looked enormously frustrated. Then, determined.

Alice looked over at the jury members, wondering what they were thinking. The barber kept scratching his head and moving restlessly in his seat. Was he listening or just hoping to soon get home, back to his business of cutting hair and shaving affable patrons? The legal clerk, what was his name? Horace Brewster. He kept stifling yawns and spent most of the time looking slightly confused. Another juror, sitting in front and dressed all in black, seemed quite dour and severe. There was no reading his face; it looked always the same.

*D*aisy was standing at the bottom of the courthouse steps, frowning, her eyes searching the exiting crowd. She was dressed in a silk gown of pale blue and hugged close a cape of the softest white wool Alice had ever seen. People walking by were mostly giving her respectful greetings, the men tipping their hats. But there was an edge to some glances, a sharpness in some eyes, a few whispers. Not all today were dutiful admirers of the Fiske family, not with the rumors circulating.

Daisy pretended not to notice and brightened with relief when she saw Alice approaching.

"It's quite exciting to be watching all this, don't you think? I wonder—" she said in a rush, stopping when she saw Alice's blank look. "I'm sorry, I know, this was a friend of yours who died, what a dreadful thing for me to say. Now you'll just think I'm a vapid idiot again."

Alice held her tongue. Her impatience with this woman had

softened; it seemed no longer to matter. She tried to stop herself from looking around for Samuel, but Daisy caught her search.

"He's not here," she said. "That's why he asked me to come, so our family always has someone in the courtroom." She glanced nervously at a scattering of men, obviously mill workers, standing outside the crowd, walking back and forth, shouting about safety at the mill. Her mouth tightened in distaste.

"Why isn't he here?"

Daisy pulled herself straight, reluctantly getting to the point. "I'm not happy about being his messenger, I must tell you. I think all of this between you two is ill advised. But he wants to see you. He asked if you could meet him this evening out by the bridge leading to the mill."

"But—why isn't he here?" Alice pressed.

"He wants to tell you about—some developments," Daisy said firmly, clearly not intending to give any more information. "Goodbye." She clutched her white cape close and turned to go back into the courthouse. She stopped, glancing back at Alice. And then, seeming not to know what to say next, she hurried away.

Alice stared after her with growing apprehension.

$\mathcal{M}$ary-o was next on the stand. Her face was pale. She kept biting her lower lip as she looked out over the crowded courtroom, constantly smoothing down the folds of her best gingham dress.

"You are Mary Dodd, is that correct?" Greene began, keeping his voice gentle.

"Yes, sir, and a friend of Lovey's. I worked near her at the mill."

"You were a member of Ephraim Avery's flock and attended his revival meetings, I understand. And you were the first person to witness the initial connection between Avery and Sarah Cornell?"

"Yes, sir, I was."

"Tell us about that."

"I could tell he liked her. He kept glancing at her when she stood with us because she wasn't praying, just standing there watching, while the rest of us were moving back and forth, singing—"

"Prostrating yourselves before preacher Avery?"

Mason was on his feet, shouting an objection, but Mary-o, flushed, had already blurted her answer. "Yes, sir, though I would never do the like again."

Haltingly, she told how Avery had come over to talk to Lovey after the meeting, how they had chatted conspiratorially.

"Did they go off alone together?"

"Not that night. But she thought he was good looking, and Lovey was a sort of a flirt, I guess. We went back a few nights later. I felt good, because I wanted her to be saved."

A guffaw from the defense table. *"Sort of a flirt?"* said Mason. "That's an understatement."

The chief justice glared at Mason. "Watch out, Mr. Mason," he said. "That kind of outburst again and I'll hold you in contempt."

Proceeding slowly, Greene drew out the details from Mary-o. Avery sat still throughout the testimony, once again in the posture of a minister of God: head bowed, hands clasped on the table before him.

There were four visits for the two of them, with Lovey disappearing one night for a very long time, Mary-o said. And there was her darkening mood. Finally her announcement that all the fervor of the tent revivals was hypocrisy, that Avery's evangelists were using God to drain money from people who didn't have much and using power as seduction. "There were no jokes from her anymore," Mary-o said firmly. She kept her eyes averted from the defense table, refusing eye contact with the line of Methodist church officials staring at her. Avery, hands still clasped, shook his lowered head slowly from side to side.

"Can you tell us a little about her last full day of life?" Greene asked finally.

"Well, we saw Alice off to Boston on the stagecoach. And then I asked Lovey if I could borrow pocket money to buy fabric for an apron," Mary-o began. "Lovey dug in her pocket right away and gave me a handful of pennies and asked if I would get her some, too. I told her thank you, that my work apron was so stained and torn, I couldn't wear it anymore. And then she laughed and gave me a kiss and said if I would wind a bundle of yarn for her that evening, she would make the aprons on the weekend."

Mary-o stopped for breath and looked around. Alice caught her eye, and they exchanged wan smiles. The two of them were among the very few in that courthouse who knew how Lovey's voice sounded when she laughed, who knew how lighthearted and generous she could be.

"She wasn't sad that day," Mary-o explained. "She seemed like whatever had been bothering her was taken off her shoulders, finally."

"Thank you, Miss Dodd," said Greene, sounding satisfied. No one surely could doubt now that this girl had every intention of living to the next day—and beyond.

A relieved Mary-o scrambled down from the witness chair as Mrs. Holloway was being called to the stand. How small the older woman looked outside the context of Boott Boardinghouse, number 52, Alice thought. There she loomed large; here in this court, she appeared almost fragile.

Greene began gently, asking what Lovey's final day was like.

"She worked a half-day shift and had an early supper," Mrs. Holloway said. "Then she changed her frock, putting on a better one she used for church, said she would be gone until very late. I left the door unfastened; shouldn't do that, but I thought, just this one time."

Greene was checking his pocket watch and hardly seemed to be listening—until abruptly changing the subject. "You found some surprising evidence at your boardinghouse recently, is that correct, Mrs. Holloway?" he asked.

"Yes, sir."

"And what was it?"

Jeremiah Mason, who had been whispering to his client, stiffened, instantly watchful. Avery's head snapped up, his eyes on full alert.

"There was a note she signed saying Reverend Avery would know where she was if she went missing. And some letters to her. We found all of them in Lovey's trunk."

Greene pounced, quick as a cat. "Notes linking Miss Cornell with the Reverend Avery, is that correct?"

"Yes, sir."

"Objection!" yelled Mason.

"Let's see where this goes, and then I'll rule," said the judge.

"Those letters are unsigned, Your Honor," said Mason. "He's trying to get them into evidence, and he can't do that!"

"Who were they written to?" Greene shot out.

"They were addressed to Lovey."

"Your Honor, these letters are meaningless! What proof is there that they are in my client's handwriting?"

"We will provide you with an answer to that, my dear Mason." Greene was grinning as he thanked Mrs. Holloway and called his next witness, a man of small, stooped stature—Barnabas Leech, a postal clerk at the Lowell post office. Choosing his words slowly, he told of the tinted letters, particularly why the yellow letter was important—he had seen Mr. Avery drop it in the box, and when he retrieved it for delivery, he saw it was addressed to the unfortunate Miss Cornell. "Yellow letters aren't so common, sir," he said. "I know, my brother sold the only box he had of that kind the week before."

"And who bought it, Mr. Leech?"

Leech pointed toward the now stone-faced Avery. "He sits right there, Mr. Greene."

Mason slammed his hand down on the desk and jumped up. "Your Honor, this trickery is outrageous!" he bellowed.

"There's no trickery about it! Your Honor, we have discovered the pages exactly match the stationery Avery owns and uses," Greene shouted back triumphantly, drowning out Mason. "They conclusively show he had a relationship with this woman. They conclusively show he was reacting to her news that she was expecting his child. They conclusively show he was confirming the time for a meeting. It is clear he intended to do her harm!"

Now the chief justice was banging his gavel, calling for order. He beckoned both lawyers to the bench, where the argument continued. Alice tried to catch a frightened-looking Mrs. Holloway's eye, eager to reassure her. You could tell, looking at the jurors, that they were impressed.

Finally both lawyers retreated. The judge cleared his throat and spoke to the court. "The note Miss Cornell wrote about whom to approach if she went missing will be admitted as evidence she was not contemplating suicide. But the letters purporting to be from Mr. Avery to Sarah Cornell are rejected. There is no proof they were written by him and are therefore circumstantial."

Greene looked stunned. Still on his feet, he said nothing at first.

Alice held her breath. The most incriminating material against Avery was being dismissed. Greene would find a way to fight this.

She watched him sink into his chair, staring at the judge. After a long moment, he rose again and spoke in a strong but funereal voice.

"Your Honor, the prosecution rests its case."

A gasp rippled through the courtroom.

And Alice could not miss the slowly spreading grin on Avery's face.

CHAPTER EIGHTEEN

*T*he shouts of children playing drifted up from the playground as Alice made her way to the mill bridge—a careless, exuberant mix of voices that spoke of normalcy and safety, which she usually enjoyed hearing. But they were only faint background noise this evening.

She saw Samuel first. His form was in shadow as he paced back and forth in front of the bridge, hands clasped behind his back. His steps were quick and short, the walk of an impatient man.

It had been so long since they were alone. She felt her breath quicken as they approached each other.

"Hello, Alice," he said.

The pause that followed was awkward.

"Something bad has happened?" she asked.

"No, on the contrary." Samuel straightened his back. He must keep this calm. He could not think about more until after this trial.

"I was afraid you would tell me we were losing." She stopped, watching his eyes shift away slightly, then come back. Something was wrong; there was reason for worry. Why had Albert Greene seemed to give up today? The evidence putting Avery near the crime scene was strong. Wasn't it enough to convince the jury?

"There are new facts emerging," Samuel said.

His voice was curiously flat for a man conveying good news. "What is it? What's happened?" she asked.

"My brother is the missing witness," Samuel said heavily. He nodded toward a bench by the rushing river. "Sit down, Alice."

*A*lice was unaware of holding her breath as she listened, only of the stinging waves of pain radiating up her arms from her tightly clutched hands. She anchored herself on Samuel's face, noting the stubble on his usually well-shaven chin as he spoke. He held her gaze, never flinching as he told the story.

The always restless Jonathan had been heading for a tavern on the path toward the Durfee farm the day of the murder, when he spied Lovey. Abandoning his original plan, he had approached her and begun trying to coax her into joining him for the evening. But he was greeted with no ready smile, no flirting or teasing. She seemed tense, oddly controlled. "You're meeting someone else," he had said, the truth dawning. She nodded, then looked past him and asked him to leave.

At that point, Samuel said, Jonathan saw a tall, thin man wearing green eyeglasses striding toward them, a wary, hostile expression on his face. He almost didn't hear Lovey's wry comment: "So the Reverend Avery shows up on time today."

"What did your brother do?"

"Turned on his heel and got out of there," Samuel said. "The last thing he wanted was an encounter with some pious fool who might see fit to denounce him to Father."

"He saw them *together*? Why hasn't he come forward to testify?"

"He thought no one would believe him," Samuel answered. He heard his own voice, watched the impact of his words reflected in her eyes. Could she see it from Jonathan's point of view? "He wasn't brave, Alice. Father had already warned him to stay away from the mill girls—told him if he didn't, if he got into any more trouble, he would cut off his monthly stipend. But he kept pursuing Lovey. He wasn't wrong about one thing—it would be easy for the revivalists to accuse *him* of murder. They would celebrate that, oh, quite jubilantly. Anything to taint our family with scandal."

Alice barely heard him. "He would do that? He would let Avery get away with murder?" She was stunned. All along, through all this pain and grief, it was Samuel's *brother* who could have convicted Avery? She stood, unable to sit still. "Greene gave up today. What now?"

Samuel didn't know why Greene had rested his case, but he hesitated to admit it.

"The trial is far from over," he said. "We have solid evidence of Avery's guilt. Don't discount the fact that Greene always has a backup plan. He knows how to play a jury. And now he has Jonathan as his star rebuttal witness. It will work." He stood, too, reaching out, then stopping, not sure whether she would welcome his touch. "I want to assure you, Jonathan *will* testify." It had taken long hours of persuasion, but it was done.

"And how did you get that promise from him?"

"He gave me his word."

There was a tightening at the side of Alice's mouth that he couldn't fail to notice.

"Are you sure you believe his version of events? There are other stories going around."

"You're asking whether or not he could be lying to cover his own guilt."

"Yes, I am."

"I know him, Alice—he is my brother. I've known him all his life. He is shallow and, yes, vain, but he is no murderer." For once, Samuel felt he had said the right words to strengthen his brother's backbone. Jonathan would face his dilemma, finally, like a man. He had mustered the strength to promise he would testify, regardless of the consequences.

"Alice, believe me. He's not lying. He's scared to death, but he isn't lying."

Relief flooded through her. Still, it nagged; Jonathan had not come forward voluntarily. "What would you have done in his place?" she asked.

"I would be afraid. But I hope I would have the courage to step forward. Look, I promise, we'll get this done. But we shouldn't talk about it, not yet. Not until the defense rests its case."

The conviction in his voice was calming. "You will do the best you can to make it happen," she managed.

"Yes," he said, his voice steady. But he couldn't stop there. "Though nothing is certain except my feelings for you."

He had shifted the terrain, just like that.

Samuel reached out for her, pulling her gently toward him, inhaling the sweet scent of lemons on her breath. She yielded, resting her head against his chest, and he hoped she could feel the rapid beating of his heart. She lifted her face to his, and his nerves relaxed. It would be all right; she believed him.

Still, he asked, "Do you trust me, Alice?"

"Yes," she whispered, trying to keep her voice from shaking. "Samuel, I do—but anything more for us is an impossibility, and we both know that." With an effort, she stepped back. "I need time to think," she said.

A jolt of alarm. "Am I not promising what you want?"

She smiled faintly, her voice slightly strained. "I want the man who killed my friend to spend the rest of his life in prison," she said. "Please make it happen."

"I will." It was a vow like none other he had ever made. He pulled her back—one more kiss, deeper this time. And for a long, hungry moment, holding tight, they clung to each other, shielded from care.

Then together, they trudged back up the hill, silent, noting only the sound of crunching gravel under their feet.

Tilda, bundled up, was sitting in a rocker on the porch at Boott Hall when Alice arrived back at the boardinghouse. She looked as tiny as a doll, her chin barely above the cocoon of blankets. Her face was gaunt after all the long nights of labored breathing. There had been less coughing lately, though, a good sign. She had seemed more engaged in the last few days, joking and laughing, playing with Ellie. The doctor had even said she might be able to go back to the looms in another week.

"Tilda, you look like an Eskimo," Alice teased as she ascended the porch stairs. "Are you warm enough?"

"Of course, I am, I'm bundled up to my eyeballs," Tilda said. She pointed upward with a hand grown scrawny from her weight loss. "It's such a gorgeous night, look at all the stars, Alice. How could I stay inside on a night like this? Will you join me?"

Alice sat on the porch rail this time, gazing upward. "I used to sit out here with Lovey every night," she said.

"I know. I was a little jealous of you both."

"Really?"

"You seemed so comfortable with each other." Tilda looked again at the sky. "Wouldn't it be nice to be able to fly up there and visit a star? Buzz from one to another like a bee gathering pollen?"

"I love that," Alice said. "And then we could visit the man and the woman kissing on the moon."

"You seem happy tonight. Am I guessing correctly as to why?" Tilda said quietly.

She couldn't share the news yet about Jonathan, not until there was a plan to get his testimony before the court. But that wasn't what Tilda was asking about. Alice felt herself blush. "Is it that obvious?" she said.

"I think we've all seen it. Perhaps even sooner than you did."

Alice straightened, bringing her gaze back to earth. "It's true," she said. "I think about him every day. But there is so wide a gap between us. And with all of what is happening at the mill—" She didn't finish the sentence.

"You're fearing disloyalty, Alice. It's not disloyal to reach for a better life. Do you love him?"

Did she? Oh, it cried out from inside of her: *yes*.

"I don't know—I am overwhelmed." Her words were false; no, they were true. It was hopeless, they were both. How strange to be talking about this with Tilda; she had shared her feelings only with Lovey before.

"Don't be a coward," Tilda said. "Take chances. We all have to do that, once in a while."

There was a sharpness in her voice that surprised Alice. "You are feeling better, aren't you, Tilda? You've been improving, the doctor says. Is it true?" she asked.

Tilda laughed. "You all keep asking that question in various polite ways, and I love you for caring, but I will not answer too politely. I feel closer to those stars tonight than I do to the friends sleeping inside this house, and that's why I am out here. But that's just tonight."

"Should you be going home?" Alice tried to say it gently.

"There is no home to go to. Isn't that the situation for you, too?"

It was true. She would never go back to the farm, to her father, to his determination to break her will. "Home" was a sentimental idea, no less ephemeral than those stars above her head; she knew that.

"Yes, it is," she said.

"So we need to find new ones." Tilda pulled her shawl closer and began rocking gently back and forth. "Tomorrow is Saturday. Let us both get going on that." She sighed. "I love it out here."

"It's chilly, let's go inside."

"The doctor said if I was bundled well, I could stay out here longer. I love being under the stars."

"Yes, ma'am." Alice smiled in the dark. Like most of the girls, Tilda would have it her own way. There was pride in that for all of them.

Samuel walked into the parlor of the family hotel suite and froze at what he saw. Every gas lamp was lit, sending restless shadows licking up against the walls; the room shimmered in heat and sweat. Jonathan was crumpled into a chair, face buried in his hands, not looking up. His waistcoat, the fine silk one of which he was so proud, lay in a lump under his feet. Daisy had shrunk into a corner, staring at their father with frightened eyes.

Hiram, still powerful in frame, towered over his younger son, whirling toward Samuel like a striking snake at the sound of the door opening. He raised his fist, a gesture Samuel had never seen directed at him.

"So there you are, you ungrateful scoundrel—my son? My son has done this?"

"Father—"

"How dare you? You had no right to wrench that useless promise from your brother. How dare you risk everything because of your infatuation with some mill girl? How dare you jeopardize this family's future? *By sacrificing your brother?* Who are you?"

Samuel had to steel himself against stepping backward, away from his father's wrath. He shot a glance at Jonathan. His brother looked like a boy again, his face ashen as he stared at a stack of documents on the table.

Samuel followed his brother's gaze. On top of the stack was an unfamiliar deposition. It couldn't be one of the prosecution witnesses; he knew all their names, and he didn't recognize this one.

"I'll set your curiosity to rest," his father said, picking up the deposition and waving it in Samuel's face. "This is the statement of some chicken farmer near Cooper Island, name of Turnbull, the result of some overzealous witness hunting by our friend Greene. Fortunately I put a stop to it." He thrust the paper into Samuel's hands.

Samuel stared at the page: Charles Turnbull had seen two men with a young woman on the path leading to Durfee's farm on the day of the murder. One matched the repeated descriptions of the Reverend Avery. The other man had stayed but a moment with the girl and Avery and then quickly walked away. Mr. Turnbull was ready to swear that the man who walked away—often seen at neighborhood taverns—was Jonathan Fiske.

It was exactly what Jonathan had told him. "This is just what we need; it strengthens Jonathan's story," Samuel exclaimed, looking up in confusion. "Why wasn't he called to testify? He's a perfect backup witness; he's been there all the time. Jonathan, we have an agreement—"

"Like hell you do," his father cut in. "If Jonathan testifies, he will be vulnerable to everybody—the newspapers, the mill workers eager for an excuse to attack us, and every damn Methodist in New England. And if they go after him, they do it to the whole family. Are you out of your mind?"

"But Jonathan's testimony is crucial," Samuel shot back.

Hiram slammed his fist onto a table next to him so violently it seemed it might break in two. None of his children had ever seen him so angry. "My own son would do this," he roared, shaking his head.

Samuel looked at his brother, the whole truth dawning. "When did you tell him?" he asked.

"This morning. Samuel, I'm sorry. I had every intention—" Jonathan stopped talking, an image of dejection.

"So that's why Greene wrapped up the prosecution today," Samuel said, stunned, looking now at his father. "You told him to."

Hiram had regained some of his composure. His eyes narrowed;

he didn't hesitate. "Of course," he said. "And I will make sure the defense gets no wind of this. Rumors will be squelched; the people mumbling them will be fired or run out of town. Those ignorant preachers will do anything to shift the blame to someone else. We are not going to be smeared by this, Samuel. No matter what."

"And Greene did your bidding—even if it might mean he loses his case?"

Hiram's smile was controlled. "Of course," he repeated. "He may still win. But there's more to his career than convicting this pathetic excuse of a preacher for the murder of a mill girl."

The words sank in, leaving indelible tracks as Samuel stared at his father. Hiram's skin burned with blotchy color, and his eyes were flat as slate. He would have his way, and none would challenge him. Samuel had always been proud of his father's force and determination. This was the deeper level, served bald.

He had no excuse to be surprised. Without Hiram's iron control, there would have been no comfortable, privileged life for any of them, no travel, no expensive schools, no servants, no shield against loss and poverty. Oh, something magnificent had been built, quite assuredly. Hiram and his partners had made it possible for people like Alice and her friends to carve out better lives for themselves. Samuel was proud of this, he was still proud of it, but it was going to end. He could see it now. His father thought power was his trump card. He could make men bend to his will, he could threaten ruin for those who didn't, he could silence Jonathan, he could let Avery escape the law. But he couldn't stop the shifting ground under the surface, nor the unrest of faceless people at the mill.

"You can't squelch everything," he said to his father. "It's wrong."

"Just watch me, Samuel."

"You can't hold back evidence," Samuel said. "I'm going to Greene—"

"He does my bidding, and you know it."

"I'm going to fight you; I don't know how. But I will."

"Foolish words. You'll harm yourself, son."

"Maybe. But no matter what happens, the blade will cut both ways," Samuel said.

Dawn was breaking when Alice's eyes flew open. She turned onto her back, pulled up the covers, and tried to court sleep, but it would not come. She wouldn't be hurrying to the courthouse this morning, not until Monday. She stretched her toes, enjoying the moment of lazy luxury. She wasn't sure how it would work, but she felt more hopeful that Samuel would seal the case against Avery. That strange, cruel man would not escape. She yawned and turned again. Perhaps she and the others could go into town today, walk together, visit the store. Maybe they could coax Tilda to go with them.

Tilda.

Alice sat bolt upright. The incessant wheezing from Tilda's bed had stopped.

She jumped up, shoving her feet into her shoes, which felt cold from the night air. She scanned the room; Tilda's bed was empty, neatly made, obviously not slept in last night.

Well, of course, she had been so content on the porch; she had probably stayed there all night. Alice pulled on a sweater and, stumbling in her haste, hurried out of the room, through the parlor to the porch. She was there, there she was, bundled tight into her circle of blankets, only tousled hair showing. Really, she should wear a cap, she might catch cold, but she was still asleep, what a relief.

"Tilda?" Don't yell; she'll jump, Alice told herself.

No response.

"Tilda?" A second time. She tiptoed forward, a tingle of fear moving down her spine. She reached out her hand. "Wake up, sleepyhead," she said.

Nothing. Alice, wondering now if she had slipped back into a dream, carefully pulled back the blanket covering Tilda's face. She must be deeply asleep.

No.

Alice sank to her knees next to the rocker and began to sway slowly back and forth. She was dimly aware of a wailing, keening sound spiraling upward from the porch, curling into the morning air, shaking the leaves in the trees. Not until she felt Mrs. Holloway's arms pulling her up, gathering her in, did she realize that despairing sound was coming from herself.

CHAPTER NINETEEN

*T*ilda was to be buried next to Lovey; that was the consensus. It was fitting, Alice thought, as she stood by the open grave, staring down on the slowly lowering coffin. She was here this time; she had to be. Great piles of rich dark loam lined the edges of the open hole, only a few feet from the curved mound that marked Lovey's final resting place. Two workmen, standing discreetly back from the small cluster of people around the grave, rested on shovels, waiting for the signal to do their job. An uncomfortable-looking Episcopal minister—recruited by Samuel—hurried through a short service, avoiding the eyes of everyone. Benjamin Stanhope was there, his head bowed over a closed, shabby Bible.

Alice looked around. Jane, Delia, Mary-o, and a sprinkling of others from Boott Hall were here, though none had been excused from the looms. It didn't seem to matter right now. And what later she would remember, the sound destined to stay in her head and heart, was that coming from the billowing figure of Mrs. Holloway. She was crying openly, wiping her eyes with a kitchen napkin snatched from today's breakfast table—a lonely, tired sound that served as a sorrowing lament for them all.

The coffin was in the grave. Alice turned away, unwilling to watch the workers shoveling dirt over it, and only then saw another mourner standing back from the group. She stopped in surprise at the sight of Hattie Button.

"I thank you for coming," she said, reaching out a hand.

"I did it for myself," Hattie said. She did not take Alice's hand, choosing instead to tightly cross her arms in front of her chest. "She was the best of all of you, in my opinion."

"I won't argue it," Alice said. She was too tired for anger, for indignation, for any sharp retort or response. "Where are you now, Hattie?"

"I would've thought you'd be among the first to know. I've been sacked, of course." The girl's face looked worn and bitter, her thin lips almost blue.

"Why?"

"Look at that one over there." Hattie nodded in the direction of Samuel, who had taken Mrs. Holloway's arm to help her back to the carriage. "Ask him, he knows. I'll tell you, it doesn't pay to cross the Fiskes. You're fooling yourself if you think Samuel Fiske cares about you at all. He's not an honest man, and he'll abandon you in a minute to save his brother. I'm telling you, if anybody killed that Cornell girl, it was Jonathan Fiske." She gave a tired smirk. "Your beau is out to save his own kind. And himself."

"What do you mean?"

"People wouldn't like hearing about his fooling around with you; he's supposed to be the good one. We've got them both."

"We?"

"I warned you; you didn't listen. If the prosecution tries to call his brother as a witness, we'll be ready." She glanced in Samuel's direction. "I'd like to hear what he has to say to you today."

"You've been working for the defense all along."

"Of course. Good-bye, Alice." She turned to walk away and stopped, turning back. "I've got something for you," she said. She dug into her pocket and took out two objects, soft and familiar.

Alice gasped. Lovey's gray leather gloves.

"Yes, I took them off her coffin. She didn't need them anymore, and I wanted to try them on, to know how they felt. It was like—like being trapped in rubber, tight rubber. The feel of them made me choke. Not for me, I know my place." She stared directly into Alice's eyes. "I don't think you know yours. You think Samuel Fiske is your ladder up? Think again. Old Hiram will never tolerate that. Then again, maybe you'll reach the top and feel trapped, that's it. Tight, no way to breathe. Don't you understand? We have to stand with our own kind."

Her torrent of words paused. She took a deep breath and continued. "Alice, you're going to have to choose. You can't not want to avenge Tilda, can you? The Fiskes killed her." She seemed to waver, her slight figure blown by a sudden gust of wind. "I can't say I wish you well, but I'll give you fair warning—best for all of you to watch your tongues. No one around here can say what they think anymore."

Hattie turned away again and trudged off, but not before Alice saw her shoulders heave and heard a familiar cough. It chilled her heart even as she curled her fingers around the softness of the gloves.

I have something to tell you, and it is not good," Samuel said slowly. They were walking together toward the carriages by the road, the soft, damp grass of the cemetery yielding beneath their feet.

She steeled herself.

"Jonathan won't be testifying he saw Avery and Lovey together. My father won't allow it." He pushed his hands deep into the pockets of his coat, looking down at the grass.

Two steps, three. He stared at her shoes keeping steps with his own, at their worn brass buckles, which looked to be hand polished by someone who cared. He noted that her feet were small. She stopped, her feet sinking deeper into the wet sod.

"Allow?"

With effort he looked up. "He says bringing Jonathan into it now will ignite the unrest at the mill. The family will be dragged into the trial, and Mason will pile on as much innuendo as he possibly can. Our reputation will be jeopardized."

"*By the truth?* Do you agree?"

"No, of course not," he protested. "You know who I am. We're not in peril." The rest was hard to get past the lump of fury in his throat. "There's more. Greene had waiting a deposition from a chicken farmer who saw the three of them that day. He recognized Jonathan and saw him walk away from Lovey and Avery. *It would have corroborated Jonathan's story.* Damn it all, it could have sealed the case."

Her face went blank with shock as his anger spilled out.

"They had that deposition all along, and they're not using it? Is this why the prosecution rested early?"

There were no words to explain; he searched for them, but there were no words. "My father is a powerful man, and I'm not denying his influence," he said.

"So everything was decided by Hiram Fiske?"

"Alice, what can I tell you? I did not know this, believe me—but the answer is yes."

"So why aren't you fighting back?" she said, suddenly furious. More than furious, frightened—remembering Hattie's parting words.

"I'm trying." There was no use telling her he had battled with his father. Or that he had confronted Albert Greene, demanding he find a way to call the chicken farmer to the stand, to no avail. Or that he had actually hunted down Turnbull and urged the frightened chicken farmer to step forward and speak up. It was hopeless. Hiram Fiske had reached him first. Legally, his hands were tied. There was nothing else he could do.

"You mean, you won't!"

Her voice sliced deep into his chest. "I don't run the mill," he said. "My father does."

"Don't give me such nonsense, you are part of it all, surely you could have fought back," she lashed out. "So you're telling me a witness could have confirmed your brother's story, but your father actually cares so little about the truth he didn't allow it?"

"We haven't lost yet; we can still win this case."

Alice paid him no heed. "Ah, and what happens to the people—the so-called *rumormongers*—who knew Jonathan was involved?"

"They lose their jobs." He stared at his shoes sinking into the wet turf.

She nodded in the direction of Hattie Button's disappearing figure. "Like that girl, right?"

"She was one of the people passing rumors and whipping up the mill workers." He paused at the sight of Alice's disdainful eyes.

"And poor and in need of a job to boot. Her crime was criticizing the Fiskes."

What could he say? He wanted to shout out, I'm sorry, it was despicable. He wanted to vomit out the arrogance and power he had lived with so blindly all his life. But he was a Fiske, and he was caught.

"Yes," he said. "It's wrong, it's stupid." He stopped, balling his hand into a fist, hitting it against a tree.

Alice stood and pulled her shawl tighter around her shoulders. She looked at him coldly.

She was dissecting him, that's what she was doing, he realized. And he had no way to hold back her knife.

"Then I shall say good-bye." She turned and walked away.

There was no moon that night, but Alice settled onto the steps anyway, tightening herself into a ball, trying to hold in her anguish. She fingered her mother's cameo, worn today to Tilda's funeral. She traced the line of the delicate profile of her mother, knowing it by heart. But it was futile; there was little comfort in memories tonight.

Samuel, I thought you were so much more. The man who had kissed her had disappeared; reverted to form. Alice pushed back her tears. He lived in a safe world where there was no disaster that couldn't be avoided or deflected. He was alien to her, that was the truth, and to have begun to think differently was foolish. The air was still; the earth smelled sweet and dry. Her face was not.

The next morning in court Jeremiah Mason was in fine fettle, clearly smelling victory for the defense somewhere just around the corner.

"Your Honor, and gentlemen of the jury"—Mason bowed low as he began to speak—"my job here is to lay bare the prejudices of the prosecution's witnesses, that lame, straggly line of misguided souls you were forced to listen to for all these many days." He rolled his eyes, eliciting grins from three jurors. The legal clerk, a short man in owlish glasses, briefly glanced up, then went back to reading a copy of the Methodists' pamphlet defending Avery.

"Now we've got people swearing they saw the Reverend Avery, almost sure of it," said Mason "Well, they qualify it a little; they *think* he was the man they saw near the site of this woman's unfortunate—*and self-inflicted*—death. But none can say so indisputably." He glared at the prosecution table. His cold smile promised a long session.

Over the course of the day, five doctors took their turns in the witness chair, each testifying identically. The fetus found in the autopsy was too far advanced to have been produced at any of the times when Lovey supposedly knew Avery. Well, yes, it was true no one really knew what was a standard length, one admitted on cross-examination. "We'd have to peek into a lot of bellies for that information," he said jovially, sending a nervous wave of titters through the jurors' box. Mason smiled comfortably, noting that the doctor who had performed the autopsy, an older man named Benjamin Stanhope—employed by the Fiskes, of course—was recruited hastily for the job and was quite lacking in experience, one might say. "Wouldn't you put less confidence in the quality of work performed by such a man?" he asked.

"Objection," shouted Greene.

"Objection sustained," Chief Justice Eddy snapped.

But those in the jury box had heard, and the answer Mason wanted settled snugly over their shoulders, though none were aware of its presence.

By lunchtime, a heavy torpor began descending over the crowded courtroom. Yawns, stretches. Each doctor was saying about the same thing; once you'd heard one, you'd heard them all, a few people murmured to one another. As for the jurors, Alice was sure they were hardly listening.

After the courtroom refilled for the afternoon session, the thrust of the testimony began to shift away from the presence or absence of forensic evidence. Instead, witness after witness began offering stories about Lovey's reckless behavior.

"I saw her going to the privy once with a towel, and I knew what she was planning to do," said Asaneth Bowen, who claimed she had worked with Lovey in the Fall River mill.

"And what was that?" purred Jeremiah Mason.

"To kill herself, that's what. Her eyes were too fiery, red, even. A naughty, reckless type, that's what she was."

"Objection!" Greene rose to his feet.

"Sustained." The judge sighed.

But the testimony was relentless.

"Her language was different from any I had heard from a female," testified a mill foreman from New Hampshire. "Coarse, in my opinion. I began to be inclined to suspect she was partially insane."

One more, another—finally, six witnesses, all swearing they knew

Lovey Cornell. And, of course, coincidentally, they were all Methodists. And none worked for the Lowell mill.

Alice lowered her head, swallowed by weariness. As far as Jeremiah Mason was concerned, it wasn't Avery who was on trial anymore; it was Lovey Cornell. And that apparently was fine with Samuel. Oh, he was there during the morning session, sitting next to his father near the front, his fine, strong profile an arresting sight, the image of integrity. Once she had seen him quickly scan the room, looking for her. Their eyes had met; she had not blinked. His face unreadable, he had looked away. He disappeared before the afternoon testimony.

Tears slowly rolled down her cheeks. To admit it was hard, but Hattie was right.

Samuel slumped down into the carriage waiting for him outside the courthouse, instructing the driver to use as much haste as possible to get to Boston. Hiram could bear witness alone for the rest of the day; he couldn't stomach the charade. Hiram didn't care if Lovey ended up being the one "convicted" here, even if the image of the Lowell mill would suffer. He'd ride that one out, or at least he thought he could. But to fight to convict a man guilty of murdering a helpless girl? Not if it collided with his self-interest.

Samuel stared out the window as the carriage clattered out of Lowell, noting the flower baskets just installed—at his father's directive—on each lamppost. Grace notes, Hiram liked grace notes. The town he had built must look proper and vibrant, must reflect his will, his vision, no matter what realities intruded. But even now, in the middle of the day, he could see a small cluster of men on the steps of the Lowell Bank: hands in pockets, caps pulled low, talking, arguing. News of Tilda's death was everywhere; one more girl dead from inhaling cotton. Was his father blind to the mill workers' anger?

A shout—and a thud as something hit against the side of the carriage.

"Sit back, Mr. Fiske," yelled the driver, whipping his horses. "That was a rock thrown by the men from the mill. They're throwing 'em at the Methodists and throwing 'em at you, why can't they make up their minds?"

"They will," he replied. He hated the image of himself, crouching down, hiding from the people who had made the family's fortune, with nothing he could do about it. Nothing at all.

He thought of Alice. That steady, cold look on her face last night. He had put it there, and he feared there would be no erasing it.

The wheels caught sparks of light from the afternoon sun as the carriage clattered on, bouncing over rocks, twisting around corners, bearing him back home.

There was only one person he could talk to about this. He hoped she would be awake when they reached Beacon Hill.

Samuel rushed through the door of the Fiske mansion, peeling off his gloves as he started up the stairs. It was late.

"Can I get you some tea, Mr. Fiske?" a flustered maid at the bottom of the stairs said, obviously surprised at his arrival.

He stopped and turned around. "No, thank you," he said distractedly.

"Some dinner, then?"

He looked at the girl, observing her worried frown. Her duty was to cater to his every whim, something he had spent his life taking for granted.

"No, Isabelle, I'm fine," he said.

She bobbed her head, relieved, and disappeared, probably into the kitchen at the back of the house.

Samuel started back up the stairs, but something made him stop and gaze with fresh eyes at his surroundings. The flickering gaslight in the front hall added a deep glow to the gold frame holding the portrait of his grandfather. His eyes traveled to the ponderous chandelier above his head, noticing how the reflected light danced on each drop of crystal, burnishing everything in the hall—the crimson carpet beneath his feet, the gleaming pendulum swinging sedately inside his mother's old clock—all of which he took for granted.

What had all this looked like to Alice when she first mounted these steps? From his vantage point, he could see into the library, where the flickering gaslight illuminated the gold-leafed leather volumes that lined the glass-enclosed bookshelves. What had she thought when she saw those books? Had she marveled at the richness of knowledge—which he also took for granted—inside their pages? Had she thought of how inaccessible they were to her?

He steadied himself against the banister. What a difference there was in their lives. An enormous gulf separated them. Saddened, he proceeded up the stairs.

Gertrude Fiske, a mohair shawl tucked around her shoulders, lay in her bed on an exuberance of plumped-up pillows, a book, open but unheeded, in her lap. She looked up as Samuel walked into the room.

"Daisy told me what happened," she said, squinting through a pair of lopsided glasses. "Poor girl, such a fragile teacup—came back this morning and couldn't stop crying. Thinks it's Armageddon. Sounds like you tried to do the right thing, Samuel. Now what?"

He sat down heavily. "I don't know," he said.

"You're the heir apparent to the Fiske dynasty—impressive role, isn't it?" A little of her natural humor had crept into her voice.

And he was finally able to say it. "I don't belong here anymore," he said.

"My dear Samuel, in some ways, you never have," she said softly. "Neither have I. The difference is, you can do something about it."

He looked closely at her, wondering why it was so easy for all to dismiss her as a placid old lady; nothing else, no spark of rebellion. But it was there; he could see it lurking in her eyes and found himself wishing he could bring forth from her the fire of the woman she once was.

"Do you feel trapped?" he blurted, immediately astonished by his own question.

"Sometimes." She didn't seem surprised. "Oh, your grandfather was a dashing, hard-driving man, and I loved him. He was an innovator. Nothing excited him more than trying something new." She smiled a bit sadly. "Hiram was born with his father's drive. Watching him and his partners plan the Lowell mill, using Francis Cabot Lowell's drawings from England—all drawn from memory, what a feat that was. Then putting it together so the whole thing *worked*— those were wonderful times. We took chances. That's what's gone now. Among other things."

He checked himself, rolling over the as-yet unspoken words of anger in his head. "Grandmother—" He stopped.

"It's all right, Samuel." She squeezed his hand. Her fingers felt like soft silk. "I know you are furious with your father. My poor Hiram, he lost himself somewhere." She sighed. "He enjoys too much the ability to make others do his bidding."

"Without acknowledging he could at times be wrong," his son said softly.

She smiled again. "He keeps us all in fancy lace and polished shoes, doesn't he? But he never understood the joy there was for his father and me in the *act* of toiling upward. He just wanted to be at the top and stay there." She struggled to pull herself up on her elbows. "Samuel, you and your brother and sister will see change— oh, my goodness, it is coming. I wish I knew how to get Hiram to pay attention."

"What can I do? What can I say to get him to understand?" He didn't try to mask the bleakness in his voice.

"What does your young mill girl say?"

"She knows we're not going to fight for a conviction. She knows the Fiskes care only about themselves." He rubbed his face, trying to ease the tension. "She sees me as a coward."

"You are not a coward, Samuel."

"Then what am I?"

Gertrude Fiske mustered a smile. "You are a good man, and you will find a way to prove that to yourself—and move on from there."

"What about you?"

"Oh, I'm here to mop up the pieces." A flash in her eyes—of what? Sadness? "Not much of a role, when all is said and done. But I'm a tidy sort, dear."

CHAPTER TWENTY

*J*eremiah Mason was taking nothing for granted. For the next several days, he fought back ferociously against Greene's various sly ploys to link Avery with the unsigned letters in Lovey's trunk. They meant nothing. She was a crafty girl, out to die in such a way that Avery would be ruined, Mason said. "Would she manufacture evidence? Yes!" he said, facing the jury, arms spread wide. "And would she commit suicide? Of course; suicide is so common a termination of their careers that it may almost be termed *the natural death of the prostitute.*"

Those words soaked deep into Alice's heart. She scanned the faces of the jurors; none looked shocked. Nobody leaned forward, eyes narrowing, mouth tight, disapproving. No objection from Greene. No mutters from the crowd. No reaction from Hiram Fiske in his seat at the front of the courtroom. No Samuel at all. She looked at the confidently swaggering Mason pacing back and forth, sharing with all the respectable citizens of Lowell his declaration about "fallen" women. Witness after witness, climbing on and off the witness stand, agreeing with him. Winks, sly remarks, muffled chortles. And by day's end, she felt beyond a doubt that there was a current, deep and dangerous, taking not only Lovey but women like herself ever farther from a dwindling shore.

Alice sank into her seat, on the edge of despair. Just for an instant, no more. Then she straightened her spine and pulled herself up. It wasn't over; she had to remember that.

*A*lice joined the crowd pushing outward, trying to shape in her mind the report she would give of this harsh day to the others at dinnertime. She could hear shouting even before the heavy wood doors of the courthouse swung open.

"Rabble," muttered a cleric squeezing forward on her right. "They'll use any excuse to get us."

"People are throwing rocks, mind your heads," somebody cried out.

The crowd surged, this time taking Alice out the door. A rock flew by, almost hitting the cleric next to her. He swore and shook his fist at a pale young man with waxen cheeks. Alice recognized the rock thrower as one of the mill workers who hauled in the cotton off the wagons.

"We know what goes on at those campsites of yours," the young man shouted. "You pretend to be men of God, but you're seducing women, that's what's happening. It's debauchery!"

He had barely finished shouting when a policeman grabbed him by the shoulders and hustled him away.

"Good riddance, and a pox on both sides. Mercy, I hope this trial ends soon." The speaker was the wife of an Episcopal deacon whom Alice had seen frequently on Sundays at Saint Anne's. She was fanning herself vigorously, as if trying to clear all unpleasantness from the air, at least any that might attach to her. When she realized she had been talking to a mill girl, she moved quickly away.

I don't know if I can keep going to the courthouse," Alice said to her friends at dinner. "It isn't the fighting outside, it's the trial itself."

"That foul little Jeremiah Mason should have his license taken away," Mrs. Holloway said, slapping an extra plate of fresh bread and butter on the table. "No one else there represents us. Now eat, you need strength."

"'Suicide . . . the natural death of the prostitute'?" Ellie said slowly in a thin, high voice. "He said that?"

It was easy to forget the presence of this child, and yet her tiny, heart-shaped face was a constant in Boott Hall. She rarely had much to say, sometimes bouncing restlessly next to her mother when the conversation got hard to follow. At times like those, she would remove whatever scrap of ribbon or bright yarn held her hair and carefully rebraid, pulling it tight, retying her ribbon, and then—often secretively—begin chewing on the ends. Delia, without even looking at her, would press her arm, and Ellie would dutifully stop. But she always listened.

They all paused. Indeed, Ellie's eyes had seemed to reflect less wonder lately, the natural loss of childhood, no doubt. That was a sad thought, but did that perhaps make her less vulnerable? Was that good or bad? Alice didn't know.

Delia instinctively drew her daughter close, but Ellie, gently, resisted. "I know what he's saying, Mama. He's a stupid old man."

The girls exchanged weary smiles.

"Where is Mr. Fiske?" Ellie asked of Alice. "Is he still our friend?"

The child's question hung in the air. Alice felt rather than saw the instant wariness of her friends around the table. They had not probed; no one had pushed to know more about her relationship with Samuel. Their undeclared loyalty was comforting, but they knew the rumors about Jonathan. Yet she couldn't decide what more to tell them. There was their safety to consider, for Hattie's words replayed insistently in her brain. Hiram Fiske was a hard man, and if he said those who talked about his son's involvement would be sacked, he meant it. And Samuel? If he didn't have the grit to stand up against such a harsh dictum, then he wouldn't save the jobs of anybody at Boott Hall, hers included.

"I don't think he will be around here anymore," she said.

A small sigh from Ellie's lips. "He doesn't believe what Mr. Mason said, does he?"

"No," Alice answered. She rested her right hand on the table, feeling the scratchy surface of the cracked oilcloth beneath, and stared down at the pattern of bright oranges and reds. Mrs. Holloway silently buttered a piece of bread and handed it to her, but she couldn't quite move to pick it up. The rest of the dining hall had returned to its normal cheerful buzz of gossip, with occasional curious glances in the direction of the four girls and a child who huddled now each day in their own island of grief. They were alone.

No, Samuel didn't believe Mason's venom. Alice could say that much for him.

*A*cross town, in the Fiske family suite tucked away in the Lowell Inn, Hiram sat with a glass of whiskey, swirling it slowly, not drinking. Directly opposite him sat Albert Greene, also cradling a glass, but his was almost empty. Standing back from them both, hands deep in his pockets, was Samuel.

"So my son has been not only arguing with you and his brother but trying to collar that chicken farmer and get him on the stand," Hiram said lazily, flicking a glance at Samuel. "Ungrateful progeny, got any of those yourself, Albert?"

Greene stirred uncomfortably but only muttered a vague reply.

"You would talk of me as a balky child?" Samuel said evenly. "You miss what is at stake, Father."

"And what is that, Samuel?"

"You have chosen to subvert the truth." He turned and looked at Greene. "Something I would think you, sir, would find unacceptable. But apparently not."

Greene flushed, his hand unsteady as he lifted his glass to drink.

"Are we going to fight over this again?" Hiram shot back.

"It isn't over, Father."

"Oh, yes, it is. There's nothing you can do, so you might as well focus with us on the rest of our case." Hiram turned to Greene. "What more does Mason have?" he asked.

"More of the same, enough to confuse the jury, which is of course his intent."

"This should have been an easy case using the available evidence."

"We were getting there, Hiram." Greene's tone was nonaccusatory, but Samuel saw his father's eyes narrow. "And I haven't given up."

"It's going on too long; I want it concluded. Too much unrest."

"Then your man is Jeremiah Mason. He's holding the cards right now." Greene tossed back his last swallow of whiskey. "'Suicide . . . the natural death of the prostitute'? Mason gets off some wild charges, but that one is particularly memorable."

Hiram shrugged, managing to make it a faint gesture of regret. "We need to work at not letting our emotions get too involved."

"Nothing wrong with a little disgust now and then."

Hiram abruptly turned to Samuel and asked, "What are you hearing from your pretty little friend at Boott Hall?"

Ah, a lighter conversation was being proposed. Greene perked up: perhaps a bit of male banter lay ahead.

Samuel saw the expectation in his father's eyes; it was time for a change of mood, and it was his job to provide it, to engage in one of those effortless changes of subject that his family did so smoothly. Another set of marching orders.

Samuel could say nothing. He walked to the door, pulled it open, and left the room.

"My son's a bit of a brooder," he heard Hiram say with a sharp laugh.

CHAPTER TWENTY-ONE

*Y*es, it was Samuel, waiting at the top of the courthouse steps. She saw him standing there, quite still, from a distance down the road as she walked. There was a bite to the morning air, and she inhaled a lungful, quickening her step. There were few people around yet.

He had seen her now. She kept walking, but it wasn't his gaze drawing her; it was her own resolve. If one of the few strengths available to her was pride, she had it. It was strong inside her, and none of them, not the judges sitting up there looking lofty, not the jurors scratching their heads and yawning, not the befuddled or malevolent witnesses, not the deacon's wife stepping back from the contamination of a mill girl or Samuel himself, could destroy it.

She paused at the foot of the stairs, shoulders straight; then climbed.

"I can't leave it where we were," he said. His eyes were strained, lined in red, his skin pale. "It's not enough."

"It has to be," she said. "You made it clear you were not willing to challenge your father for what you know is the right thing to do. You've confirmed the Fiskes will protect their own. There's really nowhere to go after that."

"I made it very clear my father runs the family like a corporation.

Don't dismiss me so quickly, Alice. I have things I need to say to you. You can march away from me, and I will respect that, but I'm not giving up without a fight."

She looked at him warily. "What do you want?"

"I want common ground for us both. Honesty. At least a search for it."

She seemed poised to run, chin up, eyes wide. It wasn't fear that he saw, he realized. It was defense against all that would hold her back, all that diminished her. And it was that valor of spirit that had drawn him to her in the first place. He loved this woman; he knew he did. But he couldn't say that to her, not yet. "Love" was too facile, too easy an emotion, and he would fight for more.

Common ground? What a strange concept. Alice gazed at him sadly. Perhaps she had seen more strength of character in this man than he possessed. Perhaps she had built a fantasy that few could live up to. She knew now her true loyalties. They had to be to her own kind.

"I don't think we'll find it, Samuel, that's telling you true," she said.

"Could we talk—on the bench by the bridge to the mill? Tonight?"

She took a deep breath, hesitating. This wasn't just about the two of them anymore. And it wasn't just about Lovey, either. It was about his family's power to deny justice to all who worked for them, whenever they so chose.

"I can't force a man to testify, whether it's my brother or a chicken farmer," Samuel said. "But I will do all I can to get a guilty verdict out of this trial."

Words, just words. He would exert no power at all, not in defiance of his father. But she nodded. "Before dinner. I'll be there," she said, then turned away and hurried off, already troubled by her decision. She had bent his way; she was still attracted. She could not break free.

Just as Hattie had predicted.

*I*t was another deliberate and tedious day. Mason set about the systematic process of casting doubt on the testimony of as many government witnesses as possible, putting people on the stand armed with often-laughable contradictions. They included half a dozen men of the cloth who attested to seeing the Reverend Avery in a small tent at a Methodist prayer meeting. Each reported seeing him at precisely the same time in precisely the same place, and therefore he could have been nowhere near the site of the murder. Even the jurors were grinning at about the sixth witness—everyone spoke from an identical script.

It didn't matter anymore whether testimony hurt or helped the case against Avery; it was entertainment.

At one point, Greene threw up his hands in disgust. "Your Honor, my esteemed colleague for the defense is throwing in every fragment of half-truth he can find, doing his best to keep the focus off the basics of this trial. Ephraim Avery had the motive and opportunity to commit this crime, and *there are letters to prove he had a relationship with this woman and had tricked her into meeting him in an isolated spot in order to kill her.*"

"Objection!" yelled a furious Mason. "The prosecution has rested and cannot push again for new evidence!"

"You had your say, Mr. Greene," the judge said wearily. "Court will convene tomorrow. We will move to closing arguments." He looked as distracted as the members of the jury now pushing and stumbling their way out of the jury box, most probably in search of a pint or two before dinner.

*I*t was growing late when Alice began trudging home, hurrying to make it to her meeting with Samuel. She felt more weary than on the days when she tended up to six looms for a full shift. Mostly, she felt sad.

Nothing was ever going to be fine. Tilda had asked if she loved Samuel, but there was no way to answer that, not given the impossibility of separating out her feelings for him from what he represented. If Lovey were here right now, they could talk about it. She would understand the contradictions. The truth of it suddenly twisted her stomach: losing her friend had meant nothing less than losing a bridge to her own heart.

No, she couldn't erase Samuel from her mind, not instantly, but time would do it for her. And yet the very fact that she had agreed to this meeting proved he stirred her like no man ever had before. Maybe, she thought, I am the hypocrite Hattie Button thinks I am.

She approached the playground, pausing for a moment to watch the children in the soft spring twilight. The little rocking horse had been freshened with a coat of red paint, and a small boy, laughing, rocked away without a care. How short, that time of happy, uncomplicated joy. Children should have some warning, some way of knowing it was dangerous to look out at the world with unguarded pleasure. But who would want to tell them, to deprive them of those few moments of blissful ignorance that would have to last a lifetime?

Alice shrugged her shoulders, trying to shake off her gloom. What was she doing, inviting sadness every time she saw a happy child? She hurried past the playground, wincing slightly each time a small, sharp rock pushed too far into the thin soles of her aging shoes, pulling her shawl close as she walked. Her thoughts felt like fragments of a puzzle, pieces scattered everywhere.

She stopped. Coughing—she heard coughing.

She glanced over to a cluster of bushes just off the road and saw a seated woman crouched tight, head down, hand to mouth, trying to muffle the sound.

"Who are you?" she said, stepping closer.

The woman's head lifted. "You," she said, her voice hoarse. "Of all people, you."

It was Hattie Button. Alice hurried over and dropped to her knees.

"Leave me alone," Hattie panted.

"You're sick."

"No business of yours."

Hattie began to cough again, heaving deeply. Alice tried to steady her, wincing at the feel of her narrow rib cage. The girl twisted and struggled, but they both knew what had to happen next. The cotton had to come up. Alice glanced back at the road; no one was there, and it was too far to the boardinghouse to shout for help.

Hattie began to weep. She coughed deeper, harder. Alice held on. Finally, it came. A large mass, but more. Alice shivered, trying to turn Hattie's head so she wouldn't see. A clot of blood as big as the cotton ball had followed.

Hattie went limp.

"What are you doing here?" Alice said. "You need help—why are you outside?"

Hattie nodded in the direction of her old bandbox—now with a broken handle—under the tree. "I've been trying to leave, but I can't go far."

"Where have you been since the funeral?"

Hattie tried to pull away. "I don't have to tell you."

"Well, you can't stay out here. I'll take you home for tonight."

"No! Everybody there hates me. Just leave me alone."

Alice looked at her with frustration. She couldn't leave her here. "Hattie, where have you been staying?"

"I'm afraid I'll get him in trouble," Hattie said, crying again.

"Who?"

"Oh, what's the use? Dr. Stanhope. Don't tell the others."

Alice stood, pulling Hattie up as gently as possible. "I'm taking you back to the surgery," she said. Slowly, struggling under the unexpectedly heavy weight of the sick girl, Alice made her way back toward town.

*B*enjamin Stanhope's eyes showed instant relief as he opened the door and saw them both. "I didn't think she'd get very far," he murmured.

He took over the burden of carrying Hattie, leading her into an anteroom, where there was a cot with a pillow and a blanket folded at the foot of the bed.

"She's been here since Tilda's funeral?" Alice asked.

"They let her go, you know that. She had no money, and she was sick. What was I supposed to do? Leave her out in the woods to die?"

His tone was almost belligerent, and Alice was startled.

Hattie lay down and closed her eyes. "I saw the blood," she said.

I can't take this anymore," Benjamin Stanhope said quietly after he and Alice walked out of the room, closing the door so Hattie could sleep. "Please stay for a moment. I've fixed some tea."

She glanced out the window; shadows were lengthening.

"For a moment," she said.

They were sitting down now, across from each other. He dropped his head into his hands. "There are too many girls getting sick," he said.

"How did Hattie come to you?"

Only in desperation, he said. Her revivalist friends had shunned her, with some whispering that if she spied for one side, she'd probably spy for the other. And who needed a sick mill girl?

"You were good to help her," Alice said.

"I have to ask you not to say anything. I'm not supposed to treat any but those who work for the Fiskes." He raised his head. "She has a sister who is coming to take her tomorrow morning. She was determined to leave on her own. Now she knows she cannot."

Alice stood, reaching out her hand. "I'll say nothing," she promised.

"I want those mill windows kept open; that's what Samuel Fiske promised. All of them." Stanhope's voice was abruptly harsh.

Samuel. "I'm sorry, Dr. Stanhope, I have to go," Alice said quickly. Maybe there was still time.

She ran—past the playground, past Boott Boardinghouse 52. She was almost to the bridge. Let him still be there, please let him be there. She saw the bench through the night mist; was there a figure sitting there, or was it her imagination?

There was no one there.

Alice collapsed onto the bench. She opened the pouch of her bag and pulled out a small handkerchief, inhaling its freshly laundered smell and pressing it tight to her eyes. Samuel, Samuel, how long did you wait? I wanted to be here; there is no denying it. And what had her not showing up told him? That she cared not at all; that she had made a promise she had no intention of fulfilling.

A slight breeze rustled through the leaves of a small boxwood shrub to the right of the bench, and Alice held her breath. But no one was approaching.

She had decided to tell him the truth tonight. *Honesty.* He said the word so bluntly, it had reached deep inside her. But what was it? She might have revealed too much. Oh, what did it matter now, and how does anyone give up all hidden thoughts and survive?

The breeze was playing now with her hair, and she looked up to the stars, feeling some peace in gazing at so much beauty, so far away. She stood, ready to head home, and almost tripped over a long stick of wood lying at her feet. She picked it up, puzzled. It was a sign of some sort—she turned over a piece of canvas nailed to the stick and saw the bright red message scrawled on the other side:

STRIKE MEETING SUNDAY NIGHT

Alice read it, then reread. No matter how she stared at the words, they would not say anything else, and they began to calm her. There was only one thing to do. Her turmoil eased, and she walked home with a steady pace.

Samuel stood on the balcony, barely registering the stars, doing the best he could to quell his own emotions. Two hours, he had spent on that bench. At some point, he had begun to feel like a fool. He could be angry; he had a right to be angry. He couldn't have stated his feelings more plainly this morning. And he had seen in her eyes a sudden connecting spark that had given him a day of mounting hope. No, something changed, she had shifted direction, without the courtesy of letting him know.

Reluctantly he lowered his eyes and stared out toward Boott Hall. There would be no sleep tonight. He wanted now only to see this trial over, to walk away, to turn his back on all of Lowell. He curled his fists tight around the cold balcony railing. He was a dreamer, a stupid dreamer. Hiram would have a good laugh over that.

CHAPTER TWENTY-TWO

*F*inal arguments began the next morning, the crisp, clipped
voices of Mason and Greene pounding home their opposing
arguments. The case against his client was all circumstantial and
could not stand up to examination, Mason announced with scorn.
The evidence was sloppy, vague, and given by hysterical witnesses
on a witch hunt, people of weak character determined to pin a possible murder on a man of the cloth whose religious affiliation they
rejected. And was it murder? There still was no proof of an actual
crime! The unfortunate Miss Cornell, having reached the end of the
line with her easy sexual favors, had found herself pregnant. Shamed,
she had committed suicide. An old and familiar story. "If you were to
seek for some of the vilest monsters in wickedness and depravity, you
would find them in the female form," he declared.

This trial was no witch hunt, Albert Greene declared when it
was his turn. The people of Lowell had responsibly done what they
could to bring a murderer to justice—the fact that it was "a man of
the cloth" who had done the deed was irrelevant. Did Lovey Cornell commit suicide? "Impossible," he told the court. No woman
could have hung herself like that; no woman could have inflicted
those wounds and bruises on her body by herself. And though the

defense was determined to deny it, the letters found in this unfortunate girl's trunk were clearly traceable to Ephraim Avery. His motive was clear—he had impregnated her, and he solved his problem by murdering her.

Only near the end of his summation did Greene clear his throat and speak to the destruction of Lovey's character by Mason. "Nothing has given me more unpleasant feelings during this trial than the attempts to impeach the character of that young woman," he said slowly. "I find it sad and astonishing that the defense has fought so hard to blame her for her own death. This extraordinary attack—which will find its place in our legal history—is meant to tell us that a young woman like this with nowhere to turn is expendable. And that leaves a shadow on our system of justice."

The courtroom was very still. Greene stood silently, legs spread, his hands linked behind his back. Finally he looked up at the judge. "That is all, Your Honor." He sat down, but not before locking eyes coldly for a long moment with Hiram Fiske.

"Thank you," Alice whispered under her breath. She strained to catch a glimpse of Samuel, who sat with his father in their usual place up front. There he was, jaw firm as stone, without expression, looking neither to right or left. If he understood how true Greene's words were, surely he would show some sign of emotion. But his face showed nothing.

Chief Justice Eddy gave final instructions to the jury shortly before five in the evening. The jurors then filed out of the jury box and vanished through a door leading to the room where they were supposed to sit across from one another at a long table and try to sort out truth from lies. It looked to Alice as if that mantle of responsibility was falling a bit too heavily on their shoulders.

The judge banged his gavel one last time. "Court is adjourned.

When a verdict is reached, the courthouse bell will ring." He stood and, followed by the others, left the room.

*I*t was a warm evening. The crowd drifted off, many in it glancing backward as if loathe to break the invisible cord binding them to the courthouse. It would not be good to stray too far, some murmured. The verdict could come, surely, anytime.

Alice lifted her face to the waning sunlight, walking slowly, trying to exhale the musty smells of the sweat and the dust of the courthouse from her nostrils. She looked neither to right nor to left; she would not tolerate in herself any search for Samuel.

Ahead of her, she saw the doctor outside his surgery, tending his small garden. Alice's step quickened. She had a goal now.

"Dr. Stanhope, did everything work out properly this morning?"

"Yes," he said, with a small smile. "All went peaceably."

"I'm glad," she said. There was so much more to ask, but she feared being overheard.

"She has a chance," he said softly. "The sister was kind."

"Why don't you join us at the boardinghouse for dinner?" she heard herself asking.

He scrambled to his feet. "Too much to do here," he said. He looked flustered. "Dinner? Oh, I hardly—" But then he ran out of anything to say.

Alice smiled. "Please," she said.

*D*inner was calm, a swirl of slow-moving parts, all ears straining for the one sound that mattered. Stanhope, his face scrubbed to the hue of an apple, took a second helping of brisket and actually conversed with Mrs. Holloway on the value of medicinal plants. There were no jokes, no laughing. And no one sang or played the piano tonight, and all knew why. But, at least, all who cared about Lovey were together.

Alice drifted out to the porch, inhaling the crisp night air as deeply as she could. She even impulsively wrapped her arms around a pillar—this tangible place was hers, and she would try to hold on to it, come what may.

And she waited.

So did Samuel. Not watching the stars or searching for a glimpse of Boott Hall but in a darkened room hazy with the cigar smoke puffed out in agitated bursts by his brother, Jonathan.

"I couldn't have made a difference by testifying," Jonathan said. "It would have just thrown the trial into an unholy mess."

A small cough from a wing chair by the fireplace. "Can you put that cigar out please? I'm getting a headache," said Daisy.

Samuel was silent.

"Damn it, Samuel, stop blaming me, will you?" Jonathan was puffing harder than ever. He stood, paced. "The verdict isn't in, for God's sake. They'll convict him."

"I don't think so," Daisy said unexpectedly. "They don't have the courage."

"You too? You'll turn on me, my own sister?"

Daisy said nothing. She picked at a ragged fingernail and pulled herself, tight and small, back into the chair.

"Don't you feel anything for that dead girl?" Samuel said through clenched teeth.

Jonathan paled. He sat abruptly, and his fingers drummed nervously on the table next to his chair. He tried to say something, but all he could do was look pleadingly to his brother.

There was no getting around it; it was done. Samuel entwined the fingers of both hands and held them to his face. Jonathan was not a villain, not a bad man. He would replay this decision of obedience to Father all his life, or was he, Samuel, just casting an overlay that was his and his alone?

There was a sound. Jonathan stopped pacing. Samuel leaned forward; Daisy started to rise.

The door opened and Hiram Fiske walked in. "Put out that cigar," he ordered his younger son. "And stop listening for the bell. There will be no decision tonight."

Not that one, Samuel thought. But another, yes. Soon.

CHAPTER TWENTY-THREE

*T*he courthouse bells, heavy and forceful, rang at eleven o'clock Sunday morning.

Alice pulled on a shawl and prepared to rush down the stairs of the boardinghouse; she must hurry, the courthouse would be jammed. Mary-o came running after her, grasping her in a brief, tight hug, casting about for something to say.

"We will prevail," she said with shaky bravado.

Alice kissed her forehead and ran.

*F*inally," the woman next to her murmured as she slipped into a seat. Alice braced herself, staring at the bedraggled crew filing into the jury box, watching them wince as they put their bottoms down on the hard, unforgiving bench for the last time. Weeks of sitting there; soon they would be free. She could see the relief on their faces.

Now the chief justice's voice was cutting sharply into the crowd, drawing every eye and ear, stopping every whisper.

"Gentlemen of the jury, have you reached a verdict?" he said, his voice booming through the courthouse, reverberating back from every dusty corner.

"We have, Your Honor," said Eleazer Trevett, the foreman.

Avery stood immobile, back slightly stooped, fingers twisting a handkerchief.

"Mr. Foreman, is the prisoner guilty or not guilty?"

There was not a sound, not a single drawing in or exhalation of breath.

Trevett's wobbly voice cut through the stillness.

"Not guilty."

A man swore and rose to his feet, fist in the air, shaking it at the jury. All through the courthouse, people were scrambling up, some screaming at the jury, some standing on the benches to shout, others cheering the verdict.

Avery whipped around, thrust his chest forward, his expression triumphant. He was staring right at Alice. Standing now, she stared back, fighting against the surge of the shouting crowd. Avery's backers had pushed into the courtroom with a mighty roar, cheering the jury members, all of whom were trying to escape the jury box as fast as they could.

Avery was free? No, no, it couldn't be. She could not absorb it.

"Order! Order!" shouted the judge. Bailiffs were pushing into the courtroom, swinging sticks. Avery's lawyers were trying to usher him out the side door, but the crowd was hard to clear. He was so close now, Alice could see the hardness of his face, the grooves carved deep down to his chin. So close, she fancied she could inhale the acrid smell of his breath.

"You killed her," she screamed. "Admit it."

He spat.

She felt released, almost joyful, as she plunged toward him, raising her hand, raising it high.

"Alice, no!" Samuel was suddenly next to her, grabbing her arm, pulling her away.

"I want to hit him," she said, struggling to free herself.

"I've got her, don't touch her," Samuel was shouting, pushing away a bailiff, grabbing her arms. "Alice, it's me." He panted. "Let me get you out of here."

She shrieked, struggling against him.

"You're bleeding, I'm taking you to the surgery," Samuel said, half pulling, half carrying her to get her away from the uproar inside the courthouse.

"They found him not guilty," she cried. "How could they do that?"

"They are fools, stupid fools," he shouted back.

They reached the surgery, Samuel still gripping her tightly as they entered, fearing she might break away and run back. They could hear angry voices, running feet, outside. Alice collapsed into a chair, stunned.

Stanhope was suddenly there, breathing hard after making his way from the courthouse. He peered at her, frowning. "Are you hurt?" he said.

"It's just my lip, I'm fine." She almost felt again the warm spit from Avery's mouth on her cheek, and once more the urge to hit him made her shake.

A sudden sharp sound of loud voices rose from outside. "Avery had better leave town quickly," Samuel said. "Not a good day when a guilty man goes free."

This was the firm Fiske voice, the voice of authority that would give pause to anyone. An umbrella of protection for others snapped open at will—and closed at will.

"Perhaps your family should have thought of that earlier," Alice said. Her eyes were cold, and he looked away. There was nothing for him to say. Nothing was enough anymore.

A quick, hard knock on the door. Stanhope stood and tugged at his jacket as he faced Samuel. "Mr. Fiske, I'm going to be direct with you about what else is going on here," he began. A quick clearing of the throat. "Those people at the door are here to find out if I'm going to tonight's labor meeting."

"I know about the meeting," Samuel said. "What do you plan to tell them?"

"I'm going to be there," Benjamin Stanhope said quietly. "I favor reforms, Mr. Fiske, not violence of any sort. They're here to ask me to join them, and I am going to say yes. I've seen enough of young girls with ruined lungs who cough up cotton."

The room was silent. Samuel stared at him, his gaze steady. "I respect you for that," he said finally.

"Thank you." Stanhope walked to the door and opened it.

"Eight o'clock, Doctor. Are you coming?" said a strained voice.

"Yes, I'll be there." He closed the door and turned back to the others, seemingly unsure of what to say or do next. "A plaster for your lip," he said to Alice, peering at her face.

"I'll put it on," Samuel said quickly, reaching for it. Anything to touch and comfort her.

"It's not bleeding anymore, thank you."

This time, she was the one who turned away.

CHAPTER TWENTY-FOUR

By mid-afternoon the crowds had dispersed, the indignant chatter about the verdict quieted. Lowell's streets took on at least the façade of normalcy of a Sunday afternoon as the sound of organ music drifted upward to the surgery from Saint Anne's.

The sun was high as she and Samuel stood together on a slope curving gently downhill from the surgery to a stream that emptied into the Merrimack. She felt the gentle pressure of Samuel's hand on her waist, guiding her to a path that led down to the river.

"Why didn't you meet me at the bridge?" Samuel asked.

"I couldn't," she said. So short a time ago, but it felt like a lifetime, and she had lost touch with the girl crying by the bridge, there too late.

"Are you saying you forgot?"

"No." She didn't have the strength to explain.

"It doesn't matter, you're here now. Let's start over. Don't hold back, I want to know everything," he said.

There was no way to encompass "everything" in a single conversation. It was too late for that. What she must give him was honesty.

They were down now by the stream, turning fully toward each other. He drew her close. Gently, she pulled back. She had made her decision—when, exactly? She didn't quite know.

"If that had been me, if I had been the one Avery killed, they would have dissected me in that courtroom, too," she said. "When Mason said that suicide is common among prostitutes . . . more, that it is their natural death"—she drew a deep breath—"he was talking to me." She held herself still with effort. "My mother whom I loved, who was wonderful, was married to a dreadful man."

"What happened?"

"She was in love with someone else, and my father caught them. He forced her to leave. He called her a prostitute." There was no need to add that he had also said—when she abandoned the farm—that she was destined to follow in her mother's footsteps.

He tried to pull her close again. "Oh, God, Alice," he said. He wanted to comfort her. He searched her face. He wanted to erect some kind of barrier around her, something to shield her from her sadness and pain, but it went far beyond that. Saying the words suddenly became easy.

"I love you," he said. "I want to marry you. Will you marry me?"

She shook her head slowly from side to side. She felt not a tremor of doubt. "I can't. It's not possible," she said.

"Alice, I love you."

"It doesn't matter, Samuel."

Her dismissal felt like a blow to the stomach. "Why not?"

She wanted to say the words. Through this long and tortured time since Lovey's death, they had been there; they were in her now. But the dream had evaporated fully today. Lovey, Tilda—gone. Avery free; justice denied.

"All of us here, all the mill girls, we live with your family's mix of benevolence and tyranny. It's all twisted together; there's no way out of that. I can't live with conflicting loyalties," she said.

He tried to marshal his words, but his tongue felt thick. He wanted to stop her. He didn't want to hear what was coming.

"You have to know—if you and your father don't agree to reforms at the mill, I'll stand with my coworkers. I'm going to that strike meeting tonight, and if our demands aren't met, I'll join a turnout."

"Do you blame me for Lovey's death?"

She said it almost tenderly. "You couldn't give her justice, Samuel. I know it wasn't all in your hands. But—yes, I blame your family for Tilda's death and for acting like cowards and throwing away the case against Avery. If your brother had testified, that evil man would be going to prison. Instead, your family's self-interest came first."

He was incredulous. "You judge me as if I *am* my family. I am *not* my family. Alice, I don't accept this. I don't think you want to leave me, I don't believe it. You're traumatized. This has been a terrible time. You've lost much, but there are good lives ahead for us. I will take care of you, I will help you do what you want to do—" He could not curb the urgency in his voice.

She shook her head. "You may not *accept* it, but I *mean* it. I don't blame you for all that has happened. But what kind of person would I be to not stand with the others in confronting your father? You can't make him do what you want; nobody can. But I wish—I wish you had fought back harder." The full import of what she was saying hung between them.

"You really mean this? You're telling me there is no future for us?"

"Yes."

Samuel stepped back. He didn't speak for a long moment. "I'm not giving up," he said finally. "I've waited too long to meet a woman like you, and I doubt that I will find one again. But I can't force myself on you." He cupped her face in his hands in a swift gesture, then let them drop. "And I meant what I said."

"Please, please, go now," she said.

"You're insisting on good-bye."

She nodded. "Yes. Please don't try to contact me or change my mind."

So this was finally the true way she saw him—as nothing more than a pawn of his father's. "Alice, I'm trying to understand you," he said slowly.

"Please don't try," she said.

Without another word, he turned and started up the slope toward trees burnished with dappled sunlight. He stopped and turned around. "You know when I fell in love with you?" he said. "It was in the church, at Lovey's funeral. I saw you walking toward me, so straight and proud and beautiful—I was caught then, and I can't be free." He shook his head and continued walking.

She watched him go, hands over her mouth so she wouldn't betray herself and call out to him. He didn't stop, disappearing finally over the edge of the hill.

Alone, Alice walked slowly through town toward Boott Hall, through the quiet heart of Lowell. She passed the darkened, shuttered company store where she and the other girls had once tossed scarves over their shoulders, admired trinkets that flashed and sparkled on their wrists and throats, and, every now and then, laughing with one another, put down a hard-earned dollar for a dream. And there, on the other side, the bank. How could that not be a benefit to them all? That feeling of power, slipping a dollar—maybe two— into a brown envelope, sliding it under the metal bars to a teller's hands—how could that not be freedom? It was, but there was never enough money; it was dignity granted with reservations.

Her head was aching. She had sent Samuel away; Lovey was gone; Avery was free. All lightness and possibility, over. Even now, walking down the street, she could almost hear the laughter of what had been, what could be. What dreams did she own anymore? Why had Lovey been robbed of hers? Avery would be a man looking over his shoulder for the rest of his life, but it wasn't enough.

*D*id you really try to slap him?" Ellie asked in awe.

Alice nodded silently as she settled herself into a parlor chair, a deep weariness seeping into her bones. Her job as witness to the trial was done. Tomorrow morning the factory whistle would sound, and it was back to the looms. Only gradually did she realize no one was saying anything. She looked up and saw the others slowly pulling on their coats, avoiding her eyes.

"You are all going to the strike meeting," she said.

Mary-o turned and faced her, standing at the front door. Her face was pale but resolute, her hand on the doorknob. "Are you with us, Alice?" she asked quietly.

Dear Mary-o, she knew the price of what she was asking.

"Yes, of course I am," Alice said. She stood and walked to the rack, pulling on her own coat, buttoning it tight.

A general exhalation of breath, as the girls glanced quickly from one to another, back to Alice, their faces mirroring shared relief. They were united once again. Whether that would do them any good was one thing, but at least they felt the presence of shared strength.

"We'll vote on the issues and then present them to Hiram Fiske. And if he rejects them, we'll turn out tomorrow. That's the plan," Mary-o said.

A turnout—no income, no home. All in the room knew the peril they faced.

"Let's go," Alice said. Why, she wondered, was she not frightened? When she had left the farm, it was with determination but also with great anxiety. Now it was different. She would find a way. One foot in front of the other, that would be how she would do it.

"I've got enough food in the larder for a week; I've been stocking up," volunteered Mrs. Holloway.

"What about Samuel Fiske?" Ellie asked. "Won't he help us?"

Trust a child to say what her friends must be wondering. "I don't think he can," she said gently.

*T*he vote—in a muted, somber crowd—was taken at eight o'clock. There had been little argument, with many unsure how this process worked. What would happen to them? Did anyone actually think Hiram Fiske would concede anything? "There'll just be others who'll take our jobs," argued one of the mill laborers, but there was a momentum, fed by the trial verdict that very day, to speak up for themselves, to assert something.

The list of demands was sent around the room for signatures, emerging somewhat wrinkled and soiled but legible. A messenger was appointed to take it to the Fiske family at the Lowell Inn.

Mary-o reported all this back in Boott Hall, hardly able to speak above a whisper. "We did it," she said.

Alice reached out and took Mary-o's hand, feeling a sudden, fierce pride.

There was something different rolling through the air at Boott Hall that night—something both huge and invisible. They all felt it. They clustered around the piano, singing, as Mary-o pounded the keys, playing every song she knew. They sang until quite late, breathing in the unknown, growing giddy, almost drunk, on what they inhaled.

*H*iram Fiske took the document from the messenger, touching it with distaste. "They can't even wash their hands after work?" he said to no one in particular.

He scanned it silently, then passed it to Samuel. "I want you to post a notice in the morning—anyone joining a turnout is automatically fired," he ordered.

"That's a little harsh, isn't it, Father?" It was Daisy, timidly. "I mean—"

"Daisy, where is this new concern of yours for the mill workers coming from?"

"I'm reading some of the essays in *The Lowell Offering*," she said. "The stories those girls can tell—"

"That's what they are—stories. Their jobs are reality, and if they have any sense, they'll pull back on their threats."

"They write poetry, too. Like me."

Hiram stared at her, a condescending smile pulling at his face. "You?" he said.

"Not as good as theirs, of course."

"I've seen some of Daisy's poems, and I think they are quite respectable," Samuel interjected. He saw his sister's eyelids flutter as she looked directly at him.

"Thank you," she said, clearly pleased.

"Very polite of you, Samuel, but hardly necessary," said Hiram.

Daisy blushed but held her head up.

"Are you finished reading?" Hiram demanded of his elder son.

Samuel turned back to the document. He looked up at his father when he finished. "You can post that notice, but you'll lose," he said.

"You're thinking of your little friend. It's ridiculous, you're losing your bearings."

"Maybe not tonight. Maybe they'll pull back, and you'll win in the short run. The long run? You will lose."

"I've always thought you understood how this business operates, Son." A flicker of what might have been sadness passed over Hiram's face. "We have to keep costs low; we've got more competitors trying to steal business every month now. There are people from everywhere who would give their souls to work in this factory. *We can't lose.*"

Samuel looked down at the paper in his hands. "They want some shortening of their work hours and a pay increase. They want the most dangerous machinery fixed. They want to be able to breathe. Do you find those things outrageous, Father?"

No one spoke to Hiram Fiske this way. "If we had won that conviction, none of this would be happening. They'd be praising us, dancing in the streets."

"Maybe. But these issues wouldn't go away."

"What is happening to you?" Fiske said to his son.

"Decrease their daily shift by half an hour. Increase pay by ten cents a day."

Hiram stepped back. "Don't tell me what to do."

"You need to show goodwill, to meet them partway."

"No, I don't."

"Then you lose." Samuel glanced down again at the wrinkled piece of paper. "The windows by the looms stay open," he said.

"Four hours a day, that's all."

"The girls get their lungs checked every month."

"You're pushing me too far."

"How do you want your factory destroyed? By a strike or by killing the mill girls?"

"I'll think about it. I have to confer with my partners, as you well know. Don't expect anything. Are we done here?"

"Improve the machinery. One more accident, and you'll have more than a strike on your hands."

Hiram seemed to falter. "Damn it, Samuel. I said, are we done?"

"For now."

They stared at each other.

"What are you holding over my head?" Hiram asked.

"I've realized I'm your employee, too. We all are." Samuel handed the paper back to his father.

Jonathan, who had been silently cradling a glass of whiskey, put his drink down on a side table. "I'll write all that out and post it at the mill," he said eagerly. He stood, his young face flushed, looking for the first time like a man with a purpose.

"You'll do no such thing," snapped his father. "I'll make the decisions around here."

"Not all of them," said Samuel.

Hiram stiffened. "You've got something else to say, don't you?"

"Yes."

"I suspected as much. Samuel—"

Samuel lifted his hand, a gesture to stop his father's words.

The older man looked shaken. "Listen to me," he said.

"It's done."

"Well, then." Hiram pulled himself straight and looked at his son coldly. "Let's hear it."

CHAPTER TWENTY-FIVE

*T*he 4:30 a.m. shriek of the factory whistle was as loud as ever. Alice jumped out of bed and began donning her work clothes immediately, blinking her eyes rapidly to wake up. The other girls were doing the same. No sleepy, yawning laggards this morning; they had to be standing sturdy and strong for whatever was coming their way. She glanced out the window: it would be a sharp, blustery day, the kind that more often heralds winter than spring. A sign? Nonsense, she was not going to dwell on such superstition.

"No news?" Delia was the first to ask Mrs. Holloway. Her face was strained with worry as she shushed a wiggling Ellie and tugged at the ties of the child's work pinafore, pulling them tight before crowding in with the others at the breakfast table.

Mrs. Holloway shook her head. "I heard from the milkman a rumor they're supposed to be posting their answer on the mill bulletin board sometime this morning." She didn't tell them that the milkman gave her the news while eyeing her with what could not be other than pity.

"Will they throw us out right away?" Ellie asked as she spooned heaping spoonfuls of thick oatmeal into her mouth.

"It won't work like that at first," Mrs. Holloway said. She sat down heavily, folding her hands together, then resting them on sturdy, ample legs. She looked worn this morning, beyond tired, Alice thought. For the first time, she noticed that Mrs. Holloway's hair had turned quite gray, almost silver. "They'll turn us down, then wait to see what we do. Maybe bring in a few Irish to make us sweat."

"How do you know?" asked Jane.

"We tried for change, a few years ago. A small turnout."

No one asked if there had been any good results.

No laughing or giggling this morning as the girls hurried down the path toward the bridge spanning the roaring Merrimack River. Alice found herself remembering Lovey's blithe initiation on her first day, the casual way she had introduced the whole scene, giving it a kind of breathless magic. It seemed long, long ago. But what kind of fairy-tale protection had she expected? She and the others had staked their futures on the opportunities of the mill, tasting the excitement of first-time freedoms, ignoring the cost. But now they were standing up, taking a chance, risking—that was new, too.

Alice watched her friends ahead of her, holding on to the rail as they moved briskly over the bridge. Delia and Ellie, hand in hand as always; Jane, who paused for an instant at the bridge and hurriedly crossed herself—a prayer was winging its way to her God; let it do some good. Mary-o, head up, purposeful, a newly grim expression on her usually cheerful face. Braver than expected; a salute to you, Alice thought.

But for an instant she saw more. Tilda's plump figure bobbing up and down just ahead, chattering with pride about how many looms she could handle at one time.

And Lovey. Yes, Lovey—skipping and laughing, teasing the others, somehow imbued with the gift of lightheartedness—her lively face, her curious, intelligent eyes. Alice blinked, her fantasy evaporating.

They were, all of them, child-women yearning to play, to work and dream and sing—perpetual "girls" of the mill. Few of them had experienced much childhood; that was for sure. But there was always an end to the time for that, and she knew in her bones it had come.

The factory room was heavy with moist air, the windows securely locked. The machinery was especially deafening—all looms were working. Ellie was running back and forth refilling bobbins, casting anxious peeks at her mother. The girls began glancing toward one another, nervous, as time for their lunch break approached. Where was the Fiske response? Were they intended to keep returning to the bulletin board by the door, lengthening the delay, allowing them all to grow more fearful? Briggs seemed as officious as ever. Did he know anything? What about the men working downstairs?

The lunch whistle didn't ring. Five minutes, ten—still no bell. The girls worked on, unsure of what came next. Maybe this *was* the answer, whispered one to another. Hadn't they been promised a response would come midmorning? Were they being tested?

"I'm hearing the men are going to walk out any minute," one girl muttered to another. "They're taunting us, that's what they're doing."

Ellie stopped still, wiping sweat from her forehead with her apron, glancing from her mother to the others, and then suddenly dropped her bobbin tray. Even with the machinery going, they could all hear the clatter.

"All right, then, I know how this works," Ellie said loudly in a tremulous child's voice. "Somebody has to start the turnout, and I'm going to do it." She lifted her chest, smoothed her apron, and started walking toward the door. "Follow me," she said as she passed the shocked workers at the looms.

"Ellie, no, no!" screamed her mother, lunging after her. "Don't let her walk out the door," she shouted to the others. "She'll be punished, I know it, they'll take her away from me!"

Alice reached Ellie first, stopping her with a hand on her shoulder. "Ellie, you are wonderfully brave, but not now, not this," she said under her breath. "Wait, wait. They'll respond." Gently she delivered the child back to her mother.

"I'm no coward," Ellie said staunchly. "I could do it, really."

"I know you could," her mother said. And began to cry.

It was one o'clock. Suddenly Briggs strode into the room with a large sheet of paper and walked straight to the bulletin board, looking neither to right nor left. One whack on a tack with a hammer; the notice was posted. He turned and walked out. At that moment, the whistle blew.

One by one, the looms went silent as, wiping nervous fingers on their aprons, they all clustered around the notice. Alice was closest and read it aloud.

> *This is to inform all employees that no form of turnout for any reason will be tolerated. Any employees who defy this rule will be immediately terminated.*
>
> *There will be some operational changes:*
> * *For those mill employees in good standing, pay will be increased by three cents a day. Shifts will be shortened by an hour a week.*
> * *Factory windows by the looms will be opened for two hours every day.*
> * *Safety instructions for all machinery will be posted and must be adhered to at all times. There will be training procedures established that eliminate any other than careless accidents.*

The paper was signed by Hiram Fiske and Jonathan. Not by Samuel.

The girls looked at one another.

"Did we win?" whispered one.

"I don't know," said another.

"We get raises," breathed yet another.

A sound at the door. Some of the men on the voting committee were standing there. "We got some of what we wanted," one of them volunteered, looking down at the floor.

"It isn't much," said Mary-o. "And no promises to fix the machines."

The men stared at her and at one another. "We've got families," one said finally. "We have to be realistic."

"But we have strength of numbers," burst out a younger man. "This isn't enough!"

"It's uphill, lad," said the first man.

Silence, at first. Then Mary-o began to cry. Something was gone from them, taken by the meager concessions allowed by the Fiskes. There had been a momentum, a sense of power, something reached for—but not grasped.

"Someday," said the younger one.

The committee would wait until the evening to meet again and formally accept the concessions made by the Fiske family. There was both disappointment and relief, a cautious, guarded relief. They had won something. Was it enough?

Some thought so. Others wondered.

Samuel stood on the balcony of his room, looking down onto Lowell. There really was no choice, he knew that. Hiram had kept his offer as tight and minimal as he could. How could these people walk away from their livelihoods even when offered so grudging a raise as three cents extra a day? Life would calm down in Lowell. There might even be talk again of its sprightly, forward-looking culture. Famed writers and historians would still come; the girls would march with green umbrellas to impress visiting dignitaries; all as usual. All in his father's vision. But the heart of it was beating thin.

He rubbed his eyes; Lord, he was tired. Over by the door, his Moroccan leather valise, fully packed, waited. He checked the time on his gold-cased watch, his father's gift when he had graduated from Harvard Law School. The coach to the train depot would be here soon. It was time for him to start using that law degree; Baltimore—a city of energy and change, wholly removed from the strictures of New England—would be his place to start.

"You really mean this?" his father had asked last night. His voice had been on the edge of bewilderment.

"Yes," he had said as calmly as possible. "I'm not your heir anymore. This is not the life for me. Jonathan will serve you well."

"I made concessions—" Hiram had stopped. What had transpired between the two of them went far beyond that now. There was no way to mend this tear, and he knew it, too. "When you change your mind, I guarantee you, it will be too late," he said heavily. "Don't think you have the option to come crawling back."

"That would be the last thing I would ever do."

Samuel took one last look out the balcony window, letting himself wonder briefly what Alice was doing right now. With great relief, he realized no picture of her was coming up in his mind; no connecting thread was unspooled between them, no linkage. That was a start. Imagine nothing from this point on. He walked to the door, picked up the valise, and exited the room.

*T*he vote was taken quickly that evening. The offer accepted. Alice left the boardinghouse, eager to escape the strange, almost-surreal atmosphere that descended in the aftermath of the committee's decision.

So, just enough to keep them all swinging on the ropes that tied them to Lowell. Why had Samuel's name not been on that meager offer? As heir apparent, he signed every document with his father, but not this one. Something had happened between the two of them.

She would walk just as far as Stanhope's surgery, she decided. But when she reached it, she continued onward. Just to the courthouse, then back, she told herself. But she kept going.

Finally she stopped before the destination that had drawn her, though she had not admitted it to herself. The Lowell Inn. She saw the lights in a suite on the third floor flickering. A figure standing on the balcony, looking out, then turning and disappearing back inside.

A carriage waited by the front door with two restless horses stamping their feet and tossing their heads, eager to be off.

There was no use asking herself why she was here.

She had no plan.

A man in a black coat was hurrying out of the inn; she could see the flash of a gold watch on his wrist as he checked the time. She opened her mouth, but no sound came out.

The man hoisted his valise into the carriage, swung up the steps, spoke briefly to the driver, and disappeared inside. Almost instantly, the carriage was clattering away.

Alice stared after it, watching until it disappeared into the night. She then turned and slowly began walking back to Boott Hall.

She had recognized the watch.

CHAPTER TWENTY-SIX

*T*he news around town that summer was that Samuel Fiske, the heir apparent, had disappeared. Gone off to the Wild West, or planning a mill in Baltimore. Did they have the necessary rushing rivers there? Surely not. Had he fled after being caught in some scandal? Or maybe he was on a European tour; that's what people like the Fiskes did when they felt like it. A few glances came Alice's way, curious ones, holding silent questions, but she barely noticed.

She had disappeared, too. She had purged fear and longing and anger, letting go, and now—with calm interest—she waited to see what would take their place.

Some changes at the mill had come. Someone pried out the nails holding many of the windows shut one night and, strangely, there were no repercussions. Briggs would slam the windows closed again—then, strangely, they would be reopened. She suspected Benjamin Stanhope had something to do with this but took care never to ask. He did seem to smile more.

She took long walks every evening, fighting no currents, letting her thoughts sort themselves out. Summer turned to autumn, and she crunched her way through falling leaves and then plodded her way through snow, minding her looms, saving her money.

In general, she was learning to live with secrets. She thought of her mother, of Lovey, of Gertrude Fiske—of the hidden stories in their lives, of the answers that might explain everything. Answers that would never come. Everyone carried their most grievous burdens secretly and separately; she had to accept that. But she would never know the truth about them. Perhaps the only way to keep secrets from harming others was to hold them tight in the heart and never let go. Perhaps that's what her mother had tried to do. And Lovey.

It was only as she inhaled the sharp, crisp air of frosty nights that Alice began unwrapping the secrets she kept from herself. She began thinking about Samuel. She would see his eyes, be almost able to touch the texture of his skin. She could feel too much.

He had honored her wishes. He had made no attempt to contact her.

By this time, the workers of Lowell had stopped chattering about the missing scion. Why should they care? Nothing much had changed. A little easing of hours, a taste more of money, a few machines oiled and fixed—enough to calm the unrest, but not enough to stamp it out.

There was very little talk among the girls on the morning trek to the mill, either. On Saturdays, she and Mary-o, Delia, and Jane would hunch down before the wind and make their way to town and visit the bank—every week a dollar for her savings fund—then they would buy themselves a small lemon cake and sip tea at the Lowell Bakery, letting the hot brew warm their insides while pretending to be ladies of leisure.

Daisy showed up one evening, bringing supplies for Alice's cameos—and four orders from her friends. Alice was surprised and grateful. It was restful, those evenings when she was able to carve; what a splendid thing to finally have good supplies and tools. More orders were coming in. Alice allowed herself to dream of the possibility of opening a small studio in Boston, perhaps in a year or so.

She told no one of her more ambitious carving effort—a bust

shaped from clay that she was working on at Benjamin Stanhope's surgery. He had consented to be her model, seemingly content to stay still for hours without conversation.

Sometimes, on her walks alone, she mulled over what she had learned from all of this. Was she able to be brave? She would do her best. Don't tar all with the same brush—yes, she was learning that, too. Not all Methodists had tried to shield a murderer from justice; not all were pulled in by charlatan ministers.

What she could not answer was, did she ask herself the right questions? Answers were hard enough. But the wrong questions took one into wilderness.

There was another accident—no, two. The worst was when a belt of leather worn from constant friction burst into flame, almost burning the hand of a girl on a loom nearby. The girls at the mill said little about these incidents—it was the prudent course, given that the number of mill workers who still advocated resistance had dwindled. The leaders, the ones who stood up to the Fiskes, were either muted or gone. Immigrants were coming in, cheerful-enough people, but rough and rowdy, at least in Mrs. Holloway's estimation.

It took a few months, but the undercurrents of change began, finally, to surface at Boott Hall.

It began with Jane. "My parents say that, since the trial and all the unrest, it isn't respectable to work as a factory girl anymore," she announced at dinner one night. "I don't agree at all, I told them they should know my friends. But they want me to come home." She dabbed at her eyes with a handkerchief. "They aren't proud of me anymore, that's the fact of it."

"Janie, we will miss you," cried a bewildered Ellie. "What will you do?"

Jane brightened. "My pastor at home says I can be a missionary, take God to the Indians out west. He will sponsor me."

"Oh, my goodness," breathed Delia. "How brave."

"He said girls need to think more of themselves, that we all can do more than sew and weave."

A silence fell over the room as each girl pondered this.

Over the months, others began to drift away, some to marry, some to teach, but none—they told each other this with pride—to milk cows and clean out pigsties. Never again would they do that.

On a bright, windy day, Alice, filled with new resolve, marched by herself down to the Central Street office of *The Lowell Offering* with a manuscript in hand. The usual routine was to place an offering on a desk in the outer office and then leave, hoping to be notified that it would be read and published. They won't want this, she told herself as she walked inside. But I'm going to try, regardless.

She stopped, suddenly daunted. A woman sat at the desk, a pair of spectacles halfway down her narrow nose, reading silently from a tall stack of manuscripts. Alice recognized her immediately—it was Harriet Farley, the stern-mouthed, revered editor of the magazine. She herself had worked the looms when she was younger. She was one of them. Amazing, something that could only happen, as Ralph Waldo Emerson had said once, in the proud culture of the Lowell mill girls. Only recently they had all burst with pride upon hearing that. Now it felt hollow.

"You have a story for me?" Miss Farley said, looking at her over her spectacles.

"Not one made up," Alice said, stepping forward and handing her the pages in her hand.

"Then what is it? Oh, never mind, I'll find out for myself." Miss Farley glanced at the title and raised an eyebrow. "'Decorum for Daring Ladies'?" she said.

"That was what Lovey wanted. That's the title I want."

Miss Farley began scanning the document, then turned the page, reading to the end. She cast Alice a sharp glance, went back to the beginning, and began to read aloud.

DECORUM FOR DARING LADIES
The Legacy of Lovey Cornell

I want to introduce you to my dear friend Lovey, whom I have lost and will always remember. She lived a brave and exuberant life and died a violent death, as most of you know. Now that kind of tale is usually only whispered about. But the trial was a travesty of justice, and I cannot believe to this day that the man who killed her was freed. Yet that's what happened, and I fear the pursed lips of the righteous will condemn her to obscurity.

Lovey was all of what should make a girl of the Lowell Mills proud. She had grit and she took chances and she was brave. She was quick to challenge authority, even when branded a troublemaker. Yes, she made mistakes. Who among us has not? Lovey did not judge—she accepted each of us for who we were. Why do we fear contamination from the free spirits of our world? She had wonderful dreams, and I was fortunate to claim her as my friend. She reminded me to look to the sky, to find hope and not be afraid of change. To be daring.

At the time of her death, Lovey was working on what she called "A Manifesto for Mill Girls," that she hoped to have published here for all of to read. I offer you the only two declarations she had time to finish:

1. *Resolved: no members of this society shall exact more than eight hours of labour, out of every twenty-four.*

2. *Resolved, that the wages of females shall be equal to the wages of males, that they may be enabled to maintain proper independence of character.*

So here, a few final specifics on a good life: Lovey Cornell saved a child from a wicked father, not a small thing to do. She laughed, she was generous. Her fate was cruel and wrong and I will remain angry about that for the rest of my life.

"That's all?" Miss Farley said, looking up.

"What do you mean?" Alice was confused.

"I think you need another few sentences." Miss Farley picked up a pencil and wrote out:

Beyond that, beyond all injustice, her reputation was shredded to pieces in that trial. Let us all remember that and fight back against those who would allow this to happen.

"Yes," Alice burst forth.

The two women stared at each other. "We'll call this a story," Miss Farley said with a small smile. "Or, perhaps—a call to arms? I'm quite sure it will get the attention of a few people in town."

"Thank you," Alice breathed.

"You're the girl who tried to slap Avery, are you not?" Her lips twitched. "Accidentally, of course."

"I tried, ma'am."

"And you want to sign your real name to this?"

"Yes, I do."

"Good for you." Miss Farley, her face crinkled in a smile, reached across the desk to shake Alice's hand. "I was a mill girl, too," she said.

Alice grasped her hand gratefully. "I know," she said.

*H*ave you heard from Samuel?" Daisy asked unexpectedly on one of her visits as Alice labored over a cameo. She was concentrating intently, her small, pretty face in a frown.

Alice shook her head. "No, and I don't expect to."

"Neither have I," Daisy said with a sigh. "I do miss him. Father won't allow his name to be spoken in the house." Then, with a hint of disapproval, "You did cause quite a disruption, you know."

"Yes, I know."

"He's in Baltimore, he sent Grandma a postcard, by the way. Look at what he had to offer you. Weren't you tempted?"

Yes, she thought.

"I think we both did what we had to do," Alice said.

"Oh, well, probably," Daisy said in a half-regretful tone.

Baltimore—he was in Baltimore. She had no clue as to how to imagine his life.

"My grandmother is very ill," Daisy said abruptly.

"Oh, Daisy, I'm sorry," said Alice. She felt a pang of sadness, remembering the spirited Gertrude Fiske.

"Samuel was always her favorite, but she loves me, too. And Jonathan. I do wish I hadn't dismissed her so much." Daisy's eyes were filling.

"Is she dying?"

"I don't know, but her face is as pale as milk." Tears now were trickling slowly down her face. "Someone has to tell Samuel. Father is too proud to budge. We don't know how to reach him. That's why I asked."

"I'm sorry. I wish I could help."

"That's all right," sighed Daisy. "I'll just have to ask that loathsome Lydia Corland. She loves to remind me now and then that she and Samuel keep in touch."

Alice felt a sharp pang but said nothing.

I think Daisy still wonders if I've heard from her brother, even though I've told her I haven't," Alice said to Benjamin Stanhope one evening as she worked on the bust. It sat over a heavy wad of newspapers on the top of a packing box, a perfect place, easy to pull into a closet when a patient came by. Her fingernails were thick with clay as she pushed and shaped. She couldn't get this man's face—the features were all there but something was missing. He managed always to hold something back, which was irritating.

"It goes both ways, I imagine," he said.

She looked at him, puzzled. "What does?"

"He hasn't heard from you, either."

"Oh no, not you, too?" she said with a twinge of impatience. "We have had no contact for a year."

Stanhope answered slowly, barely moving a muscle. "I do wonder why not," he said simply.

Alice pushed her thumb into the hollow crevice beneath the molded clay of the cheekbones, frowning, experimenting; gaining time in the silence that followed. "You're wondering why I sent him away in the first place?" she asked.

"I know how shocked you were by the verdict."

"It is some comfort knowing that Avery will never walk safely in Lowell again. People will not forget."

"So we leave Avery to history. And I know you wanted to stand with the rest of us for reform. But after that?"

Her thumb dug deeper. "He didn't fight hard enough to get his brother on the stand. He buckled under to his father."

"From what I know, he did all he could."

She looked up. "What are you talking about?"

"He tried to get Albert Greene to stand up to your father. He even hunted up the chicken farmer who saw them and tried to get him to come forward."

"He never told me that."

"Why would he? He failed."

"But he tried."

"Perhaps he didn't think that would mean enough to you."

There was a momentary silence.

"I'm supposed to be the timid one, Miss Barrow. Might you not share some of that trait?"

His directness jolted her. "Well, I couldn't see myself living the kind of life Gertrude Fiske does," she said quickly. "It's so—caged."

"Perhaps she doesn't feel it's a cage," Stanhope said.

"But I think she knows it is, and I saw how she was tolerated, and she had the most wit and intelligence of them all." She tried to explain, poking at the clay. The cheekbones were improperly aligned, threatening to ruin the shape.

"Do you think Samuel Fiske would have put you in a cage?"

She waited a long time before replying. "Not on purpose," she said.

"A lack of trust, not a good thing."

It was too hard to explain. Oh, she could still conjure up fantasies of what it would have been like to marry Samuel and live amid the luxuries of the Fiske mansion. She could place herself there, sleeping under the softest sheets, wearing silk, with Samuel next to her, the warmth of his arms around her. She could imagine telling him, from the depths of her heart, that she loved him. She could lie awake at night and wonder. But in the light of day, she knew the Fiske mansion would never have been a home for her. Those were not her ancestors lining the walls; that was not her world. Samuel would have finally realized the truth and drawn away.

And, feeling the soft texture of the clay beneath her fingers, she took comfort in the fact that she was doing what she wanted to do. Later, there would be hot soup at Boott Hall, a blazing fireplace, a friend playing the piano—even here, at Stanhope's surgery, there was a rhythm and peaceful continuity to work in a casing of gleaming white drawers and cupboards housing knives and needles and potions; grief and healing. All of this was her world, surely, where she could learn. She thought of her notebooks, filled with scribbled material from the Lyceum lectures she had attended this year. Fifty cents well spent, and she hadn't missed a one. Learning, she decided, was a form of saving, too. Theologians, not just ranting preachers; philosophers and writers like Charles Dickens and even the famous frontiersman Davy Crockett. And musicians—which might surprise the elegant Miss Lydia Corland.

So why was she crying? She wiped at her eyes with a rag, leaving a smear of clay on her forehead.

"You miss him," said Stanhope.

"I like my life now," she said. "I don't need it to change."

"But it is changing," Benjamin Stanhope said. "None of us can hold things where we want them to be. It is all slipping and changing, Alice."

"Well, that's quite profound." She picked up another cloth and began to clean her tools. Maybe that was why she couldn't quite capture this man's face. She stole a glance. It wasn't just that his eyelids were heavier and more weathered than before; it was a new sorrowing in his eyes. Or, perhaps, a stoic acceptance. Something, indeed, she had missed. A feeling of surprise—he was right. He was changing before her eyes, and she hadn't noticed.

"I'm glad we are friends," she said impulsively.

"So am I."

That was all. She worked on, the two of them in complete and comfortable silence.

It was dark out by the time Alice returned to Boott Hall. She opened the door of the boardinghouse, stepping back in surprise.

"You are so brave!" Ellie shouted, jumping gleefully around the room.

Mary-o was laughing, rushing forward to hug her. "Oh, there'll be trouble now, but who cares?"

"What are you talking about?" Then she saw—the girls had strung a clothesline across the parlor and, with clothespins, attached two pages torn out of *The Lowell Offering*.

"Oh, my goodness, I forgot it came out today," Alice said.

"Maybe we'll all get fired," Ellie said with a toss of her pigtails. "Then I can lead the turnout, right, Mother?"

Instead of paling and clutching her daughter, Delia tossed back her hair, fully grown out and once again a richly burnished red, and said, almost to herself, "I teach Ellie her lessons. Why couldn't I teach in a school? That's what I'm thinking."

And through all the excitement and laughter, thrilled by the sight of her own words in print, her own name signed on the last page, Alice knew that—whatever else happened—she could not and would not live life in small spoonfuls. The pain had not disappeared; it was simply banked, and perhaps that wouldn't change. But once in a while, she could dream of the man she had sent away.

A few weeks later, Samuel leaned forward, peering out through the window of the carriage, catching his first glimpse of the Fiske home in more than a year. Looming high on the hill, it almost blocked the light. He had forgotten—or had never fully realized— how imposing it was. He wondered what Alice had felt the first time a carriage drew her up to the massive doors of this place, that day long past when she had entered his life.

"Your parents are not at home at the moment," a servant whispered quickly, looking right and left. "Your grandmother is in her usual room."

The tightly controlled atmosphere made him sad. He was used to the vibrant casualness of Baltimore, and quite absorbed in his small law practice, but to be treated as a visitor in what had long been home was to realize how distance could be measured by much more than miles.

He hurried up the plushly carpeted crimson stairs, barely seeing the oil paintings of the long-dead Fiske ancestors framed in gold that lined the staircase. As a child, he was told that they were the people of character he must emulate. But they had always seemed a brooding bunch. Once he had stared long and hard at the painting of his grandfather—imagining what it would be like to talk to him—and decided he didn't like the coldly flat blue eyes that seemed to follow him up the stairs every day. Now they had no power.

It was Daisy who opened the door to Gertrude's spacious room on the third floor. "You came," his sister said, relieved. "I knew you would, she wants you. Oh, it is so good to see you." Together they approached a huge four-poster bed sitting squarely in the center of the room, a grand piece of furniture that had set Gertrude laughing uncontrollably when it was first installed for her. "If I've disappeared some morning, send a posse to shake out the bed," she had said. "I'll be lost somewhere in the feathers." Hiram had not been pleased.

"Is it my Samuel? Lord, I've seen everyone else, it had better be you." Gertrude Fiske's voice was weak but clear.

"It is." Samuel drew a chair up to the bed and grasped his grand-mother's hand.

"I'm not going to have a lot of deathbed instructions, and I don't want to waste time on lamentations; the truth is, I'm dying, and it's about time."

Gertrude's hair was covered in a lace cap, which—even though her corkscrew curls popped out here and there—made her appear smaller than she was. But the light in her eyes was the same as ever. "All right. No lamentations," Samuel said, trying to keep his voice steady. "At least none in front of you."

"All this fuss about where you'd go, isn't it funny? I knew all along you would head for Baltimore, but Daisy was the first to ask me. That's where I sang in the saloon."

"Why do you think I chose it?" he said tenderly.

"What happened to Alice?"

She was clearly not wasting any time. "We said good-bye a year ago; we've had no contact. She told me she could never see me again. And I have been exchanging letters with Lydia Corland." The words sat awkwardly on his tongue, even as his pulse quickened at the sound of Alice's name.

"Yes, I've heard about Lydia. She's had her eye on you for a long time. You do know she'll try to pull you back under the Boston umbrella, don't you?" Gertrude said. She lay quietly for a moment, her breathing labored. "Young people are such idiots," she finally sighed. "Why in heaven's name don't you try again?"

Even his grandmother wouldn't understand. "It's just not—"

Gertrude cut him off. "Samuel, don't continue to punish yourself." She paused, out of breath, then continued, "Hiram should have let your brother testify; now the boy will live with the shame of that choice. And you are living with the unjustified blame."

All these months gone by; a new life, breaking ties, a knitting of frayed edges, accepting losses. And here was his grandmother, tearing it open again.

Gertrude freed her hand and waved it in the direction of a desk by the window. "Daisy dear, get that magazine and show it to your brother."

Daisy quickly picked it up and brought it to Samuel. He stared at it: the latest issue, it appeared, of *The Lowell Offering*.

"Page thirty," Daisy said, with a hint of excitement in her eyes.

He flipped quickly through the pages and stopped at the sight of Alice's name. There was silence as he read.

"What's your reaction, Samuel?" said Gertrude Fiske.

"I'm proud of her," he said. More than that, he was fiercely, fully proud of her, so much so he ached inside.

"That's what I was hoping you would say."

"Father is angry," ventured Daisy. "Says Alice is just stirring things up again."

"He keeps thinking the fires are banked, but they won't be for long. A few years, maybe," Samuel said.

Gertrude sighed. "My poor Hiram has lost his way." She grabbed Samuel's hand. "But you haven't," she said. "And neither has she."

Puzzled, Samuel glanced at Daisy.

"Alice was here to see her," Daisy explained. She paused at the surprise in her brother's eyes. "They are somewhat alike, you know," she said.

*T*wo nights later, the town was still in a fuss over her piece in *The Lowell Offering*. Alice, as was her habit now, walked by herself down to the playground after dark, enjoying the stillness. Swaying gently on the swing was peaceful. No voices, no clatter of machinery, no whispers around the mill, no glances—some hostile, some admiring—as news of her piece had spread about town. In the boardinghouses, she suspected, the talk would be a mix of fear and admiration, but, strangely, she didn't care. Benjamin Stanhope had said only that it might have been wise to use a pseudonym, which was his automatic protective stance, and it would never change. His cautious heart always prevailed.

She pushed the swing higher, looking up at a brilliant display of stars, remembering the swing she had fashioned as a child with a piece of board and a rope. Swinging high and daringly over the lip of the cliff and back again. She felt she could almost reach those stars tonight—yet what she truly wanted was for one to come partway and reach for her.

A sound behind her. A footstep crunching over dry leaves. Alarmed, she swiftly turned around.

"Alice," he said.

His face seemed thinner somehow, his cheekbones carved more sharply. A man so familiar, and yet a stranger. Changed. Their gazes caught and held, and everything between them hovered in the air, looking for ground. All that she was, all that he was—the pieces floated as he reached out his hand and stopped the swing. She stood, turning toward him. He was back, he was back.

"I seem to be always asking if you will walk with me," he said quietly.

She shivered, clinging to the swing chain. "Did you come to see your grandmother?" she managed.

"Yes. And now I'm here to see you. Am I welcome?"

His voice was calm—not anguished, not defensive. How she had hungered to hear it again.

"I watched you leave from Lowell last year."

"I know. I saw you standing there, across the street."

She trembled at that. "Then why are you here?"

"My grandmother made the point that I shouldn't open a new door without first closing this one firmly first."

What new one, she wanted to ask. But she knew. Close the door, slam it, hurry, she thought. I can't be here, next to you once again, and bear it much longer.

"I read your piece," he said. "I thought it was an eloquent tribute to your friend." He willed her to move forward, away from the swing, closer to him. This was a last shot; he knew it.

"Thank you, I'm sure your father isn't happy about it."

"Probably not, but I don't want to talk about him. I'd like to tell you about what I'm doing."

"Please, Samuel, I don't think I can chat as if we're just friends," she said.

He could hear the pain in her voice, and his heart jumped. He hadn't been wrong to come. She did still care.

"I'm not part of Lowell anymore, Alice. I love Baltimore. It's young and exuberant, not tight and exclusionary like New England. I've set up a law practice, and I'm doing well."

"And you are courting Lydia Corland."

"Courting?" He was silent for a moment. "Far from it. Damn it, Alice, will you tell me if it is truly all over for you? I have to know. I've made no promises or proposal, and I am not marrying anyone until I do know."

"You left me standing on the sidewalk; you knew I was there." She started to cry. Watching him leave Lowell that night, taking with him all that had been locked in her heart, had been so fully and finally an ending.

"Alice, you didn't know *why* you were there. I understood that; I knew if I walked over to you, if I told you again how much I loved you, you would have pushed me away.".

It was true. She could have called out to him, too—but there had been nothing to say.

"I have but one question for you," he said. "Where are you now?"

One chance. She could almost feel Lovey encouraging her, prodding her to reach out for what she wanted. "I love you," she said. "I have loved you for so long."

"Oh, my darling, then stop being afraid."

She searched for the right words, but they would not come. And then it didn't matter; there were no right words. She took a step forward, letting go of the chain.

"Samuel, will you take a walk with me?" she said.

While this story is wholly fictional, the bones are true. There was a real Sarah Cornell, a young mill girl whose brutal murder in 1832 sparked a sensational trial, causing an uproar throughout New England. The fact that the suspected murderer—who was named Ephraim Avery—was part of a burgeoning evangelical camp movement set the stage for confrontation between religious groups fearing scandal and the industrialist mill owners—whose reputations depended on protecting the farm girls who flocked to their mills. This came at a time when their own workers were becoming restive and angry about low pay and dangerous working conditions. The atmosphere was volatile.

The Lowell textile mill was not the only one operating in the 1830s. Francis Cabot Lowell's prodigious memory had made it possible for him to bring the British secrets of machine-made fabric back to the United States years earlier. Capitalists had bought land and water rights in 1821, and the first textile mill was built in 1823.

That's where reality ends and fiction begins.

Fiske was a common name at that time, but my Fiske family is purely fictional.

And although I have used much of the actual testimony from the murder trial of the Reverend Ephraim Avery, and several of the real names of those who testified, I have compressed some geography and time frames in the interest of the story. *The Lowell Offering*, for example, did not begin publication until 1840—but there was indeed a "Mill Girl Manifesto," submitted by an anonymous young woman who knew something about demanding her rights.

Lovey would have been proud of that.

Kate Alcott

ACKNOWLEDGMENTS

Once again, I gratefully tip my hat to a loyal group of friends who read patiently and tell it like it is: Irene Wurtzel, Judith Viorst, Margaret Power, Ellen Goodman, Linda Cashdan, and my sister, Mary Dillon.

High-fives to you, Esther Newberg, you are a dream agent.

And Melissa Danaczko, nobody edits with the wit, exuberance, and ferocity that you do. You are a dream editor.

Frank, always to you. Friend, husband, critic: you are all of it, rolled into one. No dreams, just reality.

THE DRESSMAKER

Tess, an aspiring seamstress, thinks she's had an incredibly lucky break when she is hired by famous designer Lady Lucile Duff Gordon to be her personal maid on the *Titanic*. Once on board, Tess catches the eye of two men—a kind sailor and an enigmatic Chicago businessman—who offer differing views of what lies ahead for her in America. But on the fourth night, disaster strikes, and amid the chaos, Tess is one of the last people allowed on a lifeboat. The survivors are rescued and taken to New York, but when rumors begin to circulate about the choices they made, Tess is forced to confront a serious question. Did Lady Duff Gordon save herself at the expense of others? Torn between loyalty to Lucile and her growing suspicion that the media's charges are accurate, Tess must decide whether to stay quiet and keep her fiery mentor's goodwill or face what might be true and forever change her future.

Historical Fiction

ALSO BY
KATE ALCOTT

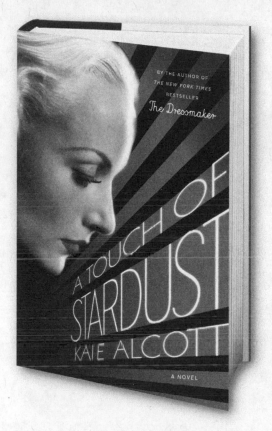

From *The New York Times* bestselling author of *The Dressmaker*, comes a blockbuster novel that takes you behind-the-scenes of the filming of *Gone with the Wind*, while turning the spotlight on the passionate romance between its dashing leading man, Clark Gable, and the blithe, free-spirited actress, Carole Lombard.

www.KateAlcott.com

Available February 17, 2015

Doubleday